CLOSE TO HOME

Selected Short Stories

by

WERoberts

Author's Preface

Though this book is the third I have published, the stories collected herein represent my earliest steps taken as a writer of fiction, and – even though they've been revised and tweaked – some of them without doubt still carry the marks of that rawness and inexperience. It is my hope, however, that over the years they were written I managed to improve in the craft of storytelling, and that in spite of their weaknesses even my earliest attempts are worth reading. I chose the title *Close To Home* because of its double meaning – nearness to the cosily familiar, and also slightly discomforting in terms of the subject matter portrayed.

Back in the early '60s I was privileged to know, and for a brief period to work closely with, the great American short story writer Raymond Carver, when we were both undergraduates at Humboldt State College in northern California. At that time Ray had not yet published any of his stories, but we all knew he was set on becoming a writer, and that sooner or later he would be recognized as such publicly. Little did we know how huge his success would be! And all of it completely deserved. I read his wonderful stories later, of course, when the lauded collections began regularly to appear, and have had them on my bookshelves ever since, wherever I moved.

For a time as a young man I dreamed, like many romantics, of becoming a writer myself, and went so far, during my high school years, as to briefly keep a journal into which I scribbled what I considered the most important thoughts and experiences of my days. When I later reread those entries, however, I was ashamed at how puerile and pompous and self-centred they were, and soon abandoned my writing ambitions. I was simply not ready then, if ever I would be.

Nevertheless over the years of maturity I have often turned my hand to various forms of writing, in an effort to broaden my freelance earning capability – adapting American novels and plays into radio dramas for the BBC, composing descriptive narrations of films for the blind (R.N.I.B.), and penning occasional jacket notes and blurbs for publisher friends. For a time I was even a full member of the Writers' Guild of Great Britain, until I let my membership lapse. But I never thought of writing fiction till very late in my life – some ten or so years ago – when, deciding to revisit some of Ray Carver's stories, I came across a short essay in his collection *FIRES* called *On Writing*, in which he states:

'It's possible, in a poem or a short story, to write about commonplace things and objects using commonplace but precise language, and to endow those things – a chair, a window curtain, a fork, a stone, a woman's earring – with immense, even startling power. It is possible to write a line of seemingly innocuous dialogue and have it send a chill along the reader's spine – the source of artistic delight, as Nabokov would have it. That's the kind of writing that most interests me...'

And later on:

'V.S. Pritchett's definition of a short story is "something glimpsed from the corner of the eye, in passing." Notice the "glimpse" part of this. First the glimpse. Then the glimpse given life, turned into something that illuminates the moment and may, if we're lucky ... have even further-ranging consequences and meaning. The short story writer's task is to invest the glimpse with all that is in his power...'

I happened to be holidaying in Cyprus at the time I read these lines, and, realizing that after more than sixty years of living I had 'glimpsed' a fair number of potential subjects for short stories, I decided to have a go. Settling myself at my laptop, over the next day or two I turned out a several thousand word piece that had a beginning, a middle and an end, and which, undeniably, was a story – whatever its merits. I gave it to my partner to read, and when she raised her eyebrows at the end and nodded, smiling, I gathered that I'd actually taken my first step as a fiction writer.

With the confidence gained from that, other stories followed, many of which are included in this collection.

Do they work? That's for the reader to decide. My benchmark of success is not set high. If one doesn't work for you, try another. And another. Hopefully you'll find gold somewhere along the line. (Or something that makes the effort worth the trouble.)

I'll leave it to Ray to have the last word, this time from his Author's Foreword in the collection, *WHERE I'M CALLING FROM*:

'If we're lucky ... we'll finish the last line or two of a short story and then just sit for a minute, quietly. Ideally, we'll ponder what we've just ... read; maybe our hearts or our intellects will have been moved off the peg just a little from where they were before. Our body temperature will have gone up, or down, by a degree. Then, breathing evenly and steadily once more, we'll collect ourselves ... get up, "created of warm blood and nerves" as a Chekhov character puts it, and go on to the next thing: Life. Always life.'

WERoberts
London
February, 2016

Table of Contents

For Emily, with all a father's love.
And for my grandsons, Luke and Julien.

WEST COAST, USA

Watershed Summer

Todd Stahlberg threw back the covers and swung his legs to the floor. Sunlight was streaming through the gap below his window blind and a glance at his watch told him he was late. He'd better hustle. He'd arranged yesterday to meet Naomi this morning for their planned climb of the hill opposite the house. He had half an hour left.

Slipping on jeans and a t-shirt, he donned a pair of clean socks and reached for his sneakers.

Two minutes later he was in the kitchen pouring cereal into a bowl for his breakfast. The car was gone from outside. Alice had probably gone to the store. No problem. He'd leave a note, tell her what they intended to do and give an estimate as to when they'd be back. He poured milk on the cereal, sprinkled sugar over it, and sat at the table to scarf it down.

Todd's dad had left before dawn, as was usual. Les Stahlberg was a truck driver, hauling lumber from the local mills down to Eureka to be shipped overseas. He worked long days and got home late. During the week Todd and his stepmother didn't see much of him, and they looked forward to the weekends when he would be around for two solid days.

Les and Alice had moved into this little house overlooking the Smith River only three months before. They'd been married six months, and

Todd was over the moon with his dad's choice of new companion. He'd met her the summer before, when he had come down for his scheduled visit with his father. Les wasn't much of a cook, and their meals had been mostly taken at Bobby's Café in Crescent City. Alice had been a waitress there. Les had taken an interest in her and started taking her out. It didn't take him long to realize what a peach she was, and a couple months after Todd's return to Oregon Les had popped the question. Todd had been delighted. Alice was soft spoken and kind hearted. She was also attractive, with long, auburn hair, a pretty face and a nice figure. Todd couldn't have asked for a better stepmom.

When the school year had finished, Todd had left his mother in Oregon (as per prior arrangements) and travelled down via Greyhound bus to spend most of the summer with his dad and his new wife in California. He'd been here now almost a month, and there was a month to go before he had to return north to prepare for the new school year.

Rinsing his cereal bowl and spoon, Todd set them on the drain board and headed for the door. There were five minutes left before his rendezvous with Naomi at the creek bridge.

He'd met Naomi only a few days before. For the first three weeks of his stay Todd had had to amuse himself, because there were no other young people living in the houses scattered along the river. Then one day, passing the large yellow house at the end of the line, he had seen a girl about his own age moping around the front yard, looking as bored and lonely as he was. He had walked on, then a few moments later, on a whim, he'd gone back to speak to her. He was too late. She'd gone back inside.

The next time he saw her he didn't miss his chance. He stopped at the wire fencing and folded his arms across the top of a wooden post, staring at her.

'Hey!' he called. 'What'cha doin'?'

The girl was tall, almost his height, with shoulder-length chestnut

4

hair and a fresh, pleasant face. She was wearing a long-sleeved cotton shirt with the sleeves rolled up, jeans, and tennis shoes. She'd been walking along the neatly kept flower beds bordering the house's lawn with her hands clasped behind her back, and had turned abruptly when he called. She peered at him suspiciously for a moment, then strolled towards him.

'Not doing anything. What're you doing?'

'Nothing. Talking to you.' He looked up toward the yellow house. 'You live here?'

'Nope. That's my grandparents' house. I live in Walnut Creek.'

'Where's that?'

'Near San Francisco. I'm only here for a couple weeks. You?'

'The same, really. I live in Oregon.' He pointed down the road. 'I'm staying with my dad and stepmom in the brown house down at the other end. On the river side.'

'Oh yes, I know it. Does your stepmom have reddish hair?'

'Yes. Her name's Alice. She and Dad got married six months ago. I'm here visiting for a while. My name's Todd. Todd Stahlberg.'

'I'm Naomi. Naomi Berryman.' She moved closer. 'Where in Oregon do you live?'

'In Eugene. I live with my mom and my sister. She's four years younger than me. And she's a pain.' He squinted at her. 'How old are you?'

'Twelve. You?'

'Twelve and three-quarters. I'll be thirteen in two months. Moving up to junior high school this year, too, when I get back.'

They had chatted thus for a few minutes, trading queries and information. Then Todd had asked if she wanted to come for a walk with him into the nearby redwood forest.

'I'll have to ask my grandma.' She started off a few paces, then turned back. 'Wait there.'

And thus it had started. First with a walk into Stout Grove, the stand of virgin redwood forest that began a quarter mile up the road and continued on a few miles over the low hills towards Crescent City on the coast. It'd been a good day and they'd found it easy to talk together – about their school life, their families, and what they liked and disliked. When they returned that afternoon Todd asked if he could see her the following day and Naomi had agreed.

Since then they'd spent most every day together, walking along the river or in the redwoods, or chatting with Alice in the little kitchen of the river house. Alice obviously liked her, too, and told Les she seemed a polite and well-brought up girl.

One day Naomi had had to go into town with her grandparents to do some shopping. All that afternoon Todd had wandered around like a lost soul. He was surprised to find himself missing her so much. He'd never spent much time with girls up to then – apart from his sister, who didn't count – and had always thought them rather superficial and silly. But Naomi wasn't like that. Naomi was thoughtful and interesting and easy to talk to. She liked to laugh and have fun. Just like a boy.

Todd picked up his pace. The creek bridge was along the road past Naomi's grandparents' house, just before the redwoods began. When the road turned slightly he saw her standing at the rail, staring down at the water. She looked up as he approached.

'Hi.'

'Hi. Sorry I'm late. I overslept.'

'That's okay. I haven't been here long. Shall we go?'

'Yeah.'

Not far from the creek bridge a trail slanted upwards toward the ridge of the tall hill. Todd had been told by his father that there was a Scout camp up there, where at weekends and during holidays groups of scouts were brought by minibuses for campouts – living in tents, cooking and eating outdoors, doing all the things scouts do on their campouts. Todd himself had had only the briefest involvement with scouting, having given up cub scouts after only two or three meetings because he didn't much like the boys in his group and had found the den mother's patronizing sing-song voice and prissy manner a bit of a pain. He didn't miss it, and thought the idea of playing at camping, wearing silly uniforms and earning badges by doing phoney 'activities,' was tedious and stupid. If he was going to do those things he'd do them properly – with his dad, or with some other grownup who really knew about hiking and camping and hunting – not with a crowd of sissies under the supervision of grownups who knew even less about outdoor living than he did himself. Still, when Todd's father had told him about the Scout campsite he'd been curious to see it, and yesterday he and Naomi had decided to climb the hill to take a look.

The morning sun was ascending into the cloudless sky as the two youngsters entered the trees along the earthen pathway, winding between waist-high clumps of bracken fern and low brush. Soon they were zigzagging upwards through a thick forest, the sound of the river only a dim murmur in the distance.

It took them half an hour to reach the split-rail fence that marked the boundary of the Scout property. When they saw it ahead of them Todd held up a hand, meaning for Naomi to wait while he checked it out. She nodded and stood with crossed arms while he went cautiously forward.

There was no one around. The two friends had the place to themselves. There wasn't much to see, really – some cleared spaces for the tents, a couple of toilet huts made from rough planks, a tank of fresh water for washing, some barbecue grills with picnic tables and benches nearby, and – off to one side – a large fire pit surrounded by a circle of seats made from cut redwood log sections resting on end. This obviously was where the scouts held their fireside powwows and told their silly stories and practiced their phoney rituals. Todd found the whole thing maddening. So much so that when he discovered a two-bladed axe stuck in a chopping block beside a stack of logs at one side, he wrenched the axe free and made for the nearest of the log section seats

'What're you doing, Todd?' his friend asked, alarmed.

'I hate these people, Naomi. They piss me off with their uniforms and their jamborees and their fireside storytelling. They pretend to know how to live in the woods like the Indians did but they don't know jack shit. They're just a bunch of city sissies playing stupid games.'

Glowering, he hefted the axe high above his head and brought it crashing down onto the log seat. The wood was well dried, the axe sharp, and the log section split easily into halves with the blow. Satisfied with his work, Todd went on to split the halves into quarters, and the quarters into eighths. And when he had finished with the first log seat, he moved on to the next.

'I don't think you should do that, Todd,' Naomi told him, frowning. 'You're destroying someone else's property. You could get into trouble. What if someone catches us?'

'No one will,' Todd returned, swinging his axe down to divide yet another log seat into pieces. 'Anyway, I'm just helping them out, aren't I? They need wood chopped for the fire, don't they? Well I'm doing it for them.'

'But those are their seats.'

'So what? They can sit on the ground then, with their legs crossed like real Indians. It'll be good for 'em.'

Naomi said no more but continued watching him. Soon the entire ring of log seats had been reduced by Todd's axe to just so much firewood. The fire circle had been completely destroyed.

Nodding his head with approval, Todd sank the axe again into the chopping block and rubbed his hands together. 'There. That'll fix the bastards.'

'Don't swear, Todd.' Naomi looked around, apprehensively. 'Let's go. I'm scared someone's gonna come and find us.'

'All right. We'll go. But I'm not sorry I did it, Naomi. So there.'

They made their way down the hill again and split up to go their separate ways for lunch, after which, and for the rest of the afternoon, they amused themselves by damming a side stream of the river –

laughing and joking as they worked – creating at length a shallow basin in which to cool their feet.

At five o'clock Todd walked Naomi back to her grandparents' house and returned home, tired but satisfied with his day. Tomorrow was Saturday. His father would be home, and even if they didn't go anywhere or do anything special he would still have the pleasure of spending time with him. He looked forward to that.

The following morning Todd again slept late. It was close to ten o'clock before he wandered through to the kitchen, where he found Alice making bread. That pleased him. Alice's fresh-baked bread was a treat. He looked forward to cutting a thick slice while it was still warm, slathering it with butter and jam before savouring every bite as it went down.

From the radio on the counter a news announcer droned on about President Eisenhower meeting with other countries' leaders at the Geneva Convention in Switzerland to discuss world peace and security. Todd wondered what Alice found interesting in that.

'Where's Dad?' he asked, pouring himself a glass of orange juice from the bottle in the fridge.

Alice turned to him, brushing flour from her hands. 'He's outside. A man knocked on the door a few minutes ago. He's out talking with him.'

'Who is it?'

'I don't know. I think he said something about being with the Scouts.'

Todd felt his stomach lurch. It had to be about the camp, the destroyed seats. But how had they discovered it was him who was responsible? Naomi wouldn't have told, he was certain.

Stepping into the living room he edged across till he could see the driveway through the front window. A pickup truck was parked across the end. Standing beside it was his father and a man in a light jacket and baseball hat. The man was tall, about his father's height, but thicker set and a few years older. And he was obviously angry. Todd could see him scowling, shaking his head and scuffing the ground with his feet. His father, too, was grim-faced, and nodded occasionally in response to what he was being told, casting occasional glances back towards the house. Once he looked straight at the living room window and Todd flinched, thinking he'd been caught watching. But then his father looked away again.

Moving back into the kitchen, Todd fixed himself a bowl of cereal, trying to calm his nerves. While he ate he watched Alice kneading the bread dough on the countertop with her rough country girl's hands. The radio was now playing music – a country-western song about love and betrayal.

He had just finished his cereal and was rinsing out the bowl in the sink when his father came in and stood in the kitchen doorway, looking at him, his lips pressed together.

'Well, slug. You had a busy day yesterday, didn't you?'

'What d'you mean, Dad?'

'That was one of the scoutmasters from the camp on the hill. He was pretty mad. Said somebody went up there yesterday and took an axe to all the log seats around the campfire pit. Split 'em into little pieces. Now they'll have to bring in a truckload of new ones.'

'Why did he stop here? Does he think it was me that did it?'

'He said he'd asked around. Everyone told him there was only one boy living along this stretch. He stopped by to see if it might've been you. Was it?'

Todd wondered if there was any way he could bluff his way out of it.

'Well, it could've been someone from somewhere else. Did he think of that? Why does it have to be me?'

Les's face was stern. 'Was it you, son? Tell me the truth.'

Todd stared down at his hand, finding something of great interest in the lines of his palm, tracing them idly with his thumb.

'I'm waiting, Todd.'

Todd looked up, met his father's eyes.

'Yeah. It was me. I did it.'

There was a long silence. Alice had stopped her kneading. Now she switched off the radio, turning to watch as Les stepped forward and pulled out one of the chairs at the table.

'Sit down, son.'

Todd did so, and Les took the seat opposite him, resting his forearms on the tabletop and clasping his hands before him.

'I want you to tell me only the truth about this, you understand? Don't make anything up and don't leave anything out. Okay?'

'Okay.'

'Were you alone?'

Todd looked up again, then down at the oilcloth table cover. 'No. Naomi was with me. But she didn't have anything to do with it. She told me I shouldn't do it. But I did it anyway.' He glanced up again. 'Don't blame her for it, Dad. It wasn't her fault.'

'Why did you do it, then?'

Todd shrugged. 'I don't know. I just don't like scouts, I guess. I think they're all goody-goodies. And the scoutmasters are a load of phoneys, too, pretending to be something they're not. I guess I wanted to bust up their stupid camp to get back at them.'

'Why? What've they ever done to you?'

There was another pause. Todd was staring at the table again.

'Todd?'

'Nothing, really.' He sighed. 'I guess it was a pretty dumb thing to do.'

'Yeah.' Les was nodding. 'I guess it was.'

Todd looked up at his father again. 'Do you have to pay for it?'

'No. Fortunately Mr. Armistad works at Simonson's mill. He can have another truckload of log trims delivered up there for nothing but the cost of the gas. I offered to pay him but he wouldn't take it. Just asked me to make sure you understood the seriousness of what you did.

And to make you promise not to do it – or anything like it – again.' He leaned across the table. 'Do you, Todd? Realize how bad what you've done is? Can I be sure you won't do anything like this again?'

'Yeah.'

It was almost a mumble.

'Yeah what?'

'Yeah, I do understand how serious the thing I did was, and I promise I'll never do anything like it again.'

Les sat back. 'Good. I believe you. But there still has to be some kind of punishment. I reckon you deserve that. It was a pretty awful thing, after all. What do think that should be, huh? Your punishment?'

'I guess no spending money for a while. And no movies or special treats.'

'Well, I kinda thought that was going happen anyway. But I think there should be something more, don't you? Something that'll help you remember your promise, so there won't ever be a next time?'

Todd looked up, suddenly alert. 'Like what, Dad?'

Les sat back and crossed his arms, frowning across at his son.

'You like that girl Naomi, don't you?'

'Yeah. She's my friend.'

'Suppose I told you you can't see her anymore this summer? That you have to spend every day from now on here on the place, by yourself?' Todd's eyes suddenly widened. 'What do you think, son? Would that be a fair punishment?'

The boy shook his head vigorously. 'No! Please, Dad. Don't do that. Don't stop me being with Naomi. I don't want to be alone anymore. I want to do things with her. She's my friend. You can make me do more chores – anything. I'll wash dishes after dinner every night from now on. But please don't do that, Dad. Please don't stop me seeing my friend!'

There were tears in his eyes now.

'But how can I be sure you've learned your lesson, Todd? How can I be sure you won't forget?'

'I promise, Dad!' the boy gurgled through his sobs. 'I promise I won't ever do anything bad like that again. And I'll do anything else you want – just tell me and I'll do it. Only please let me keep my friend.'

Todd's hands were over his face now, wiping away the shameful tears that flowed down his cheeks.

For a long moment Les stared at his son. Then he looked across at Alice, who stood watching with folded arms.

'What do you think, hon? Do you think that's a fair punishment, or not?'

Alice moved around the table to stand behind Les's chair and put her hands on her husband's shoulders, looking across at Todd, who looked back at her, appealing with anguished eyes.

'I believe him,' she said at last. 'He knows he did wrong, and I don't think he'll do anything like that again. We can find extra things for him to do around here. And there shouldn't be any spending money or movies for a while. But I don't think we should stop him seeing Naomi. Remember, she tried to stop him doing it. She's a good girl. And it's a good thing he has a friend like that to spend time with here.'

Les reached up a hand to catch Alice's fingers in his and gave them a squeeze. Then he leaned forward again, resting both arms on the tabletop.

'All right, son. I think Alice is right. And I believe you, too, when you say you've learned your lesson. But don't make me sorry for that, Todd. You've given your word, and I'll accept that. Don't ever forget what you promised.'

Todd nodded, wiping the last tears away with the back of his hand.

'I won't. Thanks, Dad. I promise I'll never forget.'

'No, I don't think you will. You're a good boy at heart.'

'Can I go now, Dad?'

'Yeah. You can go.'

Later that morning at the bridge Todd told Naomi what'd happened – the two of them leaning over the railing as he spoke, watching the water trickling through the stones below them. When he had finished Naomi turned to him.

'I'm glad he changed his mind, Todd. I wouldn't like being here on my own anymore.'

'Me neither.' Todd turned and stuffed his hands in his pockets, leaning back on the rail. 'So, what d'ya want to do now, go down to the river?'

She shook her head. 'No. Let's walk somewhere. I feel like walking.'

Todd thought for a moment. 'We could walk down to the big bridge.'

She nodded. 'Okay. Good. Let's do that.'

Together they set off past the houses and down the road towards the steel bridge that spanned the river a mile away, near the junction with Highway 199, at a point where stony cliffs narrowed the river's flow to a thirty foot width. From the bridge's railings one could look down into the deep emerald-green pool below and see schools of carp finning slowly through the shadows.

On their way the two friends talked in low voices of their siblings, their best friends, their extended families. Then, on the way back, Todd told Naomi of his parents' divorce, confessing it'd been difficult for him at first, with his father living in a room by himself across town. But both parents had tried hard to make him and his sister understand their reason for separating had nothing to do with them, that they were still loved and always would be. They just couldn't live together anymore. Naomi was greatly moved by Todd's story, and at one point reached out to touch his arm.

'It must've been awful for you. I don't know what I'd do if my parents split up. But I know I'd be pretty sad.'

Todd shrugged. 'It wasn't too hot at the beginning, but I was fine once things settled down. Now I think I'm actually better off than most kids – I've got two homes rather than just one.'

The string of houses above the river was now in sight, and Todd turned to Naomi.

'Come on! I'll race you to my driveway!'

And off they ran, squealing like kids at recess, their sneakered feet pounding the asphalt like pistons.

Over the following week Todd and Naomi were virtually inseparable, and their friendship grew more and more relaxed. With each day that passed – walking through the woods together, larking around on the riverbank, or, on the occasional rainy days, playing board games on the Stahlbergs' kitchen table (sometimes with Alice joining them, when she wasn't too busy) – Todd had grown to regard her as perhaps the best pal he'd ever had.

Then came an afternoon that changed everything.

After lunch that day the two youngsters had made their way down to the riverbank to amuse themselves at the water's edge under the hot summer sun. After a few minutes spent skipping stones across the flat river surface, they had settled themselves side by side on a patch of packed sand, lying back and shutting their eyes, letting the sun's warmth draw them into a somnolent stillness as they listened to the buzzing of bees working the wildflowers nearby, the trickle of the flowing water, and the sigh of the gentle breeze in the trees. For a long time neither of them spoke, feeling content to simply be together, sharing the moment. Then Naomi turned on her side and looked at Todd, planting an elbow in the sand and resting her cheek on her hand. Todd's eyes remained closed as she stared at him. Finally she spoke.

'You know, you'd be good looking if you only combed your hair a bit.'

Todd opened one eye to frown at her. Then he closed it again.

'Well? Why don't you, Todd? Why don't you comb your hair sometimes? And tuck in your shirt tail?'

'Why should I?'

'I told you. You'd look really nice. Handsome even.'

'Don't be silly.'

'I'm not being silly. Don't you want girls to like you?'

'What girls?'

'Any girls. The girls up in Oregon. At your school. You're going to junior high next year. There'll be nice girls there.' She paused. 'Or do you have a girlfriend already?'

'Don't be stupid.'

'Why's that stupid? It's just a question.'

'No, I don't have any girlfriend. So there.'

'Why not?'

''Cause I don't want one. Girls are a pain.'

'Am I a pain?'

He turned to look at her again. 'You're being a pain now.'

'Why? Because I asked if you had a girlfriend?'

'Yes.'

'Am I a pain all the time?'

'No. Not usually. Usually you don't act so … girlish.'

He closed his eyes again. Naomi reached out to pluck a stalk of long grass growing from the sand nearby. She chewed on the stem for a moment, watching him. Then, grasping the stem, she reached out to tickle Todd's nose with the fluffy seed end. When Todd raised a hand to brush it away – thinking it was some flying insect – Naomi hastily withdrew it. Then, after a moment, smiling mischievously, she reached out again, running the grass tip along his cheek. Exasperated, Todd swiped at it with one hand, but again she jerked it away. Finally, she deliberately poked the end of the grass stem into one of his nostrils. This time Todd growled and sat upright, rubbing at his nose furiously.

'What the…' He glowered at her. 'What'd you do that for?'

'Do what?'

'Tickle my nose. That was you, wasn't it?'

'Now Todd Stahlberg,' said Naomi, with exaggerated innocence. 'Why would I do a thing like that?'

'Because you're a dumb girl.'

Naomi frowned. 'I'm not dumb. Why are you so against girls, Todd?'

'I'm not against girls. I just want them to leave me alone. Most of 'em, anyway.'

'I think you're afraid of girls, you know? All girls. That's what I think. I think you're afraid of them, and that's why you say such awful things about them.'

'I'm not afraid of them. I just don't like them. Girls are a waste of space. They only play with dolls and talk about dumb things.'

Naomi rolled to her knees, throwing the grass stem aside. 'Is that so? Well, thank you very much, if that's the way you feel. That's a nice thing to say. And what do you suppose we girls think about you boys, then, mister smarty?'

'I couldn't care less what you think.'

'Well, I'm going to tell you anyway. Girls think you're all a bunch of babies, that's what. Running around playing dumb ball games and shooting BB guns at birds, and reading your stupid comic books. Why do you think girls hang out together, huh? Because boys are drips!'

'Oh, yeah?' Todd rose to his knees with a challenging grin. 'We're drips, huh? Want to fight about it?'

'Fight?' Naomi leapt to her feet in a sudden, eager movement. 'Sure, sissy boy. Come and get it!'

And before Todd could respond, Naomi darted forward to push him onto his back on the sand, leaping onto him, straddling his body with her legs, grabbing his arms and forcing them back onto the ground by his head.

'Hey!' Todd giggled, surprised at her suddenness and her strength. 'That's not fair! You didn't let me get ready!'

'So what, silly?' Naomi crowed, as Todd struggled to free himself. 'If you're so strong why don't you do something about it, huh?'

'I'll do something about it all right,' he gasped. 'Just wait till I get my hands on you…!'

With a determined burst of strength Todd freed his wrists and rolled Naomi over onto the sand, springing astride her, forcing her arms back onto the sand. For a few seconds the two bucked and writhed, each trying to gain the upper hand, until finally Naomi pushed Todd off to one side. Like a pair of kittens they clawed at each other, arms and legs flailing, grabbing handfuls of shirt and tugging for purchase, rolling over and over one another in the sand as they snorted and giggled.

Naomi was wearing her long-sleeved cotton shirt again, with the sleeves rolled up and the shirttail hanging loose outside her jeans. In the course of their struggles, rolling over and over in the sand, inevitably the buttons of her shirt were either accidentally undone or were forcibly pulled off by their playful wrenchings. In any case, as Naomi rolled once again onto Todd and laughingly attempted to pin his thrashing arms to the ground, her shirt suddenly fell completely open, revealing her naked chest beneath – and the two budding breasts with their pink and pointing nipples.

At a stroke their struggling ceased. On his back, Todd's eyes widened in shocked surprise. Then, in embarrassment, he looked back to her face.

They stared at one another.

Ashamed, Naomi clambered to her knees, turned away to gather the two flapping sides of her shirt together and quickly re-buttoned them.

In the stunned silence Todd raised himself to his elbows and stared at her, half-frowning. Something of monumental importance had just occurred, he knew that, although he wasn't quite sure what the consequences would be. All he knew with certainty was that Naomi could no longer be just a pal who happened to be a girl. The evidence of her nascent womanhood had rocked him to the core, and in amazement he began to sense feelings being born within him that he'd never experienced before – a kind of tenderness and caring that went far beyond the casual affection he felt for his guy friends back home.

And he realized – though he would not have been able to articulate it in so many words – that he had moved on at a stroke from being a mere boy into being a young man, with all the desires and appetites and longings that came with that advancement yet to be explored and understood. And while he was daunted by the enormity of the change he felt, at the same time there was a part of him that welcomed it, as much as he welcomed the imminent transition from his elementary school years to his junior high school years. He was growing up, and this new awareness was part of it. That much, at least, he knew. It was a challenge he embraced with eagerness. And not a little wonder.

When Naomi was decent again Todd rose to his feet and pulled her upright by one hand. Together they turned away from the scene of their epiphany and, without words, headed back towards the houses.

At some point along the way (neither of them could have said when or how), they found themselves holding hands.

And when they said their goodbyes later that afternoon at the gate to Naomi's grandparents', they knew that they were now, truly, 'girlfriend and boyfriend', and that the days spent together from here on out would be different to the days they had passed before. Sometime soon, Todd knew, initials would have to be carved into a tree trunk somewhere – framed within a heart pierced by an arrow – to give their inchoate love a voice that would speak forever. That was what was expected of him now, wasn't it?

Todd knew that he would never forget this day. And, as he watched Naomi walk up the path to turn at the door with a veiled smile and a lift of her hand, he knew that as a result of the event at the sand bar he would never again be the boy he had been before.

(London, 2010)

19

Mr. Cahill

The little party wandered slowly along the rows of the hillside vegetable garden, pausing in the warm afternoon sun to examine one vine or plant after another, chatting amiably together in low voices about fertilizers and slug repellents and the various ways to control aphids and blackfly and other common predators. Five people – two men, a woman carrying a baby, and a boy of twelve or thirteen. Weaving in and out of their feet, a pair of tortoiseshell cats kept pace with them, their curiosity piqued by the rare advent of a cluster of strangers invading their patch.

The older man took the lead in the group, drawing them down one packed earthen path after another, pointing out the blossoms on the pumpkin and squash plants, the baby cucumbers and the lush rows of chard and beet greens, pausing to delve amidst the luxuriant foliage of the climbing bean vines to pluck one or two slender specimens and handing them to his visitors to try – crunching the brittle pods in their teeth, tasting their sweet juice.

The leader was somewhere in his late seventies, of medium height and thickset body mass, and wore a plaid flannel shirt under a denim bibbed overall. On his feet were heavy leather work boots. On his balding head wisps of white hair blew about in the breeze rising from the distant river. His hands were thick-fingered and broad – the hands of a workman – and as he spoke his eyes twinkled with pleasure, for this garden was his pride and joy, and he was delighted to show it off to his appreciative young neighbours from down the hill.

He had met them only a week before when the husband had stopped by to ask if he might take a pickup load or two of topsoil from beside the forest track at the upper edge of the old man's property. He and his wife were renting the modest, single-storied house at the sharp turn of the road a quarter of a mile downhill, and he wanted some good soil to spread over their predominantly clay front yard to create some flower beds for his lady to plant flowers and shrubs in. The old man was happy to oblige ('Take as many loads as you like!'), and over the next weekend he had watched as the man and his lanky son made several trips in their well-used Chevrolet pickup up the track above his property, returning minutes later with heaped loads of loamy, redwood forest topsoil.

That Sunday afternoon, coming back from a trip to the store, the old man had stopped by when he saw the family working together in their front yard. Pulling his battered Dodge across the end of their drive, he had climbed out and ambled over for a chat.

The husband had created a string of raised beds by nailing redwood planks on edge into rectangles that bordered the driveway, the house front and the pathway to the front door. Now he and the boy were adding the new topsoil to the beds, carrying wheelbarrow loads up from the pile beside the drive and forking it into the claggy earth to create a mixture of the two that would support and nourish the roots of new plants and bushes. At one side one of the beds had been completed, and beside it the wife knelt in jeans and shirt, working fertilizer into the new soil, then depositing seeds in carefully spaced depressions, finally covering them over and wetting them down with a watering can. On the little porch nearby, strapped into a baby seat, the bonneted baby sat overlooking them all, waving a rattle and gurgling happily as she watched the activity below her.

The old man admired the little family's concerted struggle to bring colour and life to the bare ground before their house, and he told them as much. He was sure, he said, that in a few weeks they'd be amazed at the transformation all their efforts would make.

The wife, whose mane of shoulder-length auburn hair was tied back with a bandanna, turned with a homey smile to regard him closely, holding one hand over her eyes to shade them from the sun.

'Are you a gardener yourself then?' she asked.

He smiled and nodded.

'I guess you could say that. Since Arlene died – that's my wife, she died four years ago – it's become my greatest joy in life. Arlene used to be the one who kept the garden while I worked. I was millwright for Simpson's up in Smith River for years, till I retired eight years ago. When Arlene went I took over the garden and tried to keep it up like she used to. I think I have. Leastways I hope so. I think she'd be proud of me.'

The wife rose to her feet, brushing soil from her hands and stepping forward.

'I'm sure she would be. I'd love to see your garden, Mr. Cahill.' They knew his name from seeing it on the mailbox standing beside the drive up to his house. 'If you wouldn't mind? I'm trying to learn about gardening, and you might be able to give me some pointers.'

'Why, I'd be tickled to show it to you,' he'd replied, and they'd made an appointment to come up the following afternoon.

Accordingly, the next day they had arrived at the appointed time – all four of them crammed onto the single seat of the pickup – and had been effusively welcomed inside the single-story, shadowy Cahill house tucked behind its screened front porch. There they had taken seats at an oilcloth-covered table before a long window overlooking the Smith River meandering a mile or so below through the redwoods, to enjoy tall glasses of iced sun tea and slices of store-bought coffee cake. After which, the tour of the garden behind the house had commenced.

It had taken a half hour, and now it was drawing to a close as they approached the last and perhaps most majestic display in the garden

– a tall stand of sweet pea vines beside the back porch, growing up a frame of straight saplings gathered together and tied at the top with twine. From ground to tip the frame was ablaze with hundreds of multi-coloured blossoms.

The old man stood back smiling as his visitors gaped at it.

'Go on, take a sniff,' he urged them.

They did so, burying their noses in the blossoms, drinking in the sweet honeyed smell, cooing their appreciation. Digging into an overall pocket, the old man produced a pair of garden scissors, which he passed to the wife.

'Go ahead and cut a bunch or two, if you want. There's more there than I can ever use.'

The wife turned to him.

'Really?'

'Sure. Take as many as you can use. They'll just go to waste if you don't.'

'I will, then,' she said, smiling, and passed the baby to her husband. 'I'll put them in a vase on our kitchen table. Thank you so much!'

Mr Cahill reached down to pick up the largest of the cats. Holding it in his arms, he stroked its back idly as he watched the young woman selecting and clipping the stems. The great furry creature purred contentedly under his hand. Beside him, the boy knelt to pet the second cat, which writhed with pleasure against his ankles.

Minutes later the family prepared for their short drive home. In the pickup bed were boxes of new potatoes and freshly-cut squashes and beans – gifts from the old man – together with the fat bunches of sweet pea blossoms, the stems held together with rubber bands. As they turned down the gravel drive towards the road, the old man raised a hand high in a wave and everyone in the pickup waved back.

Over the following months, every time they passed one another on the road, the family and Mr Cahill would wave and smile – good neighbours, with every intention of developing their friendship further when time allowed. At the same time the young plants and shrubs in the family's rectangular beds grew and flowered and brought the hoped-for touch of colour and life to their drab front yard. Delighted, they wanted to thank the old man for his contribution, but they never got the chance.

One afternoon in the late autumn the boy returned home from school to find his mother sitting subdued at the kitchen table. Before her was a half-full cup of coffee. In an ashtray, a filter cigarette sent a spiral of smoke into the air. Across the room in the playpen, the baby gurgled happily on its back.

But the boy could see that all was not well from the distracted look on his mother's face. Pulling out the chair opposite, he slid into it.

'You all right, Ma?'

The woman's gaze seemed to come back to him from somewhere far away. Then she blinked and stirred herself, reaching for her cigarette.

'Yes, I'm fine. Just had some bad news, that's all. Marge told me. From down the road? She only just left.'

'What bad news?'

The woman took a drag on the cigarette and stubbed it out in the ashtray. Then she sighed and sat back.

'Old Mr. Cahill was found dead today up at his house. Heart attack, they think.'

The boy frowned. 'That's sad. He was a nice man. Nice to us.'

'He sure was.'

The boy leaned forward.

'Who found him? He didn't have any relatives, did he? No children?'

'No. He told us that when we visited, remember? After his wife died he was all alone in the world. Except for his cats.'

She shuddered.

'Who was it that found him then?' the boy asked.

'The people down at the store hadn't seen him for over a week.

They got worried because he always called in every two or three days. Finally they drove up and knocked on his door. His old Dodge was in the carport, and when he didn't answer, they thought something might be wrong and called the Sheriff's office.'

'The Sheriff found him?'

The woman nodded.

'Two deputies. They had to break in. He'd died in his sleep, it looks like – over a week ago.' She shook herself. 'It must've been awful.'

'Why awful?' the boy said. 'At least he didn't suffer.'

The woman looked up.

'That wasn't the worst.'

'What d'you mean?'

'The cats were locked up in the house with him. For over a week. They had nothing to eat, no food left in their bowls.'

'Did they have water?'

'Oh yes. They got water from the toilet bowl. The lid had been left up.'

The boy frowned, beginning to suspect.

'So how did they survive, then? What'd they eat?'

The woman sat forward, tracing with the tip of her index finger the flowered pattern of the oilcloth.

'Apparently they ate him. Part of him anyway. His face and neck.'

The boy grimaced.

'The *cats* did?'

'Yes.' She looked up at him again. 'But you mustn't blame them, Will. They had to eat something. They were starving. That was all they could find.'

The boy sat back, swallowing thickly. It was an image supremely horrible to contemplate, and he pitied the poor deputies who'd made the discovery.

'What'll happen to the cats now, d'you think?' he asked finally.

'They'll be taken care of.' The woman sipped her coffee. 'Given away or taken to the animal pound. Someone will probably take them.

And why not? No one will know what they did. It wasn't their fault, anyway.'

Which was true enough.

But for the rest of the boy's life the imagined image of poor Mr. Cahill lying dead in his bed in his silent house up the hill – with half his face eaten away by his beloved pets – was something he would never be able to forget.

(London, 2010)

North Bank Road

He hadn't intended to stop. Over the years he'd passed the place a couple dozen times and had never once felt inclined to arrest his through journey to touch briefly upon the long distant past. But this overcast July afternoon something tugged at his sentiments, and as the little green-painted shake house loomed up out of the redwoods on the right he slowed the hire car and pulled it to a stop on the broad opposite shoulder.

The afternoon was warm, and the driver's window was open. For a few moments after he'd turned off the engine he sat behind the wheel, listening to the ticks of the hot metal under the hood as it cooled, exploring the view around him – once so familiar. A light breeze caressed the side of his face, bringing the cool scent of the river a quarter of a mile away.

At the right, across the asphalt – situated on a bank above the road – the little green house looked uninhabited, which surprised him. The last time he'd passed there were still people living there.

At the left, outside his open window, a high thicket of blackberries completely obscured the front porch of the somewhat larger single-storey clapboard dwelling that had once housed the family of his closest friend, Bobby Nelson. Now it cowered beneath the vines, windows boarded over, its pale yellow paint cracked and peeling – a sad empty wrack, giving way year by year to the encroachments of nature and the weather. The roof looked good yet, though. That at least had lasted.

He opened the door and stepped out. In the distance the harsh cry of a jay bruised the air.

Looking around, he pushed the car door to until it clicked shut. He was careful not to slam it. Something demanded that he be as quiet as possible here – so as, perhaps, not to disturb the sleeping ghosts of the abandoned houses.

He checked his watch. 2:30. She wasn't expecting him until 3:00 or later. He had time.

Turning first toward the tangle that surrounded the Nelson house, he stepped along the gravel to what had once been the drive at the right hand side. When Bobby and he were teenagers there'd been an old barn-like shed there, opposite the house. It was in that shed that Bobby and his father, Bob senior, had constructed the boat that had pulled them all on water skis every summer over the emerald-green Smith River. He smiled at the memory.

But the shed where the boat had been built was gone. There was nothing there now but more blackberries – not even the hint of a foundation.

At the side of the yellow house an inset open porch was protected from the elements by the main house roof. He stepped up the rickety stairs and tried the back door. Locked. On the wall opposite the door was an electric outlet, and pipes for hot and cold water – where the washing machine had been fixed, he remembered.

For a moment he stood on the little porch, examining the walls and boarded-up windows carefully, looking for some other sign left over from all those years before. There was nothing.

Stepping down the steps again he moved around to the back of the house – or at least as far as the massed blackberry vines allowed. The windows at the back were boarded over, too. He'd hoped to get a glimpse inside at least, to remind himself of the layout of the interior.

But that was not possible.

He turned to look down the hill beyond the house, searching for the pathway that had led through the trees to the river and the little dock where the boat had been moored in the summers, and where they had lolled away the free summer afternoons and occasional nights – swimming, water skiing, camping together with other friends around crackling driftwood fires, drinking secreted beer and talking girls and sports and fast cars. All so long ago.

The path, too, was gone. A curtain of salal and tan oak formed an impenetrable barrier at the tree line.

There was nothing here anymore of young Bobby Nelson, or of his tall, slender mother Marge (with the dark eyebrows and the kind face), or of the heavy-set little man that was Bobby's millwright father (who'd always worn bib overalls and an engineer's billed cap). It was as if they'd never been there.

At a high school reunion a couple years before he had heard that Bobby was now living somewhere around Portland. There was an address for him in the reunion book. He made a mental note to write him sometime, to tell him about visiting his old house and to find out what he'd done with himself for the last fifty years. He wanted to know that – and to know that Bobby was okay still.

Pulling out a cigarette, he retraced his steps to the road and the car. He lit the cigarette with a lighter from his pocket and for several minutes stood smoking and staring across the road at the forlorn green house that had once been his home.

No cars came by. There was no sound, save for the calling of crows and jays in the distant woods.

Finally he flipped the cigarette into the gravel at his feet, ground it out with his toe, and stepped across the asphalt to the sloping driveway.

It flanked the house on the left, and ended at a timber framed garage at the back corner, doorless, and only just wide enough for one vehicle. Like the house, it was clad in green-stained redwood shakes. At the left of the drive – where once there had been a split-rail redwood fence and rhododendron bushes – an untidy hedge of myrtle closed off the view of the lower pasture. At some point someone had pushed a road around past the garage, towards the stand of second growth redwood and young Douglas fir beyond.

When he lived there a magnificent virgin redwood forest had stood behind the house, stretching away for miles over the hills. Only a stone's throw from the back door, these massive trees had offered him then a cathedral place of sanctuary and peace, the shadowy silence seemingly filled with the reverberant mystery of the ages. But Simpson Lumber Company had put an end to all that.

Coming home for Christmas his first year at college he discovered that the area behind the house had been turned into a wasteland of gargantuan stumps, broken limbs, mud and brush that seemed to go on endlessly. The redwoods were gone. The cost of progress, he guessed. It broke his heart.

But that was years ago. Time enough had passed since for a thick forest of second growth to blank out the scars of the brutal clearcut. If you hadn't seen it, that decimation, you wouldn't know it'd ever happened – or that those majestic trees had ever existed here.

At the front of the house – surrounding a modest rectangle of yard with a waist-high redwood stump planter prominent in one corner – a wire mesh fence sagged between redwood posts. On the driveway side a gate swung loosely on its hinges. The grass – which he well remembered mowing with a push mower as a boy – grew now ankle-high in clumps and knots, couch grass and coarse weeds bunched untidily together. He remembered that lawn after a mowing, soft to his bare feet – comforting to lie back on to watch the fluffy clouds crawling by overhead on the long, lazy summer afternoons.

Tentatively he pushed open the gate.

There was no walkway from the gate to the porch now. In his day a boarded walk led up to the front steps, though the family always entered from the door at the back of the house. Now there was nothing – not even a worn track through the grass. Even redwood eventually rots away, he guessed. And half a century is a long time.

Stepping into the front yard he turned to close the gate – out of old habit – and found the latch on the post had gone.

He turned back to the house.

The two windows to the left of the front door looked into the bare kitchen. He stepped forward – standing where once his comely stepmother (long since dead and gone) had knelt to plant irises and gladioli and nasturtiums – and pressed his face against the dirty glass, tunnelling his eyes with his hands. Inside worn linoleum covered the floorboards. There was no furniture. Dust and litter had collected in the corners.

An empty light socket hung suspended from the ceiling. On the back wall a door led to the back porch and the woodshed. Beside the door the small sliding window was positioned still above the sink. As a boy he had washed the dinner dishes at that sink. (He remembered watching their German Shepherd playing out back with the little girls while he did so, hearing their squeals of delight and the excited barking of the dog, smelling the smoke of an Old Gold cigarette wafting from behind him as his stepmother sat thumbing idly through the latest Montgomery Ward catalogue at the kitchen table.)

Not much had changed in the arrangement of things, but still it seemed strangely unfamiliar to him, as if those who had passed through in the interval had wiped away all trace of that earlier tenancy with the trivial repetition of their own domestic routines.

Money had been scarce in those years. His father (dead twenty years now) was then driving tanker or freight trucks, and sometimes even logging trucks out of the woods, or flatbeds hauling freshly-milled lumber from the local mills down to Eureka to be shipped across the sea to Japan and the Far East. But there were months at a time when there had been no work for him, and the family's meagre resources were stretched to their limits. In those times, he remembered, great pots of beans or cabbage stews or thick potato soup sat simmering on the woodstove, with maybe a few bacon chunks or a ham hock added to enhance the flavour. Great stuff – especially when dipped into with slabs of fresh homemade bread slathered with real butter churned from the milk of the cow they'd kept for a year or two. Things had been tight at those times, yes, but they'd always eaten well. His stomach rumbled at the memory.

Once his father had returned from town with the old green and white '56 Chevy pickup's bed crawling with a dozen giant King crabs – live gifts from his wife's fisherman brother-in-law (they all helped one another in those days). They ate exceptionally well that night.

Then there was the garden at the back of the house, filled with succulent vegetables – chard and corn and beans, squash and carrots, lettuces and tomatoes, a cornucopia of produce that kept the family hale and healthy through the summer and into the autumn (it had been his annual spring job to turn the earth before the planting). The canned surplus got the family through the winters, too, and sometimes those winters had been long and bleak.

In those days, he remembered, his stepmother wasn't drinking so much. She was happy then, and worked hard for all of them, and for herself.

The house front door opened directly into the kitchen. Stepping around the small porch with its worn wooden steps he moved to the two windows in the centre of the house, where the tiny living room was situated. Drawing close he peered inside.

The space was even smaller than he remembered, but there was still a stuffed chair in one corner where as a boy he had sat to do his homework (not the same chair, of course). In those days there'd also been a mahogany stereo suite (his dad had spent some money on it, he recalled) that played 33 1/3 RPM vinyl records daily – Mantovani and Lawrence Welk, and from time to time good music, too: Beethoven and

Mozart and Bach. It was his stepmother after all who had introduced him to the classics.

And opera. She'd always been a sucker for opera. All the sentimental ones: *La Traviata* and *La Bohème* and *Madame Butterfly*. Some days, when his father was away working and she was alone in the house with the little girls, she would turn the sound up loud so she could hear it wherever she happened to be, inside or out – making beds or weeding in the garden or sewing on her machine at the kitchen table – and she would sing along with it, 'la-la'ing her way through the incomprehensible foreign lyrics. He remember being outside at those times, playing alone (or with Bobby) at frontiersmen and Indians in the trees, and hearing the strains of Butterfly's aria 'One Fine Day', or Roger and Mimi's '*O Soave Faniculla*' wafting across the distance with his stepmother's thin voice as a counterpoint, and pausing to wonder.

The country-bred girl had always wanted, at least once in her life, to see an opera sung live upon the stage, in San Francisco or Portland. But that had never happened. Raised in the Nevada desert, she feared and distrusted cities, hated spending time in them. And anyway, money was always too scarce.

At the right front of the house was his parents' bedroom. For some reason a faded beige curtain had been left hanging askew over the windows, preventing a clear view of the inside. Not that there would've been much to see. In the old days there'd only been a chest of drawers and the large double bed with a small bedside table and lamp, and, in one corner, a small closet. He moved close again, straining to see beyond the curtain and the begrimed glass...

• • •

33

He had decided to take her into their bedroom because his own bed was just a single and the other bed in the room – the one shared by his half-sisters – was covered with stuffed toys and childish clutter. Not the kind of place conducive to making love, he had reckoned.

'You sure they won't come back?' the girl had asked, with raised eyebrows.

'Nah. They've gone to Brookings to do some shopping. They won't be home for hours.' He reached for her, pulled her into his arms. 'Come here, you.'

She lifted her face, smiling, and he kissed her then, deeply. She responded readily, grasping handfuls of the back of his shirt. After a moment, she pulled back.

'It feels funny, being here. In their room. You sure it's okay?'

'Why wouldn't it be? Who's going to know, anyway? I'll take you home in an hour or so and no one'll be any the wiser.'

He reached for her again.

'Wait a minute.' She pulled away. 'Don't be so pushy. There's no stopwatch, you know. It's not a track and field event.'

On the top of the chest of drawers a few framed photographs caught her eye. She wandered over to them, picked one up – a photo of the boy's father, wearing a broad western hat and cowboy shirt and sporting a dark handlebar moustache. He was climbing out of a sleek black '49 Buick convertible with its top down, and had a cheeky smile on his face.

'He's good-looking, your dad. I like the moustache. When was this taken?'

The boy stepped closer and ran his arms around her from behind, pulling her against him as he glanced over her shoulder at the picture.

'At the rodeo, when he and Laura were first going out. He grew the moustache specially. Laura likes that picture. Says it's of her own private cowboy.'

'Hmm.'

Carefully she returned the picture to its place. Passing over a framed photo of the two little girls taken beside the nasturtium-covered stump in the front yard she picked up the studio portrait of Laura herself – her long auburn hair falling to her shoulders, her face peering out in that half-smile the boy always found so alluring.

'She's younger than your dad, isn't she?'

'Yeah,' he muttered, nibbling on her earlobe. 'Fifteen years.'

'How did they meet?'

He tried to turn her around.

'Never mind all that. Come on. We don't have much time...'

'No!' She shook him off, and stepped away to sit on the bed, still holding the photograph. 'Tell me. I want to know.'

Sighing, he moved to sit beside her, glancing down at the picture.

'It was after the divorce. Dad moved down here from Oregon to take a job driving tanker trucks. Laura was working as a waitress at Tommy's. He liked the look of her, I guess. Took her out a few times, and that was that.'

'She's very pretty.'

The boy shrugged. 'I guess so.'

The girl turned to him, smiling mischievously.

'Don't you ever dream about her? About ... you know ... doing things to her? I bet you do.'

Blushing, the boy turned away.

'Don't be stupid.'

'I'll bet you do,' she said again, reaching to poke a finger into his ribs. 'She's got big titties. I bet you dream of getting your hands on them all the time, don't you? Come on, admit it!' She put her hand on the inside of his thigh and squeezed. 'I know what you boys think about. Don't pretend you don't.'

He pushed her hand away and stood up. Grabbing the picture, he returned it to its place on the tall chest of drawers, then swung around to lean his back against it, crossing his arms and scowling down at her.

'If you're just going to make fun of me I'll take you home. I didn't

bring you out here for that.'

Still smiling she stood and moved towards him, swinging her shoulders coquettishly.

'What did you bring me out here for then?'

'You know damn well what for. And we're wasting time. You promised, remember?'

Reaching out she pulled his crossed arms apart, snuggled herself close against him.

'I haven't forgotten. It's true though, isn't it? You do like her?'

'Laura? 'Course I like her.' He frowned. 'She's my stepmom.'

'But she's not that much older than you, is she? And she's awful pretty.' She put her arms around him, pushed her breasts into his chest, smiling up at him. 'Come on, admit it. You'd like to do things to her, wouldn't you?'

'Course I would. I'd have to be a block of wood not to ... to think about it sometimes. Anybody would. But that's crazy nonsense. What I really want is you. And right now.'

He raised his hands, cupped her face, lifted it for a searching kiss. She allowed herself to be drawn by his passion, her body stirring against his. Pushing a thigh between his legs, she could feel his firmness coming.

'Then why don't you take me?' she murmured. 'Who's stopping you?'

She kissed him again, her tongue delving deep into his mouth.

Minutes later they lay entwined together, naked on the quilted bedspread, their clothes discarded on the floor.

The boy moaned as he felt her hand move over him, his own exploring the dark secret between her legs.

'Ooooo, I want you, baby. I want you now!'

Rolling her onto her back the boy slid over her, preparing himself for the moment he'd long dreamt of, his pulse racing. But she pushed him back suddenly, with both hands on his chest.

'Wait! Stop!'

He stared at her.

'What?'

'Don't you have one of those ... things? A rubber? You better put it on now. I don't want to get pregnant, you know.'

The boy frowned.

'Don't you take those pills? I thought you'd take care of all that stuff. Anyway, I can always pull out at the last minute.'

She made an exasperated face.

'You're unbelievable! First of all, those pills are not given out to high school girls, dummy – even if you boys wished that they were. Secondly there's no guarantee even if you did 'pull out' there wouldn't be any little spermies left inside that could get me into trouble.'

He stared at her, blinking, a troubled frown on his face.

She reached up to caress his cheek.

'Look, silly, I do want you, just as much as you want me. But we have to be careful, that's all. Wouldn't your father have any lying around, in a drawer somewhere maybe? Any ... Trojans?'

The boy lifted himself off and lay beside her.

'I don't know. I guess I can look.'

'Well, you better. We're not doing anything without one. And get a towel.'

And he did look. Spent ten minutes searching through the chest of drawers, turning over clothes, lifting out and opening boxes, looking on shelves in the closet – even taking a peek under the bed. But without success. Apparently his father didn't mind living dangerously. But then, if you're a grown man, the boy guessed, you can afford to take risks. Or maybe he just knew a lot more about how to prevent unwanted babies.

Finally he stood looking down at her, lying naked on the bed with her hands behind her head, her legs demurely crossed – a dream of sex waiting to be made real. And shrugged.

'No luck.'

The girl pushed out her lip in an exaggerated pout.

'Then we can't do it. Sorry.'

She moved to get up, swinging her legs to the floor.

'Wait!' The boy sat beside her, taking her hand. 'I've got an idea. Something I think'll work. I thought about it before.'

'What?'

He hesitated, half-smiling, stroking her fingers. 'Don't laugh. You're gonna laugh sure as hell. Please don't.'

'I won't. I won't laugh.' She grasped his hand. 'Tell me. What?'

'Saran Wrap.'

The girl's hands flew to her mouth.

'Saran Wrap! You gotta be kidding!'

'No! I'm serious! If I wrap myself up in it surely no sperms can get out? Nothing can get through that. We'll be safe then.' He reached to grasp her shoulders, turning her so that she faced him. 'Come on, it's worth a try, isn't it? I do want you so.'

And he kissed her again, one hand moving to cup a breast, brushing the pink nipple gently with his thumb.

She moaned, pulling him closer.

'OK. Let's try it! Anything. I want you, too!'

Of course, it hadn't worked, and the longed for 'first penetration' didn't happen – at least not then. Not that it mattered. Her ardent caresses and the feel of her smooth naked skin against his had been enough to bring him off – an exquisite explosion of sensation he would never forget.

So long ago.

• • •

Pulling back from the window, the man checked his watch. 2:45. He'd have to go soon. There wouldn't be enough time left for a proper visit if he didn't, and he had to return to Oregon tonight.

Moving around to the right side of the house he nearly stepped on a single iris stem that poked its violet flower proudly a few inches above the grass. Pausing, he stooped to examine it – wondering if it was wild or one left over from all those years ago, one that Laura had planted. He couldn't remember a bed at this corner but he might be mistaken.

So perfect, that iris. So exact. So delicate.

On a whim he reached out and plucked it, pushing his hand into the grass to sever it at its base. Standing again, he turned the flower this way and that, admiring its intricacy, its variegated colours.

The windows of his old bedroom were new – modern plastic frames fitted into the wall. He stepped forward again to look inside.

The room was empty. In the dim light peeling wallpaper sagged here and there from the walls. In one corner the door of the tiny closet stood open.

There was nothing to remind him of the years he had spent sleeping in that room, shouting at his half-sisters when they, giggling like demons, pushed cold toys against his feet under the covers when he slept late in the mornings – which he often did. How he had howled at them! How they had laughed at him. He smiled. Both middle-aged women now, with families of their own. And grandchildren.

Time passes.

As he stepped back he caught a glimpse of himself reflected in the window. The deeply-lined face, the thinning hair, the thickness at the waist that had once been so slim. Shaking his head he turned away – to discover a small girl in a pinafore dress standing a few paces away, clutching a cloth doll in her arms and frowning at him.

He straightened.

'Hello, there. Where did you come from?'

The child pointed off behind the house into the trees. When he looked closely he could make out a worn pathway there and, beyond through the branches, the outlines of a house and outbuildings. He hadn't noticed them before. That would explain the road around the garage.

'Ahhh,' he breathed.

For a long moment they stood staring at one another. Awkwardly. Then the girl spoke.

'Mister, you don't belong here. This isn't your house.'

There was a silence. Then he smiled at her. And nodded.

'You know, you're right. I don't belong here. Not anymore.'

And extending his arm he offered the perfect iris to the child.

Minutes later – his brief glimpse into the windows of the past concluded – he was winding again down the narrow road in the hired car, with the breeze off the distant river blowing over his face. On his way to his annual summer visit with his dear old friend, the lonely widow who, as a girl of seventeen, had once found Saran Wrap so amusing.

(London, 2009)

A Small Town Event

"There are two ways of spreading light: to be the candle or the mirror that reflects it."
– Edith Wharton

(For Doris Whalen, who was both.)

Ellen Ainsley sat at her dressing table examining the sombre face in the mirror before her. Over her shoulder she could see Tom standing in the doorway behind, his arms crossed, staring at her with knitted brows.

'I mean it, Ellen,' he said. 'These people are all bark and no bite. They haven't got the guts to do anything serious. There's not a damned thing they could do that you really have to worry about.'

'I'm not worried for myself, Tom,' she countered. 'I'm worried for the girls. You know how awful kids can be to one another. Suppose people talk about me in front of their kids and they bring their parents' bad feelings to school and take it out on April and Dawn? There're lots of ways to get at me, darling. They don't have to go after me directly.'

Tom shook his head.

'Come on, honey. The whole thing's just a tempest in a teapot. I'm sure it won't come to that.'

'Well, it's already to the point where people are making threats. What's to prevent them going further?'

That afternoon Ellen had arrived home from school to discover in their roadside mailbox a seagull with a broken neck resting on a printed note. 'Beware the wages of wickedness!' it read. 'Ocean City will not allow its children to be corrupted! Desist or suffer the consequences!'

Shocked and shaken, Ellen had called Tom the minute she was inside the house. Tom had hurried home and together they'd buried the dead bird while the children were still next door at Mrs. Gale's, the neighbour who looked after them till Ellen and Tom finished work. Then Tom had called Daryl Harding, the Ocean City Chief of Police and a close friend, who had immediately come round.

'Okay,' Daryl had said, gripping his mug of coffee. 'I know most of this story 'cause I read about it in the *Clarion*. But tell me it all again if you don't mind, Ellen.'

Ellen had sat opposite him on the divan, her hands clasped on her knees.

'Well, there's not much to tell. Some weeks ago I had the idea of offering sex education as a part of my Junior and Senior Psychology classes. The kids seem to know shockingly little about these things. I mentioned it to Tom, who thought it was a great idea. He took my proposal to Gus Taney, who also supported it. I knew … we all knew … there would be objections raised. Ocean City is, after all, a small town, and small towns are not known for their tolerance towards progressive ideas. Not to mention the number of fundamentalist churches there are in this county. Which is why I went public first. I called the *Clarion* and asked them to do an article explaining my intentions, describing what I wanted to cover in the course and the way I meant to cover it. I pointed out very clearly that this part of the course would only be available to those students whose parents signed a letter of consent. All others would be given separate assignments for library work. I also offered to meet with anyone who wanted to discuss the matter with me further.' She glanced across at Tom, who stood leaning against the bar nursing a whisky and soda. 'I had no idea there'd be such a public outcry about it, such indignation. Altogether I've received a couple dozen letters – mostly from local clergy and church people – all vehemently opposed to the idea. I couldn't believe the tone of some of them. The unsigned ones were terrible, calling me all kinds of names. You'd think I was advocating reckless promiscuity the way they went on. When it's precisely the opposite I'm striving for – a mature, informed and cautious attitude to sex, realizing all of its implications and consequences.'

Daryl smiled wryly. 'If you're hoping for a rational understanding of your intentions and motives, Ellen, you're not going to find it with those types. They just see it as you turning their kids on to sex and they don't like it.'

'That's why Gus and I thought it'd be a good idea to have the public meeting,' Tom put in from the bar. 'So those members of the public who want to raise objections can do so in a formal way and have their concerns answered directly. Ellen agreed to that from the start. But that hasn't stemmed the tide of nastiness she's encountering.'

Daryl lifted the threatening note from his lap and looked at it again. 'Meaning this?'

'Not only that.' Ellen took a deep breath. 'Since the article appeared in the paper several mothers have come by the high school specially and told me in no uncertain terms they think it's not only a bad idea, but that it smacks of the devil's teaching. They question whether I've lost my mind. I get glares everywhere I go – the supermarket, the service station. People are angry. And now there's this business with the note and the dead seagull.'

'Hmm.' Daryl shifted forward. 'I don't suppose it's worth asking if anyone saw who put it in your mailbox?'

Ellen shook her head.

'I doubt it. The end of the drive is out of sight from other houses, and there's little traffic on the road. No, there's no knowing who put it there, or when.'

Tom stepped forward into the room.

'I don't think we'll find out who sent the note, Daryl. I just thought you should know what's going on in case anything else happens. Though I really don't expect it will.'

'Nor do I.' The lanky policeman drained his cup and rose to his feet. 'But I'll make sure the patrols pass your house twice every hour to keep an eye on things, just in case. The meeting's tomorrow night, right?'

'Yes,' Ellen said, also standing. 'At seven-thirty at the high school.'

'Well, I'll be there. The fundamentalists will have a chance to air their objections and then everything can settle down again. That's what I reckon will happen, anyway.'

'Me, too,' Tom agreed.

The policeman made his way towards the front of the house, followed by Tom and Ellen. At the open door, he turned to them once more.

'I want you to know, Ellen, I'm with you a hundred percent on this. We've had too many unwed mothers in this county over the last few years. Anything we can do to prevent that happening has got to be a good thing. In any case, you can be sure my Jennie will be in the class. In fact, I'm going to insist on it.'

Ellen smiled, extending her hand.

'Thanks, Daryl. I'm glad you're on my side. It means a lot to me.'

Harding shook her hand, warmly. Then he doffed his cap and stepped away down the steps to his car. In a moment, with a wave, he was out the driveway and gone, leaving Ellen and Tom looking after him.

Later that evening across town, in a comfortably appointed house overlooking the sea, Hiram Abrams, pastor of the Foursquare Evangelical Mission – one of the foremost and best attended churches in Ocean City – had just slipped into his pyjamas when the phone rang downstairs in the front room. Edith, his wife, took the call and a moment later called up to him.

'Hiram, it's Ralph Butler on the phone. He wants to talk to you. Says it's important.'

'Left it pretty late, didn't he?' Hiram grumbled, grabbing his dressing gown and heading downstairs. 'Couldn't it wait till morning?'

'Hello, Ralph,' he barked, taking the phone from his wife and pressing it to his ear. 'What's so all-fired important you have to phone me at this ungodly hour?'

'Reverend Abrams, I admit it's a bit late and I apologize for that. Fact is I've only just got home from a meeting and I wanted to talk to you before the day finished.'

'What about?'

'Well, the meeting I was at was with a few other concerned parents in our neighbourhood. We're not at all happy about that sex education class the high school's intending to offer our kids. We see it as the thin edge of a wedge that's going to bring in a lot of immoral liberal foolishness to the teaching curriculum, and we want to do something about it. We thought you might want to come on board.'

'To do what particularly, Ralph? You know I'm against the class. I've made my feelings perfectly clear publicly in my letter to the *Clarion.*'

'We know that, Reverend. But Ellen Ainsley's the principal's wife, after all. She has a lot of friends in this town, and they might be blinded to the real threat of what she wants to do. We thought if we all teamed up together – and if you'd be kind enough to speak for us – we might make a stronger impact at the meeting tomorrow night. We've got to stop this thing happening one way or another. The town's going to the devil fast enough as it is.'

'Well, Ralph, you know I agree with you about that. For what it's worth I can tell you I spoke today with the pastors of several other churches in the county and they were all unanimous in their condemnation of the plan. There're a lot of folks who are against this thing. I think if we all turn up tomorrow and show a united front we'll kill it dead in its tracks.'

'But will you speak for us, sir? You know, you can put words together better than any of us can.'

This allusion to the pastor's renowned skill as a public speaker flattered the man's exaggerated sense of self-importance and warmed his heart.

'All right, Ralph. I'll be happy to do that. This sort of thing can't be allowed to happen. It's against the law of God and human decency. One woman and her hair-brained ideas can't stand against a whole community and win, surely not.'

Ralph Butler murmured his agreement. Moments later the conversation ended and Hiram Abrams replaced the receiver in its cradle.

'Well, dear?' Edith said, peering around the kitchen door. 'What was it he wanted?'

'Oh, just more people concerned about that woman and her proposed sex classes. They want me to be their spokesperson at the meeting tomorrow and I agreed to do it. Told him not to worry, that common sense would win out in the end and it just wouldn't happen.'

'Well,' Edith said, wiping her hands on a dish cloth, 'I hope you're right. Otherwise heaven only knows what the young people of this town will get up to – when they're actually taught how to get themselves into trouble.'

Frowning, Hiram turned towards the stairs again, recalling Tom Ainsley's attractive wife, who was given to wearing daringly short skirts and sleeveless blouses open at the neck – deliberately flaunting her feminine attractions, clearly.

'Edith,' he said, turning, 'knowing that woman and her free thinking ways, I'd not be surprised if she intended to *show* them what to do, and that's the truth of it! She's got no right to force her crazy liberal ways on a community that knows better, and tomorrow night we'll make sure she understands that.'

Then Hiram went off to bed, with his teeth tightly clenched, smug in the certainty of his own righteousness and determined that no such pernicious waywardness would be allowed to take root in his patch on his watch.

Bayview High School was situated on a street parallel to and not far from the Pacific, tucked away from it and the nearby houses behind a stand of wind-blown fir trees. It was a new structure, having only been opened a few years before. Being the only high school in the county, pupils from all the far-flung corners were brought by bus and mini-bus into Ocean City for classes every day – some having to commute an hour each way to school and home again. Bayview was therefore a large school with a student population of some 2000 students, and the teaching staff under the supervision of Principal Tom Ainsley was equally large and diverse. Tom was immensely proud of them, and under his guidance the level of academic excellence the school had achieved (considering its remoteness at the north end of the state) was remarkable – several former pupils having acquitted themselves extremely well at prestigious universities within the state and nationwide.

Ocean City itself, however, and the county as a whole was not, and could not be, considered a progressive and enlightened community. The area, developed in the latter nineteenth century by pioneer families who came to exploit the natural resources then in abundance – great tracts of arable farmland, a healthy fishing industry, and extensive forests of giant redwoods to be felled and milled – had seemed a temperate paradise to the first-comers. And so in a sense it had been – until the commercial fishing dwindled due to over-harvesting, and the government (fearful of losing all the state's redwood forests) had put a moratorium on logging and imposed severe restrictions. Over half a century the county began to close down, as jobs dried up and residents moved elsewhere. The numbers of businesses and services shrank to accommodate the reduced population, and as the fortunes of the county suffered so did its interest in enlightenment and cosmopolitanism. Ocean City's residents exemplified the small town mentality in all too many ways – in spite of an energetic contingent of intellectuals (professionals, educators, etc.) who desperately sought to keep abreast of new ideas and developments. In short, Ocean County was – for the most part – pureblood redneck country, and new ideas of any sort were generally met with scorn and mistrust, if not outright hostility. It was into this demographic minefield that Ellen Ainsley had, for the best of reasons, introduced her scheme for teaching basic sex education to her fifteen and sixteen year old students – with, of course, the consent of their parents. She had known she would encounter objections, but the degree of hostility she experienced surprised even her. She had never believed Ocean City was quite so reactionary.

Accordingly, it was with genuine trepidation that she climbed onto the passenger seat of Tom's Volvo the following evening and watched her husband take his place beside her to drive to the high school and the public meeting, a confrontation which she now dreaded.

'You okay, honey?' Tom asked, as he closed his door and reached to start the engine.

'I'm fine. A little nervous, that's all.'

'Completely understandable, under the circumstances.' He squeezed her knee. 'It'll all be fine, Ellen. Believe me.'

She smiled at him. 'I hope so. We'll still have to live in this town, Tom, when it's all over.'

For the time of year – April – the weather that day had been glorious, warm and bright. By the evening, however, the wind had changed direction, the temperature had dropped and there was a haze of low cloud and fog that hugged the sea, slowly making its way landwards and reducing the ambient light to a dull grey pallor. Though she was used to such conditions, having lived in the county for almost ten years now, Ellen found the dwindling light oppressive and depressing. Wryly she realized how closely the conditions matched her mood as Tom swung the car into the high school parking lot and made for the staff parking area. Then her awareness snapped to attention.

'Tom! Look at all these cars! It's as crowded as during the day.'

'Yep. It's full all right. And people are still coming. I hope Vern put out enough seats.'

The meeting was to be held in the school cafeteria, with the lunchtime tables and benches collapsed and stored away and rows of folding chairs set out for the public seating.

'It isn't just older people, either, Ellen. Look at the number of kids who've come along. I must say, I didn't expect that.'

And it was true. Here and there, amidst the groups of adults that stood about talking together, clusters of students lounged by their parked hotrods and old bangers, or leaned against the walls near the school's main entrance. Seeing the Ainsley car moving past them, many turned their heads to smile and wave. Encouragement, Ellen wondered? Or gleeful anticipation of her impending public vilification?

Tom pulled the car into his allotted space and killed the engine. Looking across, he reached out to cover her hand with his and squeezed it.

'Okay, darling. Let's go face down the dragons.'

By 7:30, the time appointed for the meeting, the cafeteria was packed. All the seats were filled and scores of people were standing around the room's periphery. At one end, at a table on the raised stage, Tom, Ellen and County Superintendent of Schools Gus Taney sat chatting quietly, eyeing the audience soberly as they filed in to take their places – some smiling up at them, others scowling with barely controlled indignation.

When Tom banged down his gavel to bring the meeting to order he was pleased to see Daryl Harding and one of his officers at the back of the room, leaning with folded arms against the walls on either side of the door. Their presence would insure nothing untoward could happen if tempers flared. At least, Tom hoped so.

'Good evening, folks,' he started, after the crowd murmurs had dwindled to stillness, 'and welcome to this public meeting. We all know why we're here, and I'm sure none of us want to spend any more time discussing this matter than is absolutely necessary. I know you all have things to do at home. So the way I thought we'd handle things tonight would be for Ellen … Mrs. Ainsley … to speak first to explain what she wants to do and why. Then District Superintendent Taney will say a few words, followed by myself. At the end we'll take questions from the floor. I hope that works for everybody. Ellen?'

Nervously, Ellen pushed back her chair and stood, smiling out at the sea of faces before her.

'Firstly, I want to thank you all for coming,' she began. 'It pleases me to see that Ocean City's parents take such an interest in their children's education, and I shall do my best to answer your questions and to address your concerns. I'm sure we all know by now what my intentions are, for I outlined them as carefully as I could in my article in the *Clarion* ten days ago. Basically, ever since I started teaching here at Bayview, I've been aware that the level of ignorance regarding sexual matters among some sections of our student body is quite alarming. And while I certainly believe the prime responsibility for offering instruction and advice on these things should rest with the parents, it seems to me that there's a reluctance, or an embarrassment, in some parents to accept that responsibility – creating a situation which, at best, leaves their children in a haze of uncertainty and misunderstanding about the subject, and at worst results in consequences that can be disastrous for the young people themselves and for their families. It is this haze of misconception and ignorance that I hope to eliminate by offering, in my psychology classes, a two week course of basic sex education, designed to explain fully the physical aspects of sex and reproduction, while also – and perhaps more importantly – emphasizing the moral and ethical responsibility that sexual activity demands.'

From here and there in the audience, murmurs of unrest could be heard, prompting Ellen to raise her voice slightly.

'As I have repeatedly said, this seminar will only be available to Juniors and Seniors whose parents approve of the idea. All other students will be given research projects in the library for those two weeks, and will not suffer in any way academically. Frankly I cannot see how anyone can object to the plan. If a parent disapproves, all they have to do is not sign the consent form.'

'That's surely not the issue, Mrs. Ainsley, and you know it isn't!' a male voice boomed from the hall. 'The fact is a high school classroom is no place for any discussion of sexual matters. That's the business of parents and religious leaders only, and should be dealt with, if at all, in the home!'

Looking around, Ellen found the speaker.

'As I said, Reverend Abrams, I totally agree with you. But unfortunately there are many young people at Bayview whose parents – for whatever reason – choose not to address this sexual ignorance, and that omission all too often leads to difficult and embarrassing consequences. I don't think I need to speak any more plainly. We all know what I mean and what's at stake here.'

'Ah, but do we?' Abrams thundered from the floor. 'It seems to me, Mrs. Ainsley, that you're simply spouting a load of progressive, liberal chop-logic that flies in the face of all traditional moral and religious teaching. You're a teacher, not a preacher. You should keep your concerns limited to the subjects that are normally taught in school – reading, writing and arithmetic – and leave the rest alone!'

To this, several shouts of 'Hear, hear!' and 'That's right, Pastor!' were heard to echo around the hall.

There then followed two or three other speakers from the floor – religious leaders, for the most part, from one fundamentalist faith or another – who echoed briefly and forcefully, but less fluently and in less strident words, the sentiments of the outspoken pastor of the

Foursquare Evangelical.

At this point, Superintendent Gus Taney, leaning forward, raised a hand and turned to Tom. 'Excuse me, Ellen. Tom, can I say something here?'

'Please do.'

As Gus rose Ellen settled back in her chair, somewhat shell-shocked.

'First of all, with all due respect, Reverend Abrams,' Taney commenced, nodding in the direction of the irate cleric, 'you're wrong to suggest that our school curriculum avoids controversial subjects. As you should know, we've been teaching a lot more than reading, writing and arithmetic for some time now. What about civics, for example – the study of our various levels of government and our responsibilities as citizens in this great democracy of ours? What about political and foreign policy issues? What about the ethical questions that're raised by new developments in science – stem cell research, for instance, and cloning? Are we not to discuss these things with our young people? Are they not to be shown how important these things are so they can make up their own minds about them? Surely sex is just as important a subject for them, at this point in their lives. They need to know the facts about it, and to be made aware of the moral and practical issues involved. Wouldn't you agree?'

Here and there in the hall murmurs of agreement could be heard, much to the annoyance of the good pastor and his contingent – one of whom, a middle-aged woman in a worn grey anorak, could contain herself no longer and rose angrily to her feet.

'That's all different! We're not talking about democracy or science here, we're talking about teaching our kids the facts of life long before they need that information. What's she trying to do, turn them into sex fiends?'

'On the contrary, Mrs. Davis,' Taney answered patiently. 'We're trying to educate them so that they'll understand how important it is to be prudent in these matters, so that, through ignorance, they won't get themselves into trouble. I think that's a pretty moral and righteous thing to do, don't you?'

Now another voice was raised, a man's, from the back of the hall.

'My kids know better'n to mess around before they get married. They know I'd beat hell out of 'em if they ever got into trouble!'

Which evoked a ripple of laughter and another chorus of 'That's rights!' and 'You said it, brothers!' When the noise died down, Pastor Hiram Abrams, sensing his moment, rose again to his feet.

'You see, Mr. Taney?' he brayed pompously, smiling at the crowd surrounding him. 'You're wrong. Listen to the people in this hall. Just listen to what they're saying. We're all against what Mrs. Ainsley's intending. There's no need for meddling in these matters, and we'll do our best to stop you going ahead with it. How can we hope to keep our youngsters on the straight and narrow when their very teachers want to lead them down the road to iniquity?'

A veritable roar of approval filled the hall, with several irate parents leaping to their feet, shaking their fists in the air and bawling angry epithets:

'The Pastor's right! You know what you can do with your crazy ideas! Why don't you go back to the big city where you belong?'

At this point, Gus Taney, turning to Tom, shrugged and sat down, shaking his head. Tom, however, was in no mood to surrender to the bullying from the floor. Instead, standing again in the midst of the opprobrious caterwauling, he raised both hands in the air, palms out.

'Wait a minute! Just wait a minute, here!' he shouted. And when the angry cries and murmurs subsided sufficiently, he went on. 'All right. We've heard several speakers now who are obviously against the idea...'

'You better believe it!' shouted someone from the back.

'Well,' Tom continued, 'how about hearing from someone now who isn't against Mrs. Ainsley's plan? Surely there must be someone here who agrees with her and what she intends to do? Someone who sees the importance of this for the students?'

For a long moment there was silence as every pair of eyes roamed the hall, looking for someone, anyone, who might have the courage to speak out in the face of such naked anger. And when, after a few moments, it seemed that no one was going to stand to defend Ellen, Pastor Abrams turned again towards the stage with a look of smug satisfaction.

'You see? I told you. There's no one in this hall who agrees with her, and that's the truth of it! Now, will you just accept the obvious and desist from going ahead with your diabolical plan?'

'Excuse me...' came a tentative voice from behind him.

As Abrams turned, a thin young man wearing glasses, a student, in a white shirt and chinos, slowly got to his feet.

'I believe Mrs. Ainsley's right,' he enunciated, nervously. 'What's more, I think Ocean City should be grateful to her. This town needs more people like her to fight the closed-mindedness of some of our stuck-in-the-mud leaders.' Here he cast a pointed glance in the direction of the good pastor, who was still on his feet, glowering.

Across the hall a second young person stood up – a girl this time, with shoulder-length red hair, dressed in a smart blue blouse and long skirt.

'That's right, Paul. Mrs. Ainsley's trying to help us, not harm us. And if my parents sign the consent form – which I'm sure they will – I'm going to take that class myself. We need to know these things so we won't make mistakes that could ruin our lives. That's all she's trying to do, save us from doing something stupid, and there's nothing wrong with that. What's wrong with you people?' She looked about her with amazement and disbelief. 'How can you say such terrible things about someone who works so hard for her students? It's not right what you're doing. She deserves better than that.' Looking back towards the stage, she concluded: 'She deserves the best, because that's what she always gives us of herself.'

'That's right, Val,' said another young man, standing. 'I think Mrs. Ainsley's right, too.'

'So do I,' said another girl, rising in another area of the hall.

'And me,' said a third.

Suddenly all across the hall young people were standing, one after another, defiantly, wanting to be counted. Putting themselves on the line out of loyalty to a teacher they loved and respected, and for a cause they could clearly see the value of. Finally, confronted by so many young people standing to show their solidarity, and by the growing number of parents who overcame their timidity and joined them, the good pastor, Hiram Abrams, sank back into his chair, his face a mask of disgruntled frustration.

Tom Ainsley, standing behind the table on the raised stage, smiled down at his audience.

'Thank you, all of you.' Turning towards Abrams he added: 'You see, Reverend Abrams, you were wrong. There's plenty of support for Ellen's idea here this evening – not least from the very people she's hoping to help, our young people. And now, I believe, we can go ahead with implementing the plan. Thanks to all of you for coming along.'

And with that the meeting broke up.

Stepping down to floor level, Ellen found herself surrounded by a crowd of enthusiastic students and parents whose smiling faces filled her with relief and joy – and renewed her faith in her judgement as a teacher and mentor of young minds.

Some weeks later, after application forms for the controversial classes had been sent out for parental consent and a sizeable proportion of the students were given permission to attend, the classes were launched without incident. The ten young people whose parents refused to allow them to attend were given research assignments for those two weeks, and during the class time were sent off to the library, while Ellen Ainsley carried on in her classroom with her remaining students her careful exploration of the physiological, practical and moral aspects of the 'birds and the bees'.

One afternoon during the first week of the classes Tom arrived home with an unusual twinkle in his eye when he bent to kiss Ellen, marking papers in her favourite chair.

'What's with you?' she asked, intrigued. 'You look like you're bursting to tell me something.'

'I am. But let me get myself a drink first. It's been a long and … a rather amusing day.'

Moments later he returned to sit opposite her in his own large armchair in the family room.

'So?' she asked.

He smiled.

'Something came to my attention today that I thought would amuse you.'

'What was that?'

'You know the ten students whose parents refused to sign the consent forms? The ones you've sent to the library to do research projects during the sex education classes?'

'Yes? What about them?'

'Well,' said Tom, 'all but two of them were sent to me today for breaking school rules.'

Ellen sat up. 'Really? How, and why?'

Tom fought to suppress a smile.

'Bert Friel has a free hour between his algebra classes and he happened to step outside to enjoy the warm spring weather today when he chanced to see the eight students all huddled on the grass below the open windows of your classroom. Apparently they've been leaving the library every day soon after their arrival there and sneaking around to listen to your classes! So much for parental consent being required!'

'They what?' Ellen asked, now confused.

Tom sighed. 'For the last three days they've apparently left the library minutes after arriving and crawled round the outer wall of the school to your classroom windows to listen to your lectures. They only go back just before the bell.'

Ellen shook her head.

'I can't believe it!' she said, stunned. 'What did you do to them?'

'Nothing. Just told them not to do it again. That they could get you into a lot of trouble if their parents found out about it. But it just goes to show you,' he said with a smile, raising his glass to his wife in a toast. 'There's no stopping young minds hungry for knowledge – of all kinds – when they're really determined to have it!'

(London, 2013)

Fait Accompli

She found the place easily enough with the directions she'd been given – a simple, one-bedroom cottage set back from the road between two large Victorian houses with gingerbread scrollwork decorating their porches and eaves. At one time it'd probably been an outbuilding to one of the houses. Now a separate paved pathway led up to it through a sun-burned lawn and long-neglected flower borders.

Clutching her purse in one hand and her small overnight bag in the other, the girl turned off the sidewalk and started up the path.

The curtains were closed and there was no sign of life within, even though it was 10:30 on a bright summer morning.

When she reached the little porch, she set down the overnight case, pulled her jacket straight, brushed back her hair, and knocked on the outer screen door. When there was no reply, she knocked again, harder.

There was another long pause. Then the door opened and he stood there, bare-chested, barefoot, wearing hastily pulled on jeans. He blinked at her, then down at the overnight case, and frowned.

'Hey,' he said, thickly, 'what're you doing here?'

'Don't worry,' she returned. 'I've not come to stay. Sorry I woke you. Can I come in?'

He glanced behind him dazedly and scratched his head with one hand, trying to brush his long hair into some degree of tidiness.

'Unless you're not alone,' she added, lowering her voice.

He looked at her blankly. 'I'm alone. Yeah, I guess you can. Come on in.'

He moved back and she opened the screen door and stepped inside. He shut the door behind her. She stood in the middle of the small living room, glancing around at the clutter, clutching her purse and the overnight bag as he drew the curtains, letting in the light. Looking back at her, he frowned with irritation. When she turned in his direction, he smiled again, hurriedly.

'Well, this is a surprise. Want some coffee?'

'Yes, please. That'd be nice. Thank you.'

'I'll make some. Here, sit down.' He stepped across to the sofa to gather the discarded clothes and books that lay there. These he bundled into his arms and carried through into the adjacent bedroom, dumping the lot onto the unmade double bed. Grabbing up a shirt he hastily pulled it on, buttoned it and tucked it into his trousers. Then he stepped back into the living room and on into the small kitchen. The girl was now perched on the sofa, her purse resting on her skirted knees. The overnight bag was beside her on the floor.

She watched him as he rinsed, then filled the small percolator, measured several spoonfuls of fresh coffee into the drip tray, then reassembled the whole contraption and set it onto a ring on the electric range, which he turned on.

He looked the same, she thought. She hadn't seen him in almost four months, but he hadn't changed. Why should he? She was the one, after all, who had experienced all the excitement. If excitement was the correct word.

'How did you know where to find me?' he asked as he worked.

'I asked at the theatre. The box office people had a list of the actors and their addresses. I told the lady I was your sister.'

He looked at her and nodded.

'Smart move. Well,' he said again, 'this sure is a surprise.' He glanced at her, frowning slightly. 'Are you okay? You look a little pale.'

With one hand, she brushed back her hair. Then she shifted her position on the sofa.

'I'm fine. Now. Just fine.' She glanced around again. 'It just feels … strange, being here.'

'Yeah. Well, it's nice to see you. But what're you doing here? Why did you come?'

She put the purse beside her on the sofa and clasped both her hands over her knees, drawing them tightly together.

'I came because I have something to tell you that I thought you should know.'

'Oh?' He leaned against the kitchen doorframe. 'What?'

She looked down at the worn linoleum floor.

'In a minute. When the coffee's ready.'

He nodded. 'All right.'

For a moment he watched her from the doorway, her eyes still on the floor. He was surprised at how little he felt towards her now.

'When did you get here?' he asked finally, turning back into the kitchen.

She glanced towards him.

'Yesterday afternoon. On the Greyhound.'

'Are you staying with friends? I didn't think you knew anyone up here.'

Now she turned her attention to her hands, closely examining her fingernails, testing them with the nails of her other hand.

'I don't. No, I stayed in a hotel on Main Street. The Grand. Little place. Clean and cheap. Nice people.' She looked up at him again. 'I saw the play last night. You were good in it. It's a good part for you.'

He smiled and stepped to the doorway again, running a hand through his hair.

'You think? Gosh, it's nice of you to say so.'

'I always liked your work. You know that.'

'Yeah,' he said, awkwardly. 'Well... Thanks.'

Behind him the water groaned in the coffeepot as it heated towards the boiling point.

'Why didn't you look for me after?' he asked after a moment. 'You could've waited at the stage door. We could've had a coffee or something.'

'I did. I was on a bench by the side of the square when you came out with your friends. But there were still lots of people around. You didn't look in my direction, and I didn't feel right about ... about bothering you when you weren't alone.'

He stepped towards her now, hands in his pockets, looking down at her.

'It wouldn't have been a bother. It's good to see you.'

After a moment, he turned and stepped back into the kitchen, busying himself with rinsing and drying two coffee mugs.

'I followed you, though,' she said at last. 'I saw you in the tavern, through the open front door. You were in the back with your pals. Drinking beer and playing pool. Having a great time.'

'Yeah. That's what we do here. After. We have to wind down, you know? They're a good bunch of guys. We have a lot of fun together.'

She nodded. 'I could see.'

When the coffee had percolated the young man poured it into the two cups and brought them through into the living room. Handing one to the girl, he took the other and sat across the room in an armchair, draping the jacket that had been thrown down on it across the chair's back.

'How's your mom?' he asked. 'And your dad? They doing okay?'

'Yes. There're both fine. They keep busy with the garden. Dad feels at loose ends now he's retired. He misses the mill. The garden helps keep him occupied.'

'And your sister? She all right, too?'

'Debbie's fine, too. And her family.'

'And you're still in San Francisco, right? Working?'

'Yes. At I. Magnin's. Women's wear department.' She smiled, embarrassed. 'Not much of a job for a college graduate, but it's only temporary. I still want to teach.'

'You'll make a good teacher. I've always said you would. Don't give up on that.' He sipped his coffee. 'So. What is it you came to tell me?'

He watched as she raised her cup to her lips and sipped. Then she carefully leant forward to rest the cup on the small coffee table. Sitting back again, she clutched her hands on her knees as before, looking down at the floor, collecting herself. There was a moment of stillness before she spoke.

'I've had an abortion.'

She said it very evenly and clearly, straight out. Not accusingly, not as if she expected a shocked reaction or wanted one. Just as if she was announcing some commonplace event, something that everyone experiences at one time or another in their lives and it was just her turn.

He stared across at her, his brows gathering in a frown.

'You what?'

She looked up at him now, and a little shudder rippled her shoulders.

'I had an abortion. Two weeks ago. In Tijuana. It was your baby. Our baby.'

Carefully, the boy reached out to place his coffee mug on the small table beside him. Then he stood up.

'Let me understand this. You got pregnant? And it was my baby?'

She stared at him. 'Of course.'

'Why didn't you tell me?'

'You weren't around. And anyway, you told me we were through. That it was time to move on in your life, that you had no place right now for that kind of commitment.'

'Well, that's true, but...'

'I didn't want you to think I was trying to trap you into staying with me.'

The boy paced about the room, trying to come to terms with the news.

'You were pregnant. With *my* baby. And you just ... had an abortion? Just like that? You didn't even think to tell me about it?' He glared at her. 'How could you *do* that? Didn't you think I had a right to know?'

'I told you. I didn't want to trap you into a relationship I knew you didn't want. But I thought you should know that it happened. So I came to tell you.'

He swallowed, heavily. '*Why?*'

'Because it was your baby.'

'That's all? That's the only reason?'

She looked up at him, frowning. 'Of course. What other reason could there've been?'

For a long moment the boy said nothing. Then: 'Did your parents know?'

'My mother did. I had to tell somebody. We didn't tell Dad. He didn't need to know and it was better that way. He would've been ... upset. They both liked you, you know.' She touched her hair again. 'Mom was wonderful. She has a Mexican friend whose daughter got into trouble a year or two ago. The friend sent her daughter down to Tijuana to have the baby aborted. She knew about a clinic there. Mom asked her for the details. Then she took some money out of her savings account. She came with me, on the Greyhound. Waited for me in the clinic while they did it. Then we came back home.' She shuddered. 'It was awful. I started bleeding on the bus. I felt so ... unclean. So guilty.' She glanced up at him again. 'It's not easy to let someone kill your baby, you know? Especially when you wanted it more than anything else in the world.'

The boy stepped close, stunned. He knelt before her, grasping her hands with both of his, shaking his head in shocked disbelief as he stared into her eyes.

'Why didn't you keep it? Why didn't you come to me about it?

I would've done the honourable thing. You know that. I would've married you.'

'Yes, I knew that. But I also knew that wouldn't have been what you really wanted. That you would've seen the baby as a millstone around your neck, holding you down. That you'd finally come to hate me for it. And the baby. I couldn't face that. I didn't want it. For me. For the baby. It was better that it was dead. Gone. Better to have the slate clean for both of us.'

She dropped her head, her eyes wet now with tears that couldn't be held back.

The boy stared at her clasped hands, shaking his head as he stroked them.

'I'm sorry, baby. I'm so sorry. If only I'd known... If only you'd told me...'

She pulled one of her hands free and stroked his head tenderly, his long dark hair.

'Calm down. It's over now. It's all over. There was no need to involve you in it. I just thought you should know about it, that's all. So I came to tell you.'

After a moment she freed her other hand, gently pushed him away. Collecting her purse and her overnight bag, she stood upright, looking down at him.

'I have to go now. My bus leaves at noon. It's nearly eleven-thirty.'

The boy stood too, wiping his own wet eyes with the heels of his hands.

'Wait, I'll come with you. I just need to wash my face and ...'

'No. You stay here. Go back to bed if you want. I won't trouble you again. I just wanted you to know.'

'But your mother's savings. I should repay that. How much was it?'

He reached for his wallet.

'I don't want your money. I don't need it. I'll pay her back myself over time. She's not in any rush. I want it that way. This wasn't your doing, it was mine. And it's my debt.'

'Ellen ...' he said, reaching out for her. She backed away.

'No! Don't touch me. That's all over now. Don't pretend. I'll be all right. Go on with your life just as you wanted. You'll forget about it and about me and you'll go on. And hopefully I will, too. I just wanted you to know.'

The boy followed her with his eyes, dumbly, as she moved to the door, opened it, and left. Shuffling to the front window, he watched her pick her way down the walk to the street, then turn towards the town centre. When she'd passed out of sight behind the next-door hedge he returned to the armchair and sank into it.

She'd been right in keeping the news of her pregnancy from him. He knew that. It would've turned his life upside down.

But still he wondered what would've happened if she *had* come to tell him of it – just when his future seemed to hold such promise. There would've been no abortion, he was sure of that. The baby would've lived and thrived, one way or another. But at what cost?

And what would their child have been like?

Often over the years to come he would find himself thinking about that.

(London, 2010)

Regret

For her thirty-fifth birthday Gina Baldini's husband Al gave her a lavish box of chocolates and a huge bunch of flowers and took her out to dinner at her favourite restaurant. It was a wonderful gesture, and Gina very much appreciated it. The only problem was that was what Al gave her every year for her birthday, had done so for the last ten years, and she was beginning to feel disappointed he couldn't think of anything new and more exciting to honour and celebrate her special day.

'Happy birthday, honey,' he said now, lifting his wineglass in a toast to her over his starter of avocado and shrimp cocktail. 'Many happy returns of the day.'

Smiling, she reached out her own glass to touch his and together they sipped the chilled California chardonnay. Placing her glass back on the table, Gina glanced across at him as she prepared to attack the plate of antipasto before her. Al really was a handsome man, with his dark hair and eyes and his square-set jaw. Just as attractive now as when she had first met him and fallen in love in college a dozen years ago. And she was still genuinely fond of him, though the initial surge of passion had dwindled over the years, especially since the boys had been born. Now they were just good friends, really. She still loved him, of course. But not as she used to. Looking across at him now she didn't feel the same thrill she used to feel, a sense of weakness that made her knees shake, and a warmth emanating outwards from somewhere near her womb. That was all long ago. No such feelings anymore. Frankly, she missed them.

'So,' he continued, lifting a spoonful of avocado towards his mouth, 'anything special you want to do tonight? We have a couple hours before we have to get the sitter home. Want to see that new DiCaprio film at the Varsity?'

Gina shrugged.

'Not really, darling. It's just nice not to have to cook for a change, and I'm enjoying it.'

Al beamed.

'Good. So am I.' He cocked his head to one side. 'Not that I don't enjoy your cooking, I hasten to add.'

'It's not as good as yours, though, and you know it.'

Al had grown up with his Italian family in the Bay area, and had taken an early interest in learning his mother's traditional recipes for the classic Italian dishes. When they gave dinner parties for friends it was always Al who did the cooking, while Gina took responsibility for preparing the table and getting the house and the boys ready for the occasion. Which was a fair division of labour, as far as she was concerned.

'How are rehearsals going?' he asked, between bites.

Gina, who taught English and Drama at the local high school (Al was the P.E. teacher and coach of the high school track team), was currently involved in a production with the local amateur dramatic company, the Driftwood Players, of Shakespeare's 'As You Like it,' and was playing Rosalind – a role that, with her sultry good looks, long shapely legs and figure, suited her absolutely. The new company of players had met for the first time the previous week and rehearsals thus far were going well. Tonight, being Saturday, there was no rehearsal.

'So far so good. I like the new director, Tom Swift. He's a recent arrival from Palo Alto. A lawyer who's always craved a life in the theatre. Apparently he's also a good actor.'

'Mm,' Al responded, chewing. 'Any other new faces?'

'It's pretty much the same old crowd. Martha Vickers is playing Phoebe, and Barry Newman is Duke Frederick. Oh, there is one other new person – playing Orlando. We have lots of scenes together and so far he seems fine. He's just moved here, too – from back east, I think. He's a history lecturer at the university. Name's Aaron. Aaron Pierce.'

'How old?'

Gina frowned, thinking. 'Oh, I suppose my age. Maybe a year or two younger.'

Al winked, reaching for his glass. 'Don't have to be worried about him, do I?'

Gina laughed. 'I don't think so. He's not really my type.'

'Thank God for that.' Al smiled, sipping his wine.

She returned his smile. It was true, she thought. The new man seemed too quiet, too reserved – a bit full of himself, she reckoned. He was pretty good as an actor – at least his reading of the text thus far had seemed intelligent and sensitive. It would be a pleasure to work opposite him. But apart from a vague curiosity as to where he came from and what his circumstances were she hadn't really thought about him at all. It was just too much fun for her being back working with her old friends again after having taken six months off to devote time to the boys and Al.

'Oh,' Al said, wiping his mouth with his napkin, 'I meant to tell you. Dad's asked me to bring the boys down in June for a week's camping. Unfortunately I think the week he mentioned conflicts with the production dates for your play. Second week of June, from Friday the 12th? Isn't that right?'

Gina paused in her chewing, thinking. 'Yes, I think that's our opening night. Couldn't they do it any other time? I'm free the rest of the summer.'

'Apparently not. They've got Anna coming with Bart and the kids the week after for two weeks, then they're off themselves on their trip to Europe till mid August. That was the only window.'

Gina sighed. 'Well, you'll just have to go without me, I guess. It's a shame. I would've enjoyed a bit of mountain camping. Better than being stuck here all summer. Still, I know the boys will have a great time with Tony. They love him so.'

Tony was Al's father. Gina liked him, too. It was hard not to like a man whose eyes twinkled constantly and who always managed to make those around him laugh. She would miss seeing him.

'Never mind,' she sighed. 'I'll have the play to occupy me and that should be fun. It seems to be shaping up nicely already.'

'Well, we'll miss you,' Al said, reaching across to press her hand. 'I wish it could've been otherwise, but I don't think I'd better pass up the opportunity. It'll be so great for the boys.'

She squeezed his hand back, knowing he was right. Anyway, that was three weeks away. She had plenty to occupy herself with between times, what with the end of term approaching and rehearsals every weeknight. She would cope on her own during their absence. It wasn't as though it was the first time. Often in the past she'd remained at home while Al had whisked the boys away for a night of camping here or an overnight sporting event there. In a way, she actually looked forward to being alone again for a few days – a bit of R & R from job, family and the daily grind, with only the evening performances of the play to worry about. Yes, she would quite enjoy that.

'Finished?' asked a voice at her elbow.

Gina looked up to see the waitress smiling down at her.

'Yes,' she said, sitting back. 'Thank you. It was delicious.'

The woman bent to take her starter plate and Al's, then moved off toward the back of the room.

'Maybe we can go down to the Surf Room for a drink after? What do you say?' Al proposed, as he topped up her glass from the bottle.

'Sounds good,' Gina replied, thinking there was nothing else she could have said – though she wished there were.

His friends would be there, she knew – the fathers of several of his young athletes, and golf buddies from the Country Club. Al would sit amongst them and they would talk sports endlessly together, while Gina would be stuck making small talk with the wives – all nice people, to be sure, but none of them with interests that coincided with her own.

'Oh, well,' she told herself. 'Why should this birthday be any different from the others?'

But she couldn't help wishing it had been. She was too young to have to accept an annual routine that was beginning to chafe and to bore her – like so much else in her life just at present.

'If only something wonderful and unexpected would happen!' she thought wistfully, hiding her real thoughts from her husband behind a half-smile.

The waitress returned with their main courses and the dinner moved on.

Two days later, on Monday, Gina's disappointment over Al's rather tepid celebration of her birthday was forgotten as she plunged once more into the complex sea of obligations and deadlines that made up her working and home life. The only respite from it all, as her days grew even more hectic with the winding down of the spring term, were the evenings spent in rehearsals.

The Driftwood Theatre was an ancient converted warehouse at the edge of town – a rambling one-story building with a large central room that could be adapted into whatever form of staging the current play required. For 'As You Like It,' a much larger play than the group usually tackled, the set was complex and multi-levelled, and the rehearsals given over to the blocking of moves for the actors seemed endless and exhausting. Consequently it was only in the last couple of weeks that the amateur players finally began to find themselves in their roles and to act with conviction with one another. As was usual when this happened, an atmosphere of excitement and jubilation resulted, a heady sense of nearing the summit of the creative mountain they were all climbing together. And it was common, after evenings spent in such rewarding rehearsals, that the cast – or those members who were free to do so – repaired to one or another of the local watering holes to celebrate, normally choosing a quiet cocktail bar on the central plaza of the town, as opposed to one of the more rowdy beer palaces closer to the university.

On one of these evenings during the penultimate rehearsal week, after a particularly enjoyable rehearsal in which the play seemed to come alive for everyone and the feeling generally was that this might turn out to be one of their best productions ever, a large number of the cast found themselves seated around tables in 'Tommy and Jakes' cocktail bar on the plaza, unwinding and working their way through pitchers of draft beer.

As it happened, and through no conscious effort on either part, Gina ended up sitting at a corner table beside the aforementioned Aaron, with whom (as she had told Al) she shared the bulk of her scenes and towards whom, if she was honest, she had been feeling much more drawn of late, as he had proved to be an excellent actor exactly suited to his role and extremely easy for her to relate to. In spite of their nightly contact, this was the first opportunity she'd had to talk to him properly and she took advantage of it, questioning him at length about himself and his background, and how it was that he found himself here on the Pacific coast. Aaron, on the other hand, was finally able to get answers to certain questions he himself had entertained about Gina, her own history and involvements. In the meantime, in the midst of a pleasant ambiance of cigarette smoke, convivial chat and good spirits, quite a lot of beer was consumed at the tables.

'So,' said Gina, after learning from Aaron the details of his academic past on the east coast, 'I take it you're not married, is that right?'

'Not married, no,' he answered, smiling.

'But you were?'

'Yes, I was. Back in Connecticut. But I've been divorced a couple of years now.'

'Kids?'

'Two. A boy and a girl. About the same ages as your two.'

Gina had already filled him in on her own situation.

'Do you get to see them often?'

'I fly back every holiday. They're coming out to spend a good part of the summer with me after school's out.'

'Well,' Gina said, 'that'll be nice for you. And them. I'm sure.'

He smiled and Gina smiled back, not quite understanding the slight sensation of relief she'd felt when his single status was confirmed. What possible interest could that have for her?

'Your husband isn't a thespian then?' Aaron said, after sipping at his beer.

Gina shook her head. 'No. He's a sportsman. Golf and field events. He teaches PE at the high school.'

'Ah. Where you teach English and Drama, right?'

'Right.'

'Do you play golf, too?'

'Oh, no. I'm not into sport at all – except for a bit of jogging, just to keep myself in shape. No, my husband and I are not too well matched – insofar as hobbies are concerned, at least. We tend to go our separate ways.'

She looked down at her glass. Why had she said that? Aaron might think she'd meant she and Al led independent lives – implying an open invitation for him to make a pass. Heaven forbid he get that idea!

Although, she suddenly thought, what she'd told him about herself and Al was not too wide of the mark these last few years. They were tending to do more and more things separately, now. And, to be perfectly honest, their diverging tastes and interests went well beyond mere hobbies.

Gina shook herself and smiled up at him again.

'All right?' he asked, with a raised eyebrow. 'You drifted away there for a sec. Something on your mind?'

'No, I'm fine. Just tired, I guess. It's been a long day.' She raised her glass and drank the last few swallows, put it down with a sigh and smiled up at him again. 'I suppose I'd better be getting home. Tomorrow isn't going to be any easier for me and I need my sleep.'

'Me, too,' Aaron concurred, emptying his own glass and replacing it on the tabletop. 'Need a lift? Or do you have a car?'

'I have a car, thanks.'

She stood, taking her jacket from the back of the chair.

'Here, let me help you with that.'

Aaron rose to grasp the jacket and helped her slip into it. Gina liked it that he was such a gentleman, and didn't miss the lingering of his hand on her shoulder before he stepped back.

'I'll walk you to your car,' he said now.

'That's nice of you. Thanks.'

It took them a couple of minutes to say their goodbyes at the various tables; then they made their way out onto the neon and streetlamp lit plaza.

'It's down there, around the corner,' she told him, and turned down the street in that direction. Aaron walked at her side.

'I have to tell you,' he said quietly, 'I really am impressed with your Rosalind. You're terrific. And so easy to act with. You make my job a whiz.'

Gina smiled across at him. 'Likewise, sir. It's going to be a real pleasure doing this show for those three weekends.'

'It certainly will be for me,' he assured her, smiling.

When they reached the car Aaron waited while she unlocked the driver's door. Then, when she turned to him, he held out his hand.

'Nice to have finally had time to talk with you, Gina,' he told her. 'I look forward to doing it again, and soon.'

'Me, too,' she said, grasping his hand and squeezing it. 'Until tomorrow night, then.'

Climbing inside, she started the engine and drove off.

Glancing at her rear-view mirror, she noticed that Aaron had not moved and was still watching her.

The final production week for any theatre company is a time of great stress and tension. There are so many things that must be put right before presenting the new creation to outsiders, and not only in terms of the acting performances. Technical details regarding costumes, lighting, scenery, even individual choices as to makeup and hairstyles require concentrated attention and finessing on the part of everyone involved, and it is only with the final dress rehearsals that (hopefully) everything magically coalesces into a work that the director and cast finally feel confident enough about to offer, apprehensively, to the general public.

It had been thus with Gina and the rest of the '*As You Like It*' cast – a time for smoothing short tempers, stifling irritability, worrying as to whether things would finally work or not, feeling exhausted by the constant repetition of scenes and technical effects done and redone until they were executed correctly and consistently. At the end of rehearsals late in the evening everyone was generally so drained by their efforts that only a few people felt inclined to have a drink at the bar and unwind – that for most would have to be done at home. So it was not until after the opening night that there was any new opportunity for Gina and Aaron to spend further time progressing their growing interest in one another – other than moments of whispered conversation snatched during rehearsals, and that usually about matters relating to the play and their scenes together.

To add to this, this week coincided with the last days of Gina's high school spring term, with exams to be set and corrected and final reports offered for her students' progress. To make matters worse, schools closed for the summer break on the Wednesday and Al was to take the boys off on their camping holiday with his parents the following Friday – the very day the play was to open – making Gina's life even more complicated, what with helping the boys to pack and making sure they and Al had all they would need for the week they'd be away.

So that by the time she arrived at the theatre an hour before curtain time on opening night – which was, she'd been told, a sell-out – Gina was a jangled bundle of nerves. Relying on her years of experience with first nights, however, she did her best to collect herself while seated at her mirror, carefully applying her makeup and arranging her shoulder-length, honey coloured hair into an appropriate (and previously agreed to) style for the period. And to a certain extent her efforts paid off. She began to feel a bit better, or at least more focussed. It helped that the other ladies in the dressing room were feeling much the same nerves as she, and that – being women – they could sympathize with and offer moral support to one another for the sake of their common objective.

When the final call was made by the stage manager, and Gina and the other starters took their places for their first entrances, all thoughts but of the play flew from her mind. From that moment on, and for the next two and a half hours, her attention remained fixed on the task of making her Rosalind attractive and believable to the audience, many of whom she knew.

And it was only when her last lines were spoken, and the lights dimmed at the close of the play's final act – to be followed a few seconds later by a burst of energetic and sustained applause – that Gina could believe she had done well enough to finally allow herself to relax. Sidling into place with the others for the curtain calls in a line across the stage front, taking the company bows, she was aware of a great feeling of relief and euphoria, as if a weight had suddenly been shifted from her shoulders, or she had just stepped from the darkness of an oppressive cave into a shaft of bright sunlight.

And afterwards, backstage, when the well-wishers and friends poured through to the dressing rooms from the front, she basked with the others in the waves of effusive congratulation that were lavished upon the production as a whole and upon the work of certain actors therein, including herself. Hugs and winks, pats on the back, grasps of the arm, warm shakings of the hand, and smiles, and smiles, and smiles. Smiles in all directions. And one of the biggest the director's, Tom Swift's, pleased that he had proven himself in his new community.

Half an hour later, when the crowd had finally gone from backstage and the cast were left to themselves at last, Gina found herself face to face with Aaron outside her dressing room door, a great smile emblazoned across his face. Without a word, and to her great surprise, he suddenly pulled her toward him in an impulsive hug, lifted her momentarily off the ground and swung her in a wide circle – depositing her at last on her feet. Then, grasping one of her hands, he grandly kissed its back.

'Congratulations, my lady,' he told her then. 'You were magnificent. A true princess!'

'Ah,' she laughed, 'but I'm not a princess. The closest thing to a royal character in the play is Duke Frederick.'

'That may be,' he returned. 'But for me, there's one true princess in this production, and that's you!'

And, smiling, he turned away to disappear into his own dressing room – leaving Gina a little breathless, and secretly thrilled at the way in which he had, with his high spirits and sheer physical strength, literally swept her off her feet.

Afterwards, as planned, came the proverbial cast party, held in the theatre itself, with tables of food and drink arranged in the foyer, and the space before the stage converted into a small dance floor with a few random spotlights crisscrossing it to create a night clubby ambience. For the occasion, the husbands, wives and significant others of the cast were expected to attend, as well as certain members of the community who had – either through direct grants or gifts in kind to the theatre –

become part of the Driftwood Players support team. The building was pulsating with throngs of humanity, drinking and talking animatedly or dancing to the music played over the theatre's sound system. In the midst of this hurly-burly Gina, laughing and happy, passed from one circle of friends to another, talking loudly over the noise of the competing conversations, revelling in the release of tension after the weeks of hard work, basking in the sense of a job well done and the realization that her own contribution had been vital to the success of the performance.

As the minutes ticked by towards midnight – feeling the effects of the several glasses of wine she'd been enjoying – Gina suddenly noticed, across the heads of the crowd, Aaron's eyes locked on hers, watching her as he spoke to Tom Swift and the local newspaper reviewer. He smiled as he caught her eye.

Moments later he was at her elbow, where she found him as she turned away from a finished conversation with a colleague from the high school.

'Hello,' she said. 'Having fun?'

'Very much so,' he smiled back at her. 'Fancy a walk? I'm dying for a cigarette.'

'Sure.' She looked around her. No one seemed to be taking any interest in the two of them just now. Which was good, she thought. 'I'll just make a quick stop at the ladies and meet you outside.'

'Excellent.'

Five minutes later, having refreshed herself and her makeup, Gina stepped out into the balmy June night at the front of the theatre to find Aaron leaning against a car under a streetlamp, his arms crossed and a lit cigarette in one hand. She moved to him. He smiled and stood upright.

'That was quick.' Producing a pack of cigarettes from a jacket pocket, he held it towards her. 'Cigarette?'

She hesitated. 'Normally I don't smoke,' she told him. 'I gave it up three years ago. But tonight, why not?'

She reached to pluck one from the pack and brought it to her lips. Instantly Aaron produced a lighter, struck it, and held it for her to use.

'Well,' she said, exhaling, 'I think it all went pretty well, don't you?'

'I certainly do. As I said before,' and here Aaron's eyes bore down upon her intently, 'you were truly magnificent tonight. I really mean it. I think I might even have … fallen in love with you a little. You were that good.'

'Oh,' she said, suddenly embarrassed, 'don't. As long as I did my job well enough, I'm happy.' She glanced back towards the theatre entrance. 'Shall we walk a bit?'

'Sure.'

Falling into step they turned together into the centre of the empty road, moving away from the last streetlight and into the shadows – towards the distant silhouetted cluster of derelict buildings that was the old Forbes plywood mill a hundred yards further along. Though the night was moonless, the stars spread across the firmament imparted a slight glow, enough for them to see by.

'I didn't see your husband tonight,' Aaron said. 'Was he there?'

'No.' She glanced across at him. 'I thought I told you. He's taken the boys off for a week of camping. They left this morning. No, he'll see the play when he gets back in its last week.'

'Ah.'

'He's not much for theatre in any case. It's hard enough for me to get him to take me to a show in San Francisco when we're there together. If there's not a ball or running somehow involved he doesn't seem to have any interest.'

'That's a shame. You're so good in this. He should be proud of you. I would be.'

'We'll see what he thinks in a couple of weeks. I have a good idea now what he'll do. He'll give me a pat on the back and suggest we head for a bar so he can talk to his friends about sports. He doesn't care much what I do, anymore. Whether it's good or bad. He only comes at all because he feels he has to, for appearance sake.'

'That's sad.' Reaching out, Aaron grasped her hand. 'Do you mind?'

Gina thought of pushing him away. Then decided against it.

'No.'

They strolled on along the centre of the deserted road, hand in hand, smoking and not speaking – until in unspoken agreement they turned together through the entryway into the yard of the abandoned mill and, pressing on, came eventually to a vast, empty, open-sided shadowy storehouse where at one time units of freshly milled plywood had been stacked. Now the building stood in the darkness like a great eight-legged behemoth, its high roof blocking out the stars above their heads.

'It's so quiet,' Gina whispered, leaning her back against one of the steel roof supports. 'You can't hear anything from the town here.'

'No, you can't.' He was standing quite close, facing her in the darkness. 'We might be at the end of the earth here. Out of time. In a different dimension altogether.'

She could feel him watching her as he smoked. Then, taking a last pull on the cigarette, he threw it to the cement floor and ground it out with his shoe.

'Want to go back?' he asked.

'No.' Gina flicked her own cigarette away. 'Not yet.'

That was all Aaron needed to know. Stepping close he pulled her against him, forcing her to look up at him. There was hardly any hesitation before Gina's arms encircled his neck and she reached her lips to his, finding them warm and searching and very pleasant.

'This is wrong, of course,' she told herself, while relishing the tenderness of his caresses and the mounting urgency of his kisses. 'But who is to know? Anyway, it'll be over all too soon, and my life will carry on just as predictable and boring as it has been these past few years. Why not let myself go a little? Who can be hurt by it? And he is so gentle, so loving…'

Gina felt herself softening, her own yearning rising, until – sensing his aroused sex pressing against her, and feeling a passion she had not felt in years – she pulled her lips from his and slid slowly to her knees before him, her hands feeling for the zipper of his trousers. Finding it and pulling it down, she allowed herself the thrill of illicit sexual giving that she'd not felt, genuinely, for many years.

Aaron, his hands cupped around the back of her head, caressed her hair, moaning with pleasure in the darkness.

The following days were like a dream to Gina, a time out of time, seemingly from a different life dimension, as Aaron had said.

They hadn't stayed out much longer together that first night, fearing their absence might be noticed by the others. And when they had returned, careful to make their reappearances a few minutes apart, they'd spent the rest of their time at the party away from one another, talking and laughing with other friends, and made their separate ways home to their lonely beds not long after.

But late morning on the Saturday, remembering that she was alone, Aaron boldly looked up Gina's number in the phone book and called her. Gina, still sleepy and more than a little giddy from the intimacy they had shared the night before, had been glad to hear his voice, and had suggested that perhaps after lunch they could meet?

'Of course. But where?' he asked.

Gina thought for a moment. Then told him. In the parking lot of a certain seldom visited bird sanctuary that overlooked the marshlands along the bay. And there they had met, Gina leaving her car to sit with Aaron in his in the empty lot. Feeling strangely shy with one another initially, they talked casually for several minutes about off-hand, inconsequential things. Until at length, after a hiatus, Aaron reached his hand out to take hers again, and to squeeze it. And she turned to look into his eyes. In a flash they were locked again in one another's arms, their mouths fused, their passions rising. After several minutes, however, realizing the risk they were taking in the bold light of day (after all, anyone could drive up at any moment and find them thus – perhaps even someone she knew!), they both pulled back, straightened their clothes, said their goodbyes and took their leave of one another – knowing they would meet again in a few hours at the theatre.

That night, after the second performance went as smoothly, and proved to be as well received as the opening night, celebratory drinks were shared again by the cast at 'Tommy and Jake's'. Having carefully not paid any undue attention to Aaron all evening long, neither during the play nor after at the bar, Gina waited until he had finally said his goodnights and departed. And some minutes later – knowing he would be awaiting her in the plaza outside – she excused herself and took her own leave.

The minute the door closed behind her she recognized his silhouette across the street, leaning against a lamppost. She watched him pull himself upright and move slowly in her direction, then she turned and walked around the corner, knowing he would follow, and crossed the street to the small, heavily-shadowed parking lot she had deliberately chosen for her car so it would be out of sight of random passersby. A moment later he was at the passenger door and she moved across the seat to open it for him. Then the door closed and he reached for her and she for him, and they embraced and kissed again.

It occurred to Gina that she might take him back to her house. Why not, it was empty, wasn't it? It was late, and the neighbours would probably be asleep. But then a sense of decorum and propriety took hold, and instead she whispered to him.

'Wait. Let me drive us somewhere. Where we can be alone.'

And pulling away she started the car, driving out of the car park and down dark and empty side streets towards the quietest edge of town.

Minutes later, tucked into the shadow of a hulking ramshackle barn beside a long abandoned farmhouse, they lowered the front seat backs of Gina's car and made love together for the first time.

The following morning, Sunday, Gina was awakened early by the jangling of the bedside telephone. Reaching across, she lifted the receiver and brought it to her ear.

'Hello?'

'Baby, it's me, Al. Did I wake you?'

She struggled to focus.

'No, not really. I was just lying here thinking.'

She shuddered as she suddenly remembered she had considered bringing Aaron back to the house last night. If she had, he might still have been lying beside her when the call had come. How awkward that would've been!

'Ah, good. You sound a bit groggy. Too many cast parties?'

'No, I'm fine. Just enjoying a sleep-in. How are things going down there?'

Gina listened as her husband gave the news of their camping trip thus far, that the boys – who sent love to Mom – were presently with their grandparents at the little lake beside the campground, that he had taken a drive into the nearest town to buy groceries and to look for a public phone. How was she? How had the performances gone? She told him, feeling at the back of her mind a creeping uneasiness, putting more enthusiasm into her voice than in fact she was feeling.

'Well, I'm glad it's going well,' he responded. 'Are you missing me?'

Gina frowned. Why was he asking that suddenly when he never had before?

'Of course. I always do.'

'So am I, baby. Missing you, I mean. We're having a good time here, but frankly I've been thinking about you a lot the last couple of days. Fact is, I think I've been neglecting you a bit.' He laughed. 'Maybe I'm just horny. Anyway, I can't wait to be home with you again.'

Gina felt a chill pass up her backbone.

'Me, too, sweetheart. Give the boys my love and enjoy the rest of the trip. We'll be together soon.'

'I'll do that, precious. Look after yourself. And remember, I love you!'

Then he was gone, leaving Gina to slowly put the phone down, struggling with the sobering reminder of who she really was – a respected wife and mother.

By lunchtime, however, her solitude as she pottered about the empty house brought back the delicious sense of freedom she'd been enjoying over the last couple of days, and on impulse she suddenly picked up the kitchen phone and – finding in her purse the slip of paper Aaron had given her with his number scrawled on it – dialled it and listened to the purring of the ring tone at the other end

'Aaron Pierce,' came his voice a few seconds later.

'It's me,' she said.

'Ah. Good. Glad you called. I've been thinking about you. Missing you.'

'Me, too.'

'Last night was … very special. You know?'

'For me, too.' There was a pause. 'So, are you working today or what?'

'No. At least, not doing anything important. Just reading essays. What're you doing? Want to come out to my place and have lunch?'

Aaron lived alone in a cabin on a county road a couple miles beyond the university. She knew the road, and remembered the cabin from his description of it. As she recalled, it was in a pretty unpopulated area, his nearest neighbours a quarter of a mile away.

'All right. Suppose I pick up a pizza and some beer on the way?'

'Sounds good. I'll make a salad.'

Half an hour later she was pulling into the gravel drive of the cabin, and Aaron was at the door to meet her.

They had their lunch, washing it down with bottles of cold beer and laughing together over company gossip. Then they made love again on his double bed, slowly and thoroughly, revelling in the luxury of a comfortable mattress and clean sheets for a change, with plenty of room for their embraces and ardent couplings.

Over the following two days Aaron was busy with university and social commitments and Gina was left to herself, filling her time spring cleaning her house from one end to the other and reading a Michael Connelly novel curled up in her favourite chair.

Once when she looked up from her page she found herself idly wondering who she missed most, Aaron, or her boys? And what about Al? Did she miss him at all, really? She thought she did, but she wasn't sure. In any case he would be back in three days. But Aaron?...

Wednesday afternoon, when she could stand it no longer, she called Aaron at his office at the university and managed to catch him there.

'Hey,' she said, when he answered with his name.

'Hey, yourself. Hang on a minute while I close the door.' There was a pause, then he was back on the line again. 'I've been missing you. You been okay?'

'Yes. I've kept busy one way or another. But I thought maybe...'

When she didn't continue, Aaron prodded her.

'What? You thought maybe what?'

Gina sighed.

'It's just ... well, the boys are coming back Saturday and I've been thinking about us and what we've shared in the last few days, and ... well, I guess I'm sorry I shall be losing that. I really want to see you again, Aaron, before they get here. Do you understand? I want that very much. Because I don't think we'll be able to see each other again after they're back.'

'No, I don't suppose we will,' he concurred, after a moment.

'Can you come here tonight?' she asked finally.

'To your house? Is that wise?'

'If you come after dark no one will notice. Say around 10:30? I wish you could come earlier, only I wouldn't want the neighbours to see, you understand?'

'I'll be there,' he told her. 'And don't worry. I'll be the invisible man.'

And so he was. At least there was never any gossip later about a strange gentleman visiting the attractive high school drama teacher after hours when her husband and children were away. A blessing for her, as she later realized, and one for which she was to be eternally grateful.

Aaron, true to his word, appeared just after 10:30 with a bottle of wine and a small box of chocolates, both of which they consumed together as they lay in each other's arms on the living room sofa, watching the late evening news. (Gina had been careful, of course, to make sure all the drapes were pulled tight, and that there was no possible way anyone outside could accidentally see them together.) And when the news finished, and the television had been switched off with the remote, they had stayed twined together on the sofa for a time, nuzzling and murmuring softly to one another and enjoying tender kisses, until at length it was time for bed.

During the afternoon, while changing the sheets and pillowcases in the master bedroom, Gina had suffered a momentary pang of conscience about what she was planning to do. How brazen could she be in her adultery, to invite her lover to share her very matrimonial bed! But then, she thought, Aaron would bring to it more tenderness and caring in his lovemaking than she had experienced for many years. Why should she not make love with him here of all places? It was her bed, too, after all.

And they had, Gina having turned off the bedside light and opened the curtains at the side just enough to let a glimmer of light enter from the waxing crescent moon. For an hour or two they had made love and rested and made love again in the great queen-sized bed, until at last, finally sated, they'd drifted off to sleep in one another's arms.

Sometime around five AM, when daylight began to tint the eastern heavens and the outlines of the bedroom furniture became sharper and clearer, Aaron awoke from a pleasant dream of sunlight and warm seas to find the bed beside him empty.

Suddenly alert, he lay still in the strange bed, his eyes open, listening for any sound of Gina. Had she slipped away to the en suite bathroom? But beyond the open door there was no sound. He lay there a minute longer. Then, when he still heard nothing, he arose from the bed and, taking down the dark dressing gown from the door hanger (obviously Gina's husband's), he slipped it on and padded down the hall, brushing his long hair back with one hand and holding the sides of the gown tightly closed with the other.

But she wasn't in the kitchen, nor in the lounge. Nor in any of the downstairs rooms.

Then he remembered.

Beyond the bedrooms at the back of the house, a stairway led up to a converted loft under the eaves. The family room, she had called it. She had taken him there on her tour of the place after he had arrived. A large open area, he remembered, that ran the length of the house, with a huge television screen at one end, a long sofa and armchairs, and in the gable end on the rear wall a triangular window that overlooked the back garden.

Aaron padded back in that direction.

Gina heard his footsteps on the stairs, and when she knew he was standing at the top, looking across to where she sat huddled on her knees by the great back window, she turned finally to look at him.

'Hey,' he murmured. 'What's up? What're you doing up here?'

How could she tell him? He wouldn't understand.

'Come on, Gina. Come back to bed. Okay?'

'All right. I'll be down in a minute. You go back now.'

'I'll go. But don't be long. It's getting light. I'll have to leave soon.'

And he turned and disappeared downstairs again.

But she wouldn't go back. Not now. Not to him. Not ever. Not after the thoughts she'd had upon waking an hour ago in her love-scented conjugal bed, finding the man snoring beside her who, though sweet, was definitely not her husband.

She clutched the family photograph she had taken from a side table – the four of them grouped, smiling and happy, in a holiday snap – closer to her breast, wrapping her arms around it tightly in the half-darkness, feeling tears coming again, as she realized finally, and with terrible clarity, the answer to her question of several days before.

Who could be hurt by it, this casual and discreet affair with a likeable stranger?

Exquisite as it had been, it would be Gina herself who would suffer (she knew that now), quietly within herself and for all the years to come – the bitter guilt of betrayal for her secret and self-indulgent transgression.

(London, 2013)

The Leave-Taking

Eleanor stared out at the familiar drab suburbs as they swept past the Greyhound window under the grimly overcast sky. She had known this town well for decades in her early years. Now its old streets and buildings resonated with echoes of memories and she felt torn by conflicting emotions – pleasure at seeing it all again, being reminded of happy faces and good times, and sadness for what all her years spent there had come to in the end.

It had taken three hours to come up by bus from her home in northern California. Now that she was finally here the butterflies in her stomach started up again. Why had she come? Did it matter to her anymore that the man who had been her first husband was dying of cancer? Did she care? She sighed. Yes, she admitted to herself, she supposed it did matter. Otherwise why had she taken the trouble to travel two hundred miles to see him?

Also there'd been the pressure from Toby, their son, who had urged her, for old times' sake, to come to say 'goodbye'.

'Come on, Mom,' he'd said on the phone. 'I'll cover your expenses. I just think you should pay your respects, even though you don't care for him anymore. He still remembers his years with you with great fondness. Talks about you all the time, now. You were his first, after all. And he was yours. He deserves a little attention, don't you think, now at the last? Glenn can do without you for a day, can't he?'

Glenn was her present husband, an affable, kind man she had met in the lonely years after the divorce who had paid her attention, made her feel special again. She had never really loved Glenn, not in any romantic sense – though after thirty years of marriage she still cared for him, certainly. But not as she had cared for the first. For Jim. Jim was special. When she had met Jim as a teenager in Inglewood back in the 30s, he had knocked her off her feet. He had been so handsome then – three years older, tall and slim with dark, warm eyes, and black hair slicked back like a young Valentino. He had captured her heart, and at fourteen she had given him her virginity. That was the beginning. And it had been good. There'd been a lot of good years to follow. She smiled in spite of herself, remembering.

Toby was standing outside the depot when the bus pulled to a stop beside it. When she stepped down with the others he moved towards her, wrapping his long arms around her in a firm hug.

'Thanks for coming, Mom. It'll mean a lot to him.'

He stepped back and looked at her staring up at him, her face in a forced half-smile, her lips pressed tightly together.

'Come on, now,' he told her. 'It won't be as bad as that, I promise you.'

Putting an arm around her, he led her towards his parked car.

The family room at the back of Toby's house had been turned into a last bedroom for his father, equipped with a special hospital bed with an air-filled mattress that would move under him to prevent bedsores. Although nurses appeared every day to bathe the old man and to administer the drugs necessary to stave off his pain, it was Toby himself who did most of the caring. At one side of the room a low camp bed was made up, and there Toby spent the night, listening through the long hours to his father's laboured breathing, responding to his feeble appeals for assistance with the piss bottle, or to help shift his long, wasted body over from the bed onto the commode to do his other business. Toby himself did all this while his wife Audrey handled the rest of the family chores – keeping the twin boys away from their grandfather in the other part of the house, preparing for Toby what meals he was able to snatch – mostly in an armchair in the family room while he kept an eye on the sleeping form of his father.

Now, as he ushered his mother into that room, Audrey broke off reading her magazine in the armchair and came to whisper a greeting to Eleanor and to give her a brief hug. Then, taking her mother-in-law's coat with her into the front of the house, she closed the door behind her, leaving mother and son alone with the sleeping invalid.

'Where are the boys?' asked Eleanor, quietly.

'At school,' Toby told her. 'They won't get back before you go. Anyway, we'll be down to see you again soon.'

Eleanor nodded and moved to the foot of the bed, looking down at the wracked form that was once her husband. In spite of his illness he was still a good-looking man, with a thick head of dark hair, only greying at the temples. Jim was lying on his side, his mouth half open, a string of drool seeping down onto his pillow. His breathing was shallow, raspy and ragged, as if he was struggling to get his breath. Eleanor looked up at her son standing beside her.

'He looks so weak,' she whispered. 'How long has he got, do you think?'

Toby shrugged. 'The nurses say only a few more days. A week at most. No more.'

Eleanor sighed. 'Well, I can't stay long. The bus leaves at five.'

'I know, Mom. I'll wake him. He sleeps most of the time now.'

He moved to the side of the bed and laid a hand on his father's wrist, gently pushing up the pyjama sleeve and squeezing.

'Dad?' he said, with a low voice. Then, louder: 'Dad! Wake up, hoss. You got a visitor.'

Jim's open mouth closed and worked and the eyes struggled to open.

'Wha...?' he mumbled, blinking.

'It's Mom come to see you, Dad. Eleanor. I told you she was coming. You were looking forward to seeing her. Remember?'

Jim turned his head, looking up towards his son and squinting, getting his old eyes to focus.

'Who?'

'Eleanor. My ma. You asked to see her, remember? Well, she's here now.'

'Where?' Jim wheezed, frowning.

'There,' his son told him. 'At the foot of your bed. Look.'

With great effort Jim turned his body, raised himself on his elbows to face the foot of his bed, his eyes finally finding Eleanor's familiar form, breaking now into a wide smile of recognition.

'Ellie! You came!'

'Yes, Jim. I came.' She moved around the bed to the side opposite Toby and laid a hand gently on the ill man's chest, pushing him back down. 'But you just lie back. Don't get yourself all excited. I'm here, and I'll be here for a while. So you just relax. Okay?'

His eyes never leaving hers, Jim smiled again.

'Ah, Ellie. The boss. Just like old times. All right, I'll be good.'

Eleanor reached out to grasp one of his hands and squeezed it. Then she looked up at her son on the other side of the bed.

'You can go now, bub. We'll be all right. I'll call you if we need anything.'

Toby smiled, patted his father's arm and left the room, pulling the door closed behind him.

For a long time there was silence as the aged former combatants faced one another, drinking in the changes wrought by time and hard living – the wrinkles and liver spots and sagging flesh – remembering the faces they had known and loved when they were young, so many years before.

It was Jim who broke the silence after wetting his lips with his tongue.

'Can you give me a little water, Ellie? My mouth gets pretty dry.'

'Of course.'

Turning to a side table, she poured an inch of water into a plastic tumbler and held it out to him. Jim raised himself slightly and she brought the glass to his mouth. He drank a swallow or two, then settled back onto the pillow. Ellie set the glass on the side table again.

'That's better. Thanks, honey.'

She watched him as he wet the inside of his mouth with his tongue.

'Are you in much pain?'

'Not much. I would be, but the morphine keeps that pretty much under control.'

'Thank heaven for that.'

'Yeah.' He smiled. 'Small mercies. But no big ones.'

She smiled back. Then looked down.

'I was sorry to hear about … about the cancer, Jim. It's not fair.'

He shrugged. 'What's fair? Never mind. I'm old enough, and I've had a good life. I had to go one way or another. Might as well be this way.'

They exchanged tight smiles. Then silence settled again.

'How's Glenn?'

'Fine. He said to tell you how sorry he is.'

'That's nice of him.'

'He's always liked you, you know.'

Jim smiled. 'Yeah, I know. It was you that didn't.'

She tightened her jaw.

'I'm sorry. But that last time you visited was a bit difficult for me. That's why I asked you not to stop by again.'

He nodded. 'I guess even an old leopard keeps his spots, right? I tried to be on my best behaviour.'

'You can't stop being what you are, Jim.'

'It was good enough for you, once.'

She sighed. 'That was a long time ago.'

'I know.'

She looked out of the window at the trees bordering the lawn.

'I might drift off to sleep again,' he warned her. 'I can't stop myself. If I do, stay with me awhile, will you? I'll wake up again.'

She looked back at him.

'I'll stay.'

Silence again descended, as both went over in their minds the memories of their shared years.

'Why did it happen, El?' he asked at last. 'Why did you stop loving me?'

'Oh, Jim. It was all so long ago.'

'Please…'

She grimaced.

'There were a number of things. Mostly your mother. It was hard having her living with us, disapproving of everything I did – my housekeeping, the way I looked after Toby. And you were just as bad. I could never do anything right.'

He nodded. 'The problem with being an only child, and a son at that. A mother's never satisfied with her son's woman.'

'Don't I know it.'

'Then there was the war. I was away three years. You were stuck with mother and a baby all that time. It can't have been much fun.'

She looked down at the bed, her face tightening. He reached out a hand to touch hers on the counterpane.

'Now, now. I don't hold that against you, Ellie. What happened while I was away. I didn't mean to bring it up.'

She shook her head, frowning.

'Don't, Jim.'

'You had too much on your plate. And you were alone.' He smiled. 'You were also a good-looking woman. It's understandable someone would try it on with you.'

'I'm not proud of what I did, Jim. I've tried to forget about it, to forgive myself. But it's not been easy. Let's not talk about it now.'

He nodded, recalling the story told him by his mother after his return from the South Pacific. How one evening there'd been a knock on the front door and Ellie had gone to answer it. She had opened it to find an irate young woman standing there who had asked her name, then slapped her soundly across the face, declaring that if Ellie had anything further to do with her husband she'd be back again, and next time she'd be bringing something sharp with her, to mark her face as a whore. Jim's mother had heard the whole thing, had reported it faithfully to her son at the first opportunity, relishing the relating of every detail, twisting the knife into his love for this woman she had never really accepted. Hurtful as the story had been, Jim had forgiven his young wife then, much to his mother's shock and disapproval. And he still forgave her. It was a strange time, those war years. People did strange things. Shit happens.

'There's a chair by the window,' he told her. 'Why don't you bring it over and sit? There's no need for you to stand there.'

She nodded and stepped away, returning with the straight-backed chair and settling on it. Now their eyes were on a level and he turned to her, staring at her with enormous fondness.

'You were always the best, Ellie. The one I loved most. Even though I married again and loved them, too. You were the first, after all. That made us special. Don't you think?'

She nodded.

'Yes, Jim. I guess I feel the same way.'

'Good.' He reached out to squeeze her hand. 'I'm glad you came, El. I needed that. Thanks, darlin'.'

The minutes ticked by. Jim felt the weariness coming on again and could do nothing to stop it. His eyes drooped in spite of himself and he slipped again into merciful blackness.

Eleanor sat holding his hand for a long time, waiting for him to reawaken.

But he didn't.

Looking across at his worn face other earlier images of him came back like ghosts. The gangling youth in Los Angeles that had swept away her heart. The jaunty sailor on liberty in his crisp new uniform and white cap. And later, the proud father's smile when he held for the first time the son they had both wanted so much.

So many good memories. Before the bad ones came.

Eventually Eleanor's head drooped to her chest and she drifted off, too.

Until some time later, when Toby gently awoke her and told her it was 4:15, that Audrey had made coffee and a sandwich for her to have before they left to catch her return bus.

'Fine,' she told him. 'Just give me a minute.'

He nodded and left.

Eleanor rose, replaced the chair by the window and came back to Jim's bed, looking down at him for the last time, pressing the details of his ravaged face into her memory. Then she stooped and kissed his cool forehead.

'Goodbye, old friend,' she whispered.

And followed her son.

Later, on the bus that wound its way through the mountains back to California, Eleanor made a surprise decision – at least to herself.

Securing a photo of Jim from Toby after his father's passing, she kept it in her wallet from that day forward, hidden away from Glenn and everyone else. A treasured thing valued only by herself, a token of the love she had carried within her over the years, in spite of everything, for the exasperating but beautiful man that had been her first husband.

(London, 2013)

Damn Foolishness

Vern Carson and Ernie Fowler, two septuagenarian friends, were sitting together on Vern's back deck, watching the sun sinking slowly into the Pacific. The men were both widowers, retired lawyers who lived alone in adjacent houses on the bluffs of Marin County, north of San Francisco. After an afternoon spent at the golf course Vern had brought out his bottle of 25-year-old Scottish malt whiskey and the two of them were enjoying drinks together before retiring for simple, separate dinners and an early night.

The May weather was warm, the sky emblazoned with fiery streaks of cloud that stretched from horizon to horizon. For a long period neither of the old friends spoke, each lost in reveries of the past generated by the view before them. Then Ernie leaned forward, chuckling, as he poured another finger of whiskey into his glass from the bottle on the table between them.

'What's tickling you?' Vern asked, sliding his own glass towards him. 'And you might as well put a drop in mine too, while you're at it.'

Ernie did as he was asked, then took a sip of his drink and settled back into his cushioned deckchair.

'I was just remembering the damn foolishness I got into when I was young. Makes me wince now to think of it. What an asshole!'

'What kind of foolishness?'

'Oh, you know. You remember your student years? I did some pretty crazy things in those days. I'll bet you did, too.'

'Well,' said Vern, 'I was pretty boringly conventional as a student, Ern. My Catholic parents kept me under a pretty tight rein. I never really felt free of their restraints even after I left home. But what were you up to then that tickles you so much now? Share, amigo.'

Ernie sipped his whiskey and smiled.

'I don't think I've ever told another soul about this. You're the first one to hear it.'

He took another sip, placed his glass on the table and sat back again, clasping his fingers over his stomach and watching the sun as it commenced its descent through the sea's horizon.

'It was while I was in law school at USC. I was twenty-two or twenty-three; living alone in a little apartment that was paid for by my GI Bill money. The studies were going well, and I was pretty much enjoying life. But I hadn't had a girlfriend for months, and for a time I got pretty lonely.' He chuckled. 'Hell, I was just 'horny', I suppose. I had all these youthful juices flowing and no way to get rid of them. Anyway, one night on a whim I stopped by a strip bar that had just opened up nearby. *The Corral* it was called. This was long before pole and lap dancing clubs.' Now he laughed. 'Christ, these days we've got strip joints everywhere. You keep stumbling over them. But in those days it was new – the licensing laws had just been relaxed – and I was curious. So I stopped one night and went in. I was alone, of course. Opposite the bar there was this little stage for the girls, and spotlights, and they'd do a little dancing act to taped music while they bumped and ground their way down to G-strings, and then finally to nothing at all. I bought myself a beer and settled at one of the tables near the front.' He chuckled. 'It was stupid of me to spend time gawking at a bunch of good-looking naked women, horny as I was. But that's what I did. And for a few weeks it became a habit. I was there almost every night for an hour or two.'

'Hm,' Vern grunted. 'Must've cost you a bit. There was a cover charge, surely?'

'Oh, yeah. There's always a cover charge. But I'd buy one beer and nurse it. And I'd find out the girls' schedules, so I could turn up just before my favourite gal's act was due to start.'

Vern shook his head, smiling. 'You had a favourite girl?'

'Sure did. Her name was Dolores. Never forget her. Chicano girl. Mid-to-late twenties. Long black hair and a body to die for. Caught her act every single night. Threw ten-dollar bills onto the stage as tips to get her attention. Even spoke to her once or twice after, when she was heading out with her driver to the car – off to do a turn at another club.'

'Did you ask her out?'

Ernie turned to Vern.

'You gotta be joking! Date a stripper? What would my parents have thought? Or my classmates?' He took another sip from his glass. 'But I came close to it, I have to confess. As it happened, it was a good thing I didn't get as far as actually asking or I might've had my nose rearranged.'

'How is that?'

Ernie shook his head.

'One night I steeled myself to talk to her. I wanted to get her to meet me somewhere so I could get to know her better, find out what she was really like. I had this stupid idea we would find one another magically compatible. Anyway, that night I allowed myself two beers instead of the usual one, for Dutch courage. By that time I had a hell of a crush on her, silly ass that I was. I'd go back to my apartment after watching her and try to study, but I'd keep thinking of her brown body rolling around on that stage and I couldn't concentrate. I was becoming obsessed!'

'So what happened?'

'Well, this one night I was determined I'd catch her outside after her act, and I waited by the back entrance till I saw her and her driver/minder coming out. When they passed me I called out to her. She held up and waited for me while the driver went on to unlock their car.'

'What'd you say to her?'

'Not much. She remembered my name and thanked me for being there every night. I told her it was easy with such a gorgeous lady performing on the stage. She seemed to like that, and I was just about to ask her for that date when her driver walked up beside her and glared down at me. He was a big fella, probably ex-Marine. Tattoos on his arms, the whole bit. Anyway she then said, "Ernie, I'd like you to meet my *husband*, Dave. Dave, this's Ernie – one of my best fans." Well, I nearly fell on my ass. I had no idea she was married. I would never have expected her husband to be driving her from club to club, helping her to show off her scrumptious ass to the world. Anyway he stuck out his big hand, and somehow I managed to shake it. Then Dolores apologized for having to go, said a quick goodbye, gave me a peck on the cheek and she and Dave got into their car and drove off.'

There was a silence. Then Ernie laughed once, sharply, emptied his glass, and sat it on the table beside him.

'That was the end of that. The end of my non-starter romance with Dolores, the beautiful – married – Latina stripper!'

He continued to chuckle, shaking his head as he poured himself another finger of whiskey. Vern, meanwhile, was watching him, smiling tightly.

'So, what'dya think?' Ernie asked, looking across. 'Pretty pathetic, wasn't it?'

Vern raised his eyebrows, but said nothing.

'What about you, Vern?' Ernie went on, after a silence. 'No embarrassing stories you can lay on the line for me, your old friend of thirty years? Truth time, pal. I showed you mine; now you show me yours. I won't tell a soul. I swear.'

'There's no one left to tell, Ern. No one that matters anyway. So you needn't worry about that.'

'Go ahead then. Confession time, Vern. It's your turn to tell me something you did you wish had never happened. You gotta have one of those, at least. You may've been strait-laced but you can't have been that pure.'

Vern shifted in his seat, re-crossing his long legs the other way round. On the horizon the sun was just winking its last before sinking into the sea.

'Well, there was something. Once. Something that happened back while I was married to Connie, my first wife, in the late sixties/early seventies.'

Ernie leaned forward. 'I knew there would be. Go on, Vernie boy. Elucidate.'

'I wasn't as young as you were when you met your Dolores. I was in my mid-thirties then. Doing pretty well. On the brink of becoming a junior partner with Pestana and Kidwell in Hollywood. We were living in a fancy split-level up in Topanga Canyon, with a deck and a modest pool. My daughter Faye was about eight then, and we decided – since Connie also worked (as a society reporter for the *Times*) – that we needed an *au pair* to look after Faye when she came home from school, and during the evenings when we had social engagements to go to.'

'I should know,' Ernie confessed, 'but I don't. What's an *au pair*?'

'It's French. You know, those young foreigners who come to America to learn English, in exchange for living with American families and looking after their kids part-time? Anyway, Connie made the arrangements through an agency, and after a couple weeks this girl turned up – Mexican, from a small coastal town near Mazatlan. Her family were both professionals – father a dentist, mother a teacher – so she spoke pretty good English already. They wanted her to improve it so she could get a management job in tourism when she got home.' He sipped his drink, watching the last of the sun's glow fading from the western sky. 'Her name was Maribel. Maria Isabel Garcia. And she was nineteen years old.'

There was a pause as Vern sipped his whiskey.

Ernie leaned forward, raising his eyebrows. 'Was she …' he spread his hands, '…nice? This girl?'

Vern frowned at him. 'You mean attractive? Yeah. She was. Five-seven or eight. Shoulder-length black hair. Dark skin. Eyes like burnt almonds.'

'And the body?'

Vern nodded. 'Nice in that department, too. Not, you know, voluptuous. But nicely rounded. Very pleasant to look at.'

Ernie sat back again, sipping his drink.

'I'll bet you did a lot of that when you could get away with it. Looking.'

'Oh, I did. I may be strait-laced but I've never passed up the chance to gawk at a pretty girl.'

'So what happened?'

'Nothing much really. She spent a year with us. She fit in very well. We all liked her. So much so that at Christmas we went down to stay in her village and share the holidays with her family. Had a great time. She was a sweetheart. A real sweetheart. Her parents were nice, too. Fine, decent people.' He downed his whiskey, then turned to add another finger to his glass. 'It was because of that trip that I decided to study Spanish.'

'Why was that?'

Vern shrugged.

'I guess I fell in love with Mexico. Wanted to fit in. I hated having to nod and smile at people when they tried to speak to me. It was embarrassing. And frustrating. So when I got home I started listening to Spanish language tapes, studying the grammar. Pretty soon with Maribel's help I was doing pretty well. Sometimes she'd make me to talk to her in Spanish – long conversations about who we were and what we wanted out of life – and it was good practice. She was very patient. And understanding, when I made mistakes. Sometimes when I was writing up the lessons in my exercise book she'd come and stand over me, leaning over my shoulder to point out the errors I'd made in my answers.'

Vern snickered.

'Seems to me you were getting pretty familiar with this girl.'

'She was a member of the family. We'd watch television sometimes together in the den, after Faye had gone to bed and Connie was off finishing some article. Maribel would sit near me on the floor, leaning back against the sofa, her long black hair only inches from my knee. I had to stop myself from touching it.' He paused. 'But I never did. Anyway, we were very easy together.'

'And nothing happened between you?'

Vern frowned at him again.

''Course not. Don't get the wrong idea, Ern. This girl was a kid. A virgin. Never even had a boyfriend.'

Ernie leaned forward again, squinting.

'Are you trying to tell me, Vern Carson, that you never entertained the slightest improper thought about this girl? Come on, man. That ain't even possible.'

It was a while before Vern spoke again.

'I guess to be honest I did have those thoughts. It was hard not to when she used our pool almost every day, and I would see that brown body flexing in the sun. I remember thinking how lucky the young man would be who would be loved by her one day, who would be given the gift of that body.'

Ernie was looking a bit confused.

'So ... what is it about this story that embarrasses you? What'd you do that was so all-fired foolish?'

Vern shook his head, averting his eyes.

'Well, it was nothing really.'

'Come on, Vern!'

'All right.' Vern sighed, sitting upright again. 'I guess I kinda fell in love with her. This girl. A stupid, hopeless, crush – the kind that's no use to anybody. Fell in love with someone half my age who was in our house as my daughter's nanny. To speak truth I became obsessed with her, just like you did with that stripper. Looked forward to seeing her every morning when I came downstairs, and to renewing that contact in the evening when I returned from work. It became one of the most important things in my life. Of course, I tried to hide it from Connie. And I think I succeeded. At least, she never mentioned anything.'

'So what did you do? What happened? Did the girl realize what you felt about her? Did you ever tell her?'

Vern raised his eyebrows and exhaled sharply through pursed lips.

'I only told her at the end, the night she was packing her bags to go home.' He got up and carried his drink to the rail at the edge of the deck, then turned. 'Connie was in the kitchen with Faye and I made some excuse to go upstairs to see her. I knocked on her door and Maribel let me in. I stood there for a time, watching her packing her clothes into a big case on the floor. Neither of us said anything for a couple minutes while she packed. Then she looked up at me and smiled. "Did you want something?" she asked me.

'I told her then. Told her I was sorry, that I didn't want to cause her embarrassment or anything but that over the months she'd been with us I had come to feel ... something very special towards her. I stammered like an idiot, I remember, confessing how awkward I felt telling her this, that I didn't mean to frighten her or to put her under any pressure. I just wanted her to know my feelings. Wanted her to know, when she went back to Mexico, that there was someone left behind here in the good old US of A who cared for her. Cared for her a lot.' He took another sip of whiskey before continuing. 'Oh I said other things, too. Told her that if I was ten years younger and single I would've followed her in an instant. But I wasn't single. The whole idea was stupid, and I knew it. But I wanted her to know, all the same. That I loved her.'

There was a pause. Then Ernie spoke softly from his chair.

'What did she say to that? After you told her.'

Vern stared up at the darkening sky. 'She was very good. She didn't say anything initially. She just got to her feet and stood looking at me, her hands hanging by her sides. "I'm sorry," she said eventually, with big sad eyes. "I'm very sorry, Vern." That was it. There was nothing more she could say. I nodded, smiling stupidly at her, and went downstairs, my heart pounding in my chest. The next morning she said her goodbyes to all of us and took a taxi to the airport. She wouldn't let me drive her.'

'And you never saw her again?'

When Vern didn't answer, Ernie pressed his question.

'Come on, tell me.'

'I saw her once more. Three months after she'd left I found an excuse to take Faye down for a week's visit with Maribel and her family. To do some swimming and sightseeing. A little vacation. Connie was tied up covering a celebrity wedding in Santa Barbara so Faye and I went alone. Daddy and daughter time.'

'How did it go? How was Maribel?'

Vern shook his head, staring at the floor in great discomfort.

'She took sick, almost the moment we got there. I hardly saw her at all. She kept to her bed, spent almost every day in her room, being looked after by her mama.'

'Ha!' Ernie shook his head slowly. 'It must've been a long week for you.'

Vern nodded, soberly.

'It was. Faye and I filled our days with sightseeing trips and visits to beaches along the coast. We had fun, made memories. But I always came back in the evenings hoping to see Maribel, to spend time with her. I hardly ever did. She took her meals in her room, only occasionally wandering through to the front in her pyjamas. It was pretty obvious to me that my being there had made her sick. Or at least made her feign sickness. At one point Faye said to me, "Dad, you've got to let her go, you know? She's not for you." This from my nine-year-old daughter.' He chuckled. 'I guess she could tell from my hangdog expression.' He raised his glass and drank it off, then shook his head. 'It was awful. I felt ashamed I'd caused Maribel so much embarrassment. And mortified that my daughter had caught me out.'

'Did the family realize what was going on?'

'I never knew. I suspected the mother might've known, that Maribel might've told her of my confession in her room that night. But if she did Maria didn't hold it against me. In fact, I can remember her on several occasions reaching out to touch my arm, or my hand, as if commiserating with me for my infatuation. As if she understood and forgave me. But the father never knew, I'm sure. Augustine was always a very gracious and generous host. I liked him.' Vern studied his empty glass. 'Tragically he died a year later in an air accident. Maria wrote to tell me. In Spanish. I sent a letter of condolence.'

'And you never saw Maribel again?'

Vern shook his head.

'Not after that visit. And apart from the letter from her mother about Augustine's death I never heard from the family again either. I don't know what became of Maribel. I often wonder where she is and if … if she's had a good life. If she's happy.'

There was silence as the night settled slowly over the two old friends. Finally, slapping his hands on his knees, Ernie rose and stretched and reached for his cell phone.

'Well, old timer. That was a touching story, but I'm going home now, to make my dinner. Then I'm watching Letterman in bed. It's been great, dude. I'll see you at the club tomorrow, yes?'

Vern nodded. 'I'll be around. Give me a call when you're *compos mentis* and we'll plan the day. If you become *compos mentis*, that is.'

With a laugh Ernie turned and, raising a hand, disappeared down the deck stairs towards his own back yard.

After his own meal had been prepared and eaten, Vern did the washing up and put food down for the cat. Then he watched the news on CBS. There was nothing new. Only the usual mayhem and horror. The world going to hell in a handcart. Had it always been thus?

When he felt the urge for bed he made sure the doors were locked, turned off the living room lights, and stood for a moment in the darkness at the sliding door overlooking the deck. Outside fluffy clouds partly obscured a near full moon that sent a shimmering path of silver across the Pacific.

It'd not been a bad day. With Ernie's help he'd gotten through it without feeling gutted by Elaine's absence for more than a few minutes. She'd been dead eighteen months now, and it was still pretty difficult. The house seemed so empty without her.

Passing into his bedroom he approached his desk, where the table lamp and the computer were still on. Tomorrow, he thought. Tomorrow I'll do the emails to the grandkids and the well-meaning friends. Tonight I'm just going to sleep.

Leaning forward he closed down the computer. From beside it he picked up his favourite picture of Elaine in its silver frame, raised it to his lips and kissed it. Then he set it down again.

He stooped to turn off the desk light, then stopped and straightened. Turning to a nearby shelf, he reached out to lift a framed faded photo down into the light. It was of a girl sitting on a wooden chair, wearing a frilled red party dress with a scooped neckline. Her legs were crossed, and on her feet were white high-heeled shoes. She was leaning back against the chair with her hands clasped in her lap. Her long black hair curled at her shoulders, and there was a faint smile on her face.

Vern had had the photo for thirty years. Maribel's mother had pressed it into his hand just before he'd left their village that April. 'Take it,' she'd whispered. 'It was taken the day of her fiesta for finishing college. She looks beautiful, no?'

He had nodded, and slipped the picture into his inside jacket pocket – more grateful than she would ever know.

Maribel looked beautiful to him even now, even though the sun's rays had taken most of the photo's definition away. A ghost from the past. Long gone, but never forgotten.

Lifting his hand Vern reached out to touch the image, letting his fingers trace the fall of her dark hair.

A gesture of his enduring affection.

Then he replaced the photograph on the shelf, turned out the lamp and began his laboured preparations for sleep.

(London, 2010)

The Swimmer

Bradford Buckleigh bent his legs and leaned forward into the surf, feeling it close over his shoulders, cool and refreshing after the humid stickiness of the summer night. Pushing off, he commenced a slow crawl out and away from the beach.

Behind him the small bay was empty under the moonlight, and in the distance beyond only occasional sets of car headlights moved left and right along the coastal highway, the drivers oblivious to his presence here. He was completely alone and unobserved at this hour, and that was the way he wanted it.

Pulling himself steadily forward into the gentle Pacific surge he made for the path of light that danced across the surface before him, thrown by the beams of the full moon. Soon he had his usual rhythm going, the steady, machine-like synchronization of arms and legs and breathing that he'd spent a lifetime perfecting. And he was in shape for it, in spite of his years and the nagging pain in his side. In his youth Brad had been a champion swimmer, competing in two separate Olympics for his country, and though he'd not won medals he had come close, had been a respected member of the US Swimming Team. Ever since then he'd continued his faithful routine of swimming three or four times a week, keeping his body in shape, maintaining his special relationship with the water, that comforting familiar world that had brought him so much joy, so many good times. For Brad had won many competitions along the way, even though he hadn't succeeded at the top of his chosen sport. In state and regional tournaments as a young man he'd always placed high, if not appearing in the winners' circle, and he had loved the attention his prowess had earned him, the respect shown by his peers and trainers. He was proud of that, and that pride had given him the confidence to become a high achiever in school and university. He had done well, enjoying as a result an enviable career as a producer and then director of films and television series. Tinsel Town had welcomed and nurtured him, and now, in his seventies, Brad Buckleigh was recognized as one of the best and most revered 'characters' of the movie business – even if in recent years he'd been less active in his work than he had been earlier.

There'd been good reasons for that, he reflected, his mind pursuing its own pathway as his body surged effortlessly onwards through the water.

Firstly the loss of Adam in the Desert Storm conflict. Such a promising young man, a son to make any father proud, taken suddenly by the fickle lottery of waste that was war.

Then, five years later, the suicide of his wife Nadine, the life-partner who had been his stalwart support and confidant since they'd first met at Berkeley in the flower power years of the sixties. At the time of his son's enlistment Brad had of course considered the horrible possibility that Adam could meet with some tragic end in Iraq or elsewhere (God forbid). But Nadine's death had come as a complete surprise, even though he well knew how much she had felt Adam's loss – probably even more than he did. Mothers always suffered these bereavements more acutely, didn't they? And Adam was her only child. Nadine had doted on the boy, looked forward eagerly to the grandchildren he would one day bring her, after his impulsively chosen career as a professional soldier had paled on him and he returned to make the successful life she knew he would make, with a wife who matched his intelligence and capabilities. But a roadside IED had taken all that away in one devastating flash. And all her dreams were gone. All her expectations.

Brad had come home one day to find her lying dead on their bed, a half-filled tumbler of gin and a dozen near-empty pill bottles arranged on the night table beside her. Her still form was surrounded by a circle of open photo albums charting Adam's growth through the years. It had broken his heart finding her thus, looking so peaceful in her death sleep. He had stayed cradling her body in his arms for some time before he had finally picked up the phone to call their doctor.

Brad felt his throat tighten and dampness fogged the inside of his swimming goggles. He forced himself to stop the tears. If he didn't he wouldn't be able to see anything unless he halted to rinse them out. And he didn't want to stop. He couldn't stop. He had to keep going, keep going. Till he reached the finish line.

Think about something else. Something happy. Better times.

Lifting his arms one after the other he laid them carefully before him in sequence, turning his face from the water after every other stroke so as to breathe, his feet constantly scissoring behind him, pressing him relentlessly forward.

For some reason his first film success came to him – 'Dark Water, White Light', a drama written by a friend and adapted by the two of them into an award-winning screenplay. The explosive public reaction at the first showing, the glowing critical acclaim once it had been released, had been a wonderful surprise. Then came the press interviews and public appearances and endless congratulations. The film had propelled its two young stars into positions of prominence they never thereafter lost. For him it represented the watershed between being an unknown director who had had to fight for finance for his projects to a hot property that everyone wanted on their pictures. The money flowed, and as the years passed his work grew in stature, as did his reputation. Soon he had won a Golden Globe, had been nominated as Best Director at the Oscars. The long run of demanding, high-quality, high-return work had left him exhausted but happy. He had seldom felt stress, and if he had he'd worked it out in his regular swimming sessions, soothing away the tensions through the forced exhaustion of his muscles, stripping it all away and leaving him open for the deep rest he needed to prepare for the fresh challenges of another day.

There were so many friends in those years, close friends that he and Nadine had frequently met with for dinner, or poker games, or trips abroad, or just hanging out together by the pool. It was an idyllic life in so many ways. He thought of them now, those old friends, ran them through his mind like images from a high school annual, familiar faces and voices, many of them now dead and gone, all of them once loved and regularly seen, almost like family – a good thing, since he had lost his own parents so young.

After Adam's death their social life had closed down. Nadine couldn't face other people, had no desire to make a pretence of being social when she couldn't be, locked as she was in her grief. So they had stayed home, and Brad had started to drink. Work offers tapered off. Old friends were timid about calling, not wanting to disturb their grieving, afraid of being drawn into it themselves. Brad did get occasional work offers and he accepted them, but nothing that would take him away from Nadine for more than a few hours at a time. He had remained in Hollywood, working from home, returning every night to the atmosphere of loss and longing that haunted the Buckleigh house like a bad smell.

A houseful of ghosts.

So much for happy thoughts.

Sensing his lungs reaching the limit of their endurance Brad stopped his swimming, rolled over onto his back in the water to rest, gasping for air, gently fanning his spread hands to keep afloat, staring up at the faint stars in the moon glow. Twisting his body he looked back briefly toward the shore, saw the white slash of the sandy beach a mile or so away, the road beyond. Knew his Porsche was up there somewhere, parked under a tree on one of the access roads. Knew his carefully folded clothes were still piled on the rock where he'd left them. A part of him wanted to go back, to wear the clothes again and to drive the Porsche fast along the twisting seaside road, to rejoin life. But that wasn't possible anymore. Not since yesterday. Not with what he knew now.

He turned his attention back to the orb of the moon above him, lolling back into the water, catching his breath. Reaching up a hand he pushed up the goggles, massaged his eyes, then wiped the water away and pulled the goggles into place again.

Time to go on. Resting did no good; it only delayed the inevitable. Why put it off? Onward to the finish.

Gathering himself, he rolled over in the water and picked up his steady crawl seaward again, along the beam of moonlight.

It had started as a dull ache in his right side. He'd thought it was just his liver complaining about the nightly doses of alcohol it'd had to contend with for the past several years, and he'd left off drinking for a few nights to give it a break. But the ache had not improved, had in fact gotten worse. Finally Brad had made a doctor's appointment.

Franklin Peabody was one of those old friends from the past, a golf partner and former frequent player (with his wife Eleanor) at the weekly poker parties. Franklin had also delivered their son, and had served as family doctor and counsellor/advisor to the Buckleighs for as long as they had been in Hollywood.

Brad went to see him and they had chatted amiably while Frank had given him a thorough examination. At the end, when he had dressed himself again and sat in the armchair opposite the desk in his friend's office, Frank had suggested he undergo a series of tests to further explore the cause of his mysterious ache.

'Not that I'm too concerned,' Frank assured him. 'You're one of the fittest men I know, even if you do drink too much these days. Your swimming helps that enormously. I can't imagine anything being really wrong. But I think it's an idea to have the tests done all the same, just so we can rule out certain things, if you know what I mean.'

Brad had known what he meant, and had gone along willingly to the hospital for a day of blood-taking and scanning and general technical prodding and probing and had not thought another thing about it.

Until a few days later – the day before yesterday – when he'd had a call from Franklin asking him to drop by the office the following morning. Brad could tell there was something wrong from the rather tentative way Frank spoke, but he hadn't allowed himself to think the worst. After all, he was only seventy-two. He should have years ahead yet. He'd even started to make plans to kick-start back into life his dormant career. There couldn't be anything seriously wrong with him, could there?

Then he was back in Frank's familiar office again, with the photos of Eleanor, their children and grandchildren on the desk. The medical certificates and diplomas framed beside the window overlooking McArthur Park. Frank's face, frowning.

'Brad, I'm afraid I've got bad news…'

And there it was. Inoperable cancer of the liver/pancreas. Signs of it already spreading to the lungs and colon. A death warrant with no reprieve.

'How long?' Brad had asked, stunned.

Frank had shrugged. 'Two months. Maybe three. But soon.' He leaned forward. 'I'm sorry, Brad. I wish I could offer a ray of hope, but there isn't any.'

'Give me the straight skinny, Frank,' Brad had replied. 'What's going to happen to me?'

Peabody had tried to prevaricate, talking vague possibilities and generalities until Brad had pressed him, on the basis of their old friendship, to speak candidly. Then Frank had described what could almost certainly be expected: the long, dreadful slide to oblivion via wasting organs and failing body functions and pain and pain and pain – excruciating pain, which could and would be controlled, but only with mind-numbing drugs that would take him out of consciousness altogether until his tired old heart finally stopped.

What kind of end was that to look forward to?

Brad's only consolation was that Nadine had been spared having to witness it. But that was a feeble consolation. Nadine herself had been dead three years now.

Brad couldn't remember how he had gotten home, but he had. And sat in a chair for hours trying to come to terms with it. Finally making his decision. The only decision possible for a champion with no dependents.

Brad felt his chest about to explode again and paused a moment, gasping and treading water. Turning back, he could hardly make out the bay now against the dark smudge of the hills behind it. He must be miles off now, surely. Too far to make it back, even if he was tempted to change his mind. But he wouldn't change his mind. The die was cast. Onward or bust. That was all there was left.

In his senior year in high school he had competed in a state-wide tournament to determine the best of the best as far as the swimmers were concerned. Brad had placed in the first three in all his heats, and had ended up in the final. That race was the one he always remembered when he thought of the struggle to win and what it cost. He thought of it now, turning again along the moonbeam pathway towards China, reactivating his tired arms and legs, straining with every muscle in his body toward the finish line he'd been too slow to reach the first time round. Then it had been second best for him. This time he was on to a sure thing. This time there was nothing but victory ahead for him. All he had to do was keep going.

With the ghost whispers of his dead wife and son urging him forward, and with the screams of the remembered crowd echoing in his ears, Brad Buckleigh crawled on steadily across the water.

Towards his end.

(London, 2013)

The Waiting Room

The old courthouse room was empty, apart from three bentwood chairs arranged against the wall opposite the two curtainless windows overlooking the street. Above the chairs a framed photograph of Roosevelt smiled into the room with the promise of a New Deal. At either end of the narrow space dark hardwood doors led off to other areas – one giving onto an echoey corridor and downstairs to the building's main entrance, the other into an inner office. In the three chairs, two young men and an older woman sat stiffly, unspeaking. The two men were in their late teens, farm boys in the dress of men who work with animals and muck and machinery. The woman, on the other hand, was wearing what was clearly her best Sunday dress, though it was now faded and worn and threadbare here and there. As the time passed the two young men sneaked surreptitious glances at one another and at the woman, under the pretext of rubbing an ankle or scratching an elbow or relieving a stiff neck. The woman, on the other hand, sat motionless and subdued, staring down at the tightly clasped hands in her lap.

After many minutes of strained silence the door to the inner office opened and a tall balding man in a white shirt and tie appeared in the frame and beckoned sternly to one of the young men, who nodded and rose. Swallowing dryly, he moved across the room to slip past the man into the room beyond. The white-shirted man glared briefly at the room's remaining inhabitants, then withdrew, closing the door behind him.

For a long moment there was silence again, a silence invaded only by the faint ticking of the wall clock hung between the windows and the occasional rumble of vehicles passing along the street outside. No sound could be heard from beyond the office door. Not even the murmur of voices.

The black hands on the clock face read 11:30. Only half an hour left, both watchers thought, before the lunch break. Maybe they wouldn't be called in before then? Maybe they'd have to come back again after? What a nuisance, the boy thought, frowning. The Old Man won't like that.

He scratched his elbow again and glanced towards the woman, twisting his face finally into an awkward grin.

'Reckon we'll make it before lunch?' he asked her.

Looking up from her hands, the woman tried herself to smile, to be neighbourly.

'Don't know,' she said. 'We'll just have to wait and see, I guess.'

The boy stood, glanced again at the wall clock, then stepped to one of the windows to look out at the trees and the courthouse lawn below. After a few seconds he turned to look at the woman again, jamming his large hands into the pockets of his faded bib overalls.

'I sure hope they can see us before lunch,' he said, shaking his head. 'My Pa's mad enough I have to be here at all when he needs me so on the farm.'

The woman said nothing, just smiled thinly across at him.

The clock ticked through another couple of minutes while the young man stood there before the window, scuffing the side of one rough work boot against the other, working his mouth, glancing at the woman now and then with a hint of a frown on his brow. Finally he could hold it back no longer.

'Goddam war!' he said, forcefully. Then he bowed his head,

embarrassed. 'Begging your pardon, ma'am. Only it's brung so much trouble to all of us.'

Without looking at him the woman nodded her agreement.

'That it has, to be sure,' she said at last, almost a whisper. After a moment she looked up at him. 'You here to ask to be excused from conscription?'

The boy frowned.

'Yes, ma'am. My brother was took three months ago and my old man can't run the farm without me to help him. He wants me to tell 'em they can't have me, that taking one son is enough.'

The woman nodded again, understanding now. It was not an uncommon request amongst farm people, though one that was seldom granted. Only time would tell if he'd be one of the lucky ones.

'What about you, ma'am?' the boy asked at length. 'Why're you here?'

'Pretty much for the same reason you are,' she said. 'To ask for an exemption for my son. Though the circumstances are different.'

'Different how?'

The woman sighed, shifted slightly on her chair, produced a hanky from a sleeve and dabbed at her eyes. When she was finally able to speak her voice was strained and tearful.

'I'm here to ask that they leave my third son be,' she said. 'He turns eighteen tomorrow. They'll want him to go off to the war like all the rest.'

'Well, ma'am. Them's the rules for most folks. Not many can get around 'em. 'Less he's sickly or crippled or not right in the head.'

'I know that,' she replied. 'Believe me, I know that. But taking my Aaron would just be plain inhuman cruel, and I'm not letting him go without a fight.'

Sympathetic now, the boy returned to sit in the chair beside the woman. Placing his broad palms on his muddy denim knees, he turned to look at her.

'So,' he began, tentatively. 'What's your excuse for wanting him set aside? Is he crippled or something?'

'No,' the woman returned, still working at calming her eyes. 'He's a fine boy, fit as a horse.'

'Well then, on what grounds do you want him excused?'

For a moment the woman sat clutching the hanky in her lap. Then she reached to the floor to her purse, extracted from it a small black and white photograph. Sitting up again, she handed the photo to the boy, who took it and frowned down at it, studying the figures pictured.

'All them your sons?' he asked after a moment.

'Yes. Those are my boys. Simon, Jacob and Aaron.' She reached across to point with her index finger. 'That's Aaron on the end. At the right. He's the youngest.'

The young man frowned.

'So where are the other two boys, ma'am? Gone for soldiers already?'

The woman nodded, tearing up again.

'They were soldiers, yes,' she said at last.

'Were?' The boy's mouth dropped open and his brow furrowed. 'You mean they're both gone? Killed in the war?'

'Yes. They're dead now, both of them. Killed on one of those French beaches during the landings two months ago. They enlisted and trained together, they were together there in that landing, and they died there together.'

'Oh, my God.'

Another long moment passed while the young man, his brow clouded, stared down at the grainy photograph of the three brothers. Then, after reaching first to touch each figure with the tip of his index finger in a kind of dumb salute, he passed the picture back to the bereaved mother, watched her bend to replace it in her purse.

'What about your husband, ma'am?' he asked. 'Why ain't he here doing the asking?'

The woman sighed, deeply.

'My husband is dead, too,' she said at last. 'He was killed in a road accident five years ago. So I'm all alone now, you see? Apart from Aaron.'

The boy stared at her, his mouth open.

'I hope they let him stay, ma'am,' he said finally. 'Your boy Aaron, I mean. I surely do. Losing two boys is enough.' Then after a beat he sat up, stuck out his chin, forthrightly. 'Hell, I'll go for him, if they'll let me. It ain't right you should run the risk of being left all alone. I know Pa could get along fine without me if he really had to, if the chips were down. And anyway he's not alone. He's got Ma.'

The woman smiled wistfully at him.

'But suppose something happened to your brother – God forbid! – and then to you? Then they'd be left all alone just like me. That wouldn't be fair, would it? And it could happen, just like with my...'

She stopped, forced down a sob, regained her composure again, blinking.

'I don't care, ma'am. I don't reckon we'd both be taken anyway. And folks are saying it shouldn't last too much longer now, so he should be home soon. I mean it, though. I'll go for your boy, if they'll take me that way.'

The woman's face slowly crinkled into a smile, and she reached across to grasp one of his rough farmer's hands, squeezing it.

'That's awful kind of you, son. But I couldn't let you do that. Not and maybe put your father into the same situation I'm in now. No, I guess we'll just both of us have to take our chances and trust to Providence to give us the right decisions.'

She squeezed his hand again, firmly. Then she released it and sat back in her chair, pulling herself erect almost fiercely.

Silence fell again.

'God-damned war,' she whispered finally.

'What's that, ma'am?' asked the boy, leaning towards her.

She looked at him.

'You were right, son. What you said before. It is a God-damned war. A taker of lives and a destroyer of families. And nobody's safe from it, even this far away.'

Seconds passed as they held one another's eyes, united in their helplessness, their frustration, their righteous anger.

Then there was a click and both turned to look as the inner office door opened again.

(Edale, July, 2015)

Reunion

From the moment Ray opened his eyes he knew this day would be the one – the day he'd been waiting for, and dreading, for the last six months.

Across the room, beyond the foot of his bed, he saw the pink light of dawn peeking in under the drawn roller blind. Through the open doorway adjacent he could see the back of Lillian's robe and her white hair as she washed herself in the tiny bathroom sink.

From outside came the rasping caws of the fat crows perched on the water tower in the lot behind the convalescent home – hovering like buzzards above a wounded animal, waiting to pounce at the moment of death.

For a moment Ray lay unmoving, taking stock of himself and of the limited world around him.

It must be early, he thought – around five or five-thirty. There were no sounds from the hallway, no murmur of voices. Everyone else was still asleep, except for the duty nurses at the front of the building.

It had been another dream-filled night for him, with image after image from his past appearing in succession to grab his attention and jerk him off on another mad fast-motion retrospective. His older brother Jake, his five sisters, the shadowy father who came and went. His little German mother, working herself half to death to make ends meet in their rough cabin in the flat South Dakota wastes. Their dog 'Ty', the faithful German shepherd who'd been the boys' constant companion during those early years.

At least there had been little pain in the night. He was grateful for that. Lillian had given him his morphine regularly – swabbing his mouth with the liquid from the tiny bottle, letting it be absorbed by the lips and tongue to deaden the sharp stabbings in his bowel and chest. The relief had been almost instantaneous each time, soothing away the jagged edges, releasing him from the discomfort of the present back into the welcoming familiarity of the past.

Lillian came back into the room now, rubbing lotion into her hands, and approached the bed. Seeing his open eyes, she smiled.

'All right, darling? Anything I can do for you?'

He struggled to shake his head, a barely perceptible movement which she nonetheless acknowledged with a nod. Sitting on the bed beside him she lifted his hand, caressing it between her own and looking down at him lovingly.

He was lucky to have found her ten years ago, he knew that. They were lucky to have found each other. A lonely widower, escaping his grief with regular bouts of heavy drinking, his life an empty waste since his wife of thirty-five years had suddenly been taken from him by a heart attack, Ray had followed the suggestion of a friend to attend a grief therapy session at the local community centre, and had found there a kindred spirit in the form of this wiry little woman who had lost her own life-long partner at around the same time. Though neither of them had expected it, a friendship had sprung up between them, and from their weekly group therapy sessions they would go off together afterwards to drink coffee at a nearby café, to talk about their pasts shared with deceased partners – helping one another to come to terms with the loss, finding to their surprise that in so doing they were building a bond of comforting dependence upon one another.

When the therapy meetings were no longer necessary the two continued to meet, and Ray took to spending more and more time with

Lillian at her house in the nearby small town. Soon they were sleeping together – finding solace in one another's arms. No matter that they weren't married. There could be no justification at their advanced ages for the smirks and insinuations of public self-righteousness.

It was inevitable that Ray should sell his lonely house in the mountains and move in with Lillian in Garberville, and this he did within a few months. For the next eight years the two of them lived happily together, discovering with their increasing affection for one another a new chapter in their lives, a time of peace and contentment – even happiness – that neither had believed possible after the loss of their spouses. Settled in Lillian's comfortable '30s wood-frame house on a side street of the town, they spent their days shopping or reading, walking arm in arm along the broad sandy beach at the coast a few miles away, sharing seafood dinners at their favourite restaurants, or receiving visits from younger relatives on both sides, growing even older together comfortably and lovingly.

Then, after a routine doctor's visit for an extended bout of painful constipation, the diagnosis of Ray's cancer came, and the months of dwindling and suffering. When he became too weak they moved into Harbor View, a convalescent home at the centre of nearby Shelter Cove, where they could both live in the same room and where Lillian would be assisted in caring for her ailing partner by a trained nursing staff and regular doctor visits.

Thus they had lived for the last three months, as Ray grew thinner and weaker and his appetites waned – for food, for diversion, for life. As he weakened he slept more, and when he slept he dreamt, and always of the same things. Of his youth in South Dakota. Of his brother Jake, his five sisters, his tough little German mother struggling to cope in the difficult days of Depression America. And of the dog Ty.

In the quiet of their room, feeling now the soothing caress of Lillian's hands on his, Ray gave a tiny squeeze in return – all that he was capable of – and closed his eyes once more, to be drawn again down the shadowy road without end.

Hurrying. Faster and faster.

Why?

A voice called from up ahead.

'Come on, Ray! Can't you keep up? If you can't move any faster I'll leave you behind!'

Jake in the distance, turning back to harangue him. Three years older, and as sleek a runner as the great Jim Thorpe himself. It was hard to keep up with him, but Ray tried for all his worth. He didn't want to lose sight of Jake; didn't want to be left behind.

'Wait! Please, *wait*!'

'Come *ooooonnn*!!'

Once when they had been playfully teasing a pair of gravediggers in the local cemetery, they had ventured too close and Jake had been grabbed by the men and forced into a pine coffin lying empty nearby. Pressing down the lid, the men had nailed it home over Jake's shouts of defiance. Ray and another neighbour boy had watched all this in speechless horror from a distance. Then, spurred by desperation, the boys had pulled sling-shots from their back pockets and sent a stream of stones flying towards the culprits, pelting them several times and causing them to abandon their hammering to give chase. Round and around the gravestones the two boys had darted, keeping the wheezing men at bay, lurching this way and that. Left alone in his terrifying confinement, Jake had battered away at the coffin lid with his hands and elbows and knees until it had slowly prised up and the nails had pulled free. Leaping out, Jake had then entered the fray, hurling a stone which struck one of the men on an ankle and set him dancing about on one leg, grasping his wound and howling with rage. When the man's partner stopped to assess the seriousness of the injury, the three boys seized their chance and scarpered over a nearby wall. As ever Jake was in the lead, racing for the cornfields where they could lose themselves amidst the curtain of green plants.

'Hurry! Run like hell before the bastards catch us!'

They ran like hell, Ray's young legs pumping like pistons, his heart thumping in his chest and his lungs straining for breath, pressing forward towards his brother.

'Faster, Ray! Faster! Come on!'

He awoke gasping for breath, with Lillian's concerned face frowning down over him.

'There, there, darling,' she cooed. 'It's all right. You're only dreaming again. Calm down and catch your breath. There's nothing after you now.'

Except that there was – something far more lethal than two angry gravediggers.

And it wouldn't be long now before it caught him.

Later in the day, after a few spoonfuls of yogurt and some sips of juice had been coaxed past his dry mouth, he slept again. And was surprised when he woke to find his middle-aged stepson looking down at him with a pained expression, holding his hand and stroking it.

'We're sure going to miss you,' the man whispered. 'I had to come, to say thank you for being such a great stepdad. You're a good man, Ray.'

He squeezed the bony hand, his eyes tearing.

Ray nodded. He'd been a good stepson, too – not too troublesome as a boy, and loyal and supportive in the later bad times. He was sorry to cause him such hurt. Sorry he'd come so far for nothing.

He closed his eyes again as the weakness and fatigue took him again, drawing him under for the last time...

Now he was walking through a frosted winter pasture, with Ty racing away before him, yipping enthusiastically, rounding up the cows for the morning's milking. Ray followed him, padding on bare feet across the frozen earth – if only they could afford a new pair of boots! – hopping when possible from one steaming cow pat to another, squelching the warm sludge between his toes, savouring momentary relief each time ... until he had to move on again. In the distance he could hear Ty barking. And Jake's irritated voice as ever urging him to catch up...

That night when Ray didn't awaken again Lillian was comforted by the nurses, who warned that the end was very close. But she was not to punish herself by remaining awake all night, they told her. She must sleep when her body told her to.

Lillian tried to stay awake. Clutching his hand, she listened to his laboured breathing, stroked his ravaged features. But in the hours towards dawn she could no longer arrest the drooping of her eyelids and the drifting of consciousness. So she kissed Ray's brow, whispered that she loved him and dragged herself across the room to lie on her narrow bed – willing herself to sleep in spite of the rasping breaths of her beloved partner, hoping against hope she'd not awaken too late and miss him.

Ray knew it would be soon now, for the images came even more quickly than before. And the voices.

After a space of restful blackness he was hauled once more into the past, this time into a world of whirling snow – acres of it in all directions as far as the eye could see, thick and wet and sticky, drifting against distant buildings and blowing like feathers in the South Dakota wind. There was a group of people with him this time – indistinct figures of youngsters bundled in greatcoats and scarves, woollen hats and mittens, gathered about a bonfire at the base of a low hill and blowing out clouds of steam with their breaths, laughing and shouting. Above them on the gentle slope others flew in couples down the scarred incline on wooden sleds. He could hear their excited laughter mingling with the barking of dogs, as they raced down the hill after the sleds. His dog Ty was at his feet, a ball of pure energy, springing to the right and then to the left, emitting ecstatic yelps, urging his young master to pull the sled up the slope again for another run. And so Ray did, grasping the rope with his mittened hands, plodding upwards once more through the swirling whiteness. Such hard work, lifting one foot after the other. Trudging uphill. Such painfully hard work.

'Come on, slowpoke!' came shrill voices from above. 'You'll never get here at that rate.'

He knew the voices and looked up – and could just about see them there. His sisters Helen and Martha – the youngest of the girls – gathered at the hill's crest with a clutch of their classmates from the little one-room school. He recognized two of the others – Abigail Kearney and Ruth Adams – not seen or even thought of in seventy years. Where were they now?

And who was that other figure, standing at the side? Another female. Older, dressed in modern clothes. Looking down at him with such yearning, such love. Willing him closer.

Not his long dead wife? Not Ginny? How could that be? But why question it? This was a dream after all. Anything was possible.

'I'm coming,' he croaked.

He was doing his best, couldn't they see that?

Those girls. How wonderful to see their rosy-cheeked faces waiting for him, beaming against the snow! Young and alive again. Instead of old and dead and in the earth, where he knew they almost certainly were. Helen and Martha definitely were. And Ginny, too, of course. (He'd attended all their funerals, witnessed their interment, had he not?) Ray carried on climbing, feeling the pain building in his legs and arms, gritting his teeth, bending forward into it, straining for dear life.

As he approached the hillcrest the swirling flakes thickened and the brightness became suddenly intense, blinding, whiting out everything. He could see no one now, and the voices were distant and muted, as if buried in a box. He stopped climbing, gasped for air. Rubbing his eyes with a mittened hand, he tried to clear them so as to see through the painful white light to what lay beyond. But he could not.

'We're here, Ray!'

The voice of his beloved mother. Faint, but undeniable. Was she there, too?

'We're all here waiting for you, can't you see us?'

'I'm here, too, Ray!'

Ginny's voice, a voice he hadn't heard for ten years. The memory of it choked him and made his dry eyes start with moisture.

'We're all here! All very close,' she coaxed, just beyond his vision. 'Very, very close. Keep trying! Keep trying!'

'Don't give up now, kid!' cried Jake. Jake the rebel, dead these dozen years from tobacco and booze and a life lived at full tilt. 'Why do I always have to wait for you, little brother? You're nearly there, just a little bit further. Come on! Give it your best shot!'

And so he did, straining forward with every tired muscle in his withered, wasted body, striving to transcend the blinding whiteness, holding his breath with the effort, pushing himself with every last calorie of energy upwards into the light...

Until the fierce whiteness suddenly imploded and the terrible struggle ceased, and merciful black oblivion wiped it, and him, entirely away.

Lillian opened her eyes, suddenly wide awake. The silence of the room was profound now. But she knew she'd heard Ray's last rattled exhalation seconds before, and knew that he was gone.

Calmly she drew herself up, then stood.

Across the room, lit by the faint glow of the nightlight beside his bed, Ray lay on his back, his arms outside the covers, extended down his sides, his fists clenched tightly in some final unknown struggle.

She stepped closer.

His eyes were open, rolled up and back, as if searching for something high above him. His whole body seemed to stretch upwards, reminding her of a high jumper pushing himself off the earth, lifting himself, arching his back to clear the bar.

Whatever he was striving for was past worrying about now. But she hoped with all her heart that he'd made it.

Moving to the telephone beside her bed, she called first through to the front desk and told them the news, asking to be left alone for a time. Then she dialled for an outside line and called her family, awaiting at the house. Her message was brief. They'd be with her in an hour.

She hung up. Pulling herself up with an effort, she crossed again to Ray's bed, looked down at his lifeless form for a long moment. Then she crawled onto the bed beside him – curling herself close, gathering him tight against her, feeling the warmth of his still body dwindling by degrees.

And wept silent tears.

(London, 2010)

BEYOND

The Wimbledon Ghost

The young man switched off the little black and white television and turned to the frail figure lying in the hospital bed across the room, her head and upper body raised on a nest of pillows.

'There, Granny. How was that? Did it bring back memories?'

'Oh, yes,' she cooed. ''Course it did. The Wimbledon fortnight was always my favourite competition. I had to give up the tournaments in my thirties, but I kept playing until my late seventies – as you know – when arthritis made it impossible to continue. I miss my tennis a lot. It was a good life.'

'Well,' he said, as he moved to the bed and took her hand, 'you certainly earned your place in Wimbledon history, even if most of the crowd out there today wouldn't know your name.'

'I only won one singles championship, Ian.'

'Yes, but you were runner-up several times.'

'That's true. But the game has moved on so since my day.' She shook her head. 'When I watch these girls now, grunting like beasts and hammering away at the ball with both hands on the racket, I realise how tame we were in comparison. We were trying to remain ladies as we played, I suppose. These girls play just like the men, and good on them for it. It's changed the women's game entirely, made it far more athletic and powerful. I'm only sorry we hadn't the courage to do that in my day. Fetch me a glass of water, will you, dear?'

'Of course.'

She watched him as he poured water from the pitcher on her side table into a plastic tumbler, then handed it to her. She drank two or three swallows, then passed the tumbler back.

'That's better. Thanks, dear.'

'My pleasure, Granny. Anything else I can do for you?'

'No. Just pull that chair over and sit by me a bit. I haven't seen you for weeks and it's nice to visit. It was good of you to bring the television so I could see the final. Very thoughtful of you. Thank you for that.'

The young man pulled the armchair from the window and sat beside his grandmother.

'I thought you'd like to see it,' he said, sitting back and clasping his hands over his stomach. 'So now what? What d'you want to talk about? You know all my news. I've already told you.'

She smiled, her face a mask of impishness.

'Did I ever tell you about the time I was beaten by a ghost at Wimbledon?'

He looked askance. 'Beaten by a what?'

'By a ghost, Ian. You heard me. In front of a full house on Centre Court.'

'How could that happen?' her grandson scoffed. 'You're kidding me, right?'

'No, I'm not. And since you've been kind enough to think of me on Ladies' Singles final day I'll tell you all about it. But you mustn't breathe a word to anyone else. It's one of the most closely guarded secrets of our time.'

And as the young man looked on in amazement the old lady told her story.

'It happened a long time ago, between the wars, while most of the western world was suffering from the effects of the Great Depression.

I was lucky enough to have been the daughter of upper class parents who recognised my tennis talents and had money to pay for my weekly lessons, in spite of the hard times. Of course I still went to school and then to university, but I never gave up my training, and I never lost my dream of playing tennis for England.

'At nineteen my chance finally came. I had managed to play consistently well over a number of months and in the summer of that year I qualified to play in the Wimbledon tournament. Of course I was over the moon and worked my hardest during those two weeks, riding on a tide of unshakeable confidence, knocking aside my opponents one after another – until that final glorious Centre Court win that gave me the silver dish that now sits on its stand on the chiffonier in your mother's drawing room.'

Her grandson nodded. 'She's enormously proud of it. Keeps it shining like a beacon.'

'Well, good. So am I. Anyway, the year after that I was the hot favourite to win the title again and I arrived at Wimbledon full of determination and energy. There was the usual list of international stars I would have to work my way through to get to the top and I was eager to get on with it. But the atmosphere at the start of the competition was clouded slightly by some tragic news. A young American girl from somewhere in the Midwest – Des Moines or Terre Haute or somewhere like that – who had won a place in the Wimbledon competition had taken a freighter from New York to Southampton and had never arrived. Apparently the ship sank without trace only a day or two out of New York. So we were all saddened by the thought of that young girl who had been so excited about coming to play in the great Wimbledon tournament, but who had gone to a watery grave instead.

'What's more, mirroring our slightly subdued spirits, the weather in the days leading up to the tournament was damp and gloomy, and on opening day we arrived at the courts wondering how long it would be before rain would halt play. Then an extraordinary thing happened.

In a matter of minutes the clouds lifted and the sun broke through to shine. We all remarked how strange it seemed, as if someone had suspended the wet weather just for opening day. And it held, that hiatus in the weather, for some time.

'Anyway, that day I was scheduled to play on Centre Court against a young Czech girl who was making her first visit to the Wimbledon tournament. As was usual with me, I spent half an hour that morning warming up on one of the outer courts and got to the changing rooms early, where I showered, changed into my match clothes, and – as soon as the call came – made my way out to the court. Sitting in my chair I busied myself arranging my rackets, towels and water bottles for the match. Meanwhile, the sky above remained clear and bright.

'Minutes went by and my opponent still hadn't arrived. The umpire was about to send a runner to track her down when, at the mouth of the tunnel leading to the dressing rooms, a wraith-like figure appeared – a girl in a white knee-length tennis skirt and blouse, her hair cut in a pageboy close to her face. She looked very pale, and her dark eyes as she stepped out onto the court looked round at the spectators as if she couldn't quite believe where she was. I put it down to nerves, to being on Centre Court for the first time, and thought nothing of it. But there was more. In her hand she carried only a single racket, nothing else – no extra rackets, no water bottle, not even a towel. Well, I thought that was a bit strange, but as I had not met the Czech girl before I naturally assumed that she was just a bit eccentric. The umpire obviously didn't know her either for she called out the Czech girl's name and, when the newcomer nodded her head, announced that play would begin after a five minute warm up. I took a handful of balls and a racket and walked to one end, where I made a few crisp service deliveries that sent the ball boys scrambling. The other girl, I was surprised to notice, went to her baseline, produced one ball and served a clean ace to the inside corner of the box. Then she stopped. That was her warm-up. While I carried on she stood silently behind her baseline, cradling her racket in her arms, her eyes still scanning the grandstands like an overawed child.

'"Time!" the umpire shouted, and we both stepped towards her. The coin was flipped to determine who was to serve and from which end of the court. When that was settled, I stopped off at my chair for a quick sip of water, while the girl marched straight to her end of the court and took up her position. I then marched to my baseline and the game commenced, myself serving the first game.

'Well, it was a hard match let me tell you. For all of being so tiny the Czech girl had an amazing fluidity of movement around the court, managing to get to and return every tactically placed volley I sent her, pounding them back at me with surprising power, forcing me to race from side to side, covering more ground with each rally than I'd ever had to with any of my previous opponents. Somehow I managed to break her fourth game, however, and then served to take the first set, which I did after a very close deuce game that see-sawed each way for several minutes before finally being decided with a clean ace.

'The second set was just as arduous for me. The girl had me running about like a gambolling puppy and my stamina was wearing thin. Though I gave it my best effort, she managed to break my fifth game, then won her next game – and the second set – to love. I think I was just too worn out by all the running around she was forcing me to do to offer any reply.

'I took my rest break perched on my chair, trying to compose myself, sipping water and trying to catch my breath before the last battle was joined. When I glanced over at her chair I was surprised to find it empty. As I said, she had brought nothing with her but her racket, and how she managed to play so hard for an hour and not be thirsty was beyond me. I looked around, and was shocked to see her standing on the far baseline awaiting the restart of the game, holding her racket before her and looking about, now with a strange half-smile on her face.

'That last set was the hardest of my career. I sweated blood to match the unrelenting volleys this Czech girl bombarded me with, trying to get the ball back over the net with some directed purpose behind it. Sometimes I succeeded in wrong-footing her and managed to sneak the occasional winner by along the sideline. But she seemed to anticipate my every idea, and sent the ball hurtling back at me with stinging force, as if punishing me for trying to outwit her.'

Ian now was leaning forward in his armchair, his eyes fixed on his grandmother's face, completely absorbed in her story.

'So what happened then? How did that third set finish, Granny? Tell me!'

'Well, she broke me in my fourth service game and won every game after that. I was lucky if I got a point. And when the last game – and the deciding set – was won and the crowd burst into sustained applause, all I could do was to stumble towards the net, where I shook the coldest hand I've ever touched, then staggered back to my chair and collapsed onto it in a daze, wondering how it'd all happened, how I had been unlucky enough to draw such a demon to play against in the very first round. During all this time the Czech girl was standing in the middle of the court, smiling brightly and looking around at the cheering spectators, many on their feet. Finally, she turned towards the royal box – empty on that occasion – and dropped into a deep formal curtsey, then rose again. Raising a hand in acknowledgement of the continuing applause and shouts of the crowd, she turned and, with a nod towards me and to the lady umpire, moved towards the tunnel mouth --- and disappeared!'

The old lady stopped speaking and stared smiling at her grandson, her eyebrows raised.

Ian leaned forward, his arms crossed over his knees. 'Disappeared, Grandma? What do you mean?'

'You heard me, Ian. She literally disappeared. One moment she was there at the tunnel mouth, the next she was gone and the tunnel was empty.'

Ian shook his head in disbelief. 'Did everyone see that, or just you?'

'Well, for many people in the stands it probably looked as if she'd just entered the tunnel and moved out of sight. It would require being in the same line of sight as I was, and close to the ground, to see what I saw. Fortunately few people were that unlucky.'

'So what happened next?'

'Well, I couldn't believe that what I had just seen was anything but some kind of hallucination brought about by my exhaustion, so I just sat there, sipping my water, staring dumbly into the middle distance for a time, trying to get myself back together again. Strangely, moments after the girl's departure, the sky darkened again, the clouds soon resembling the threatening sky of the morning. Shaken from my reverie by this sudden change, I gathered my things together and had risen to leave the court when the second amazing thing happened.'

Ian shook his head, puzzled now. 'The second thing? What second thing?'

The old lady gave her impish smile again.

'As I said, I was just about to make my exit from the court when there was movement at the tunnel mouth and a girl appeared in tennis dress and carrying a racket bag, wildly distracted and jabbering away in full voice in broken English mixed with some guttural eastern European language. Dashing past me she entered into an animated conversation with the umpire, who leaned down from her perch to listen, frowning.'

'Who was the girl? What did she want?'

'Ian, it was the Czech player I had been scheduled to play that morning. And she proved it by producing her passport. Apparently, as she explained, she, her mother and their driver had all fallen asleep simultaneously minutes before they were due to set off for Wimbledon. They just sank down wherever they were and went out like switched-off lights – she and her mother in their hotel room, the driver outside in the waiting car.'

Ian's eyes were as large as saucers. 'Why? How could such a thing happen?'

'There's no explanation, Ian. It just happened. They weren't able to get to Wimbledon until two hours after their scheduled arrival time. She had missed her match entirely and was beside herself with remorse and shock.'

'Unbelievable!'

Ian got to his feet and crossed to the window, his brows knitted in a deep frown. For a long moment he stared outside, then turned to his grandmother again.

'Then who was the girl you played? The girl who beat you that morning?'

The old lady smiled again.

'No one knows. Lawn Tennis Association staff went searching for her all around the grounds but no one came up with any clues. The other dressing room was empty and there were no reports of her being seen anywhere around the courts, either before or after the match. Even people standing near the dressing rooms said they hadn't seen her. She had simply disappeared into thin air.'

Stunned, Ian moved again to collapse onto the chair, clasping his hands before him.

'Was there never a clue as to who she might've been?'

'Not then. The tournament authorities assumed she was some stranger who'd managed to sneak past the gatekeepers and find her way into the Centre Court players' area. And that she'd made her exit the same way, undetected. They searched for an explanation as to how such a thing could've happened but came up with nothing. Finally it was simply hushed up and forgotten.'

'What happened about the match itself? She had defeated you, after all.'

'Well, since she wasn't the opponent I was scheduled to play the defeat was not even registered. The following morning I played the Czech girl on one of the outer courts and beat her easily. I went on that year to the semis, but got no further – I think because of the exhaustion I'd suffered from that first match with the mysterious disappearing player.'

Ian shook his head again.

'So who do you think she was, this girl? Do you have any theories?'

The old lady smoothed the counterpane before her with her hands, then clasped them together.

'In spite of the attempts made by the Lawn Tennis Association to keep the story hushed up, the identity of the mysterious girl was of major interest to the tabloids, as you can imagine. Of course many photographs were taken of the girl during the match by newspaper photographers, but strangely none of them turned out. Apparently the girl's image was always blurred and unclear – something they put down to being caught in quick movement. Since there were no useable pictures one paper got a sketch artist to draw a likeness of the girl, based on the memories of several of the match spectators. I saw the drawing. It was quite true to her looks. At least, I thought so.

'Some weeks later I received a telephone call from a young American requesting an interview to discuss the strange story. As I was still living at home, I invited him there and saw him in the sitting room alone. He produced the newspaper sketch of the girl and asked me if it was a good likeness of the player who had beaten me that day. I told him it was. Taking back the sketch and pocketing it, he walked to the large windows that overlooked Eaton Square and stared outside. Then he turned towards me again, clasping his hands behind his back.

'"The girl in that sketch is an absolute dead ringer for my sister, the late Abigail Thomas. You might remember her as the American tennis player who never made it to the Wimbledon tournament, who died when her ship sank shortly after leaving New York." He produced a photograph from the inside pocket of his jacket. "Is this the girl you played against that day?"

'He handed me the photograph – and I nearly fainted. The girl in the picture was definitely the one I'd faced across the net that morning. The same determined, elfin face. The same dark eyes, the same pageboy haircut. I had to sit down, I was so shocked.'

For a long moment, the ancient tennis star and her grandson remained silent, mulling over the extraordinary story. Finally the lady shook herself from her reverie, smiling across at the young man.

'And there you have it, Ian. The story of how I was defeated at Wimbledon by a ghost.'

Shaking his head, her grandson stood, dragged the chair back to its place by the window, and returned to the bedside.

'Well, it's a story I shall never forget, Grandmother. You've astonished me. But I'm afraid that now I must get myself home. Enid's giving a dinner party tonight and I mustn't be late.'

'It's been good having you here, darling.' She took his hand in hers and squeezed it. 'Give Enid my love. And thanks to you both for thinking of bringing the television so I could watch the final. I enjoyed it immensely.'

'I'll tell her.'

Bending forward he kissed the old lady on her forehead. Then, squeezing her hand and laying it down gently on the counterpane, he moved to the television and unplugged it. He was about to carry it away when his grandmother's voice stopped him again.

'There's one thing to add to that story, Ian. Something else you must keep secret and never divulge to another soul.'

'What's that?' he asked, turning back to her.

'Ever since that summer the Wimbledon courts have been haunted.'

'Haunted?'

'It's a well-known fact to anyone who has worked there, and to many who have played on those courts over the years. But the public must never know about it for obvious reasons.'

Ian stepped closer to the bed.

'What form does this haunting take? More mysterious players appearing from nowhere and beating the socks off real competitors?'

'No, that only happened the one time with me. No, the other hauntings have been nothing like as dramatic, or as obvious. Security men have complained about hearing the thwack of balls being struck on Centre Court in the dead of night – as if by a player practicing his serve. Cleaners at other times have sworn they've glimpsed a girl tennis player with a pageboy haircut just at the edge of their vision. Of course, when they investigate there's never anyone or anything there. On one occasion, however, a security man did find something curious and inexplicable after one of the nocturnal Centre Court practice sessions.'

'What was that?'

'Near the back wall behind one of the baselines he found a stray ball.'

Ian scoffed. 'A ball? Surely there's nothing surprising about that. A ball could have easily been overlooked from the day before.'

The old lady smiled.

'Yes, but not this ball. This happened only five years ago. And the ball, when examined, was an old one, typical of the kind we used in the 1930s. Clearly, the young American is still keeping up her game, even though, as the years roll on, the rest of us are all sadly falling by the wayside...'

(London, 2013)

Šolta

Jack and Peggy had been married for five years when she became pregnant. It was not a surprise – they'd been talking about having a baby for months, and had decided together she should stop taking the pill. It had only taken her a month or two after that to conceive.

She announced the news to him a week after they had buried her mother. Jack was of course delighted, and puzzled that things had worked out that way – that the coming of this new life was confirmed just as the other had been extinguished.

They had stayed with her father, helped him with the arrangements for the funeral. They had seen that through, then stayed on with him until he seemed more or less settled and content to carry on on his own. They arranged a live-in housekeeper to clean and to prepare his meals and, when they thought the time was right, they went home again – with his blessing – to their flat across town.

Jack was an actor, and had managed to secure a season's repertory work at the local theatre. When they returned home after the funeral, Jack had one more production to see through. In mid-summer his contract was to finish. He'd been offered a new contract for the autumn, with attractive casting, but had decided – after discussing things with Peggy – that it might be good for them to have a holiday beforehand. It had been a trying year.

It so happened that Peggy had a friend in Yugoslavia – a girl she had met at an international student theatre festival in Zagreb she had attended while at university. The two had remained close ever since, exchanging regular letters. Occasionally Zlata, who was a budding writer and translator, would come to London on a visit and they would get together. Jack found her intelligent and amusing, with a wry Eastern European sense of humour that was new to him – dark and quirky and slightly sinister. He liked her.

When Zlata learned of the death of Peggy's mother, she had written immediately to invite the pair of them to Yugoslavia for a two week break.

'It will do you good,' she'd said, 'to be in another country, where you might be able to concentrate happily on the coming of your baby, and not on the loss of your mother. Come in July. We will stay in Zagreb a few days, then travel down to Split and stay on an island I know near there. It will be good for you. You must come.'

Jack and Peggy decided to accept her invitation. When his work at the theatre drew to a close they made their plans, booked their train fare (via Paris), and prepared for the long journey across southern Europe with eagerness and excitement.

The trip to Paris was uneventful. Jack spent most of it with his nose buried in a thick novel. On the cross-channel ferry (this was years before the channel tunnel), Peggy left him in the lounge to walk on deck in the bracing sea air. He could see her sometimes through the windows overlooking the bow, peering over the side with her arms crossed, squinting back at Dover's cliffs, or ahead toward the hazy coastline of France. She liked boats, he knew.

In Paris they stayed in a three-star hotel just off the Rue St. Honoré, and had dinner in a nearby restaurant – three courses, with half a carafe of Beaujolais Nouveau. Peggy was not much of a drinker, but Jack enjoyed his wine. While she was content with one glass with dinner Jack worked his way through the rest of the carafe, feeling himself relaxing as the meal progressed.

The weather in Paris was gentle – partly overcast, but with no wind – so that the evening was pleasantly balmy.

On their way back to the hotel, Jack suggested they take a walk along the Seine before they turned in. Peggy demurred. The long train and ferry journey had made her tired, she said. She wanted to have an early night (their train was to leave at 10 the following morning). But she urged him to go ahead with his walk if he wanted to. It was a lovely evening, she agreed.

Jack dropped her at the hotel with a peck on the cheek, and made his way onward toward the river, striding along with his hands in his pockets, his sweater draped over his shoulders, enjoying the crimson-shot clouds in the evening sky and eyeing the people he passed – especially the couples striding along with their arms around one another, or holding hands. Truly, he thought, Paris was the city of lovers.

When he came to the river he turned eastwards, following it along until he crossed over onto the Isle de la Cité, then crossed again to the Boulevard St. Michel and the Rive Gauche.

As always the life of the Paris streets dazzled him, and with the effects of the wine pleasantly fuzzing his senses, he prowled on through the narrow winding byways of the *Quartier Latin* like a hungry man at a banquet table, absorbing everything greedily, smiling like a man drunk on life itself.

At length he found himself in an area of the city he didn't recognize, full of apartment blocks and small hotels. He had crossed the river again, he remembered. He must be somewhere near the Opera, but where?

Turning down another slightly darker and even emptier street, he noticed a young woman leaning against a wall further along. As he approached her she turned to smile at him.

'*Vous couchez seul, monsieur?*' she murmured, throatily.

She was wearing a skirt that stopped mid-thigh over fishnet tights, high leather boots, a jacket open over a low-necked top that stretched over her full breasts, and a beret perched on her short dark hair.

Jack found her attractive, and for a moment toyed with the idea of going off with her. He could imagine the feel of her warm, soft flesh, the touch of her hands upon him, her mouth. He'd never been with a whore, though he had sometimes thought about it, and wondered what it would be like to experience sex with a professional. But this was certainly not the time to find out with his pregnant wife waiting for him, tucked up in bed a few streets away. Smiling, he shook his head.

'*No, merci.*'

And walked on.

Minutes later he found himself in his street and entered the hotel. Peggy was asleep on her side of the bed, having left the bathroom door open and the light on. Jack undressed, washed and brushed his teeth, turned off the bathroom light and crawled in beside her, putting out a hand to feel the slight roundness of her belly under the nightdress. Snuffling lightly in her sleep, she grasped his hand in hers.

For a long time he couldn't sleep. Probably the wine, he thought. Or the stimulation of the walk.

He tried to think of the logistics of the rest of their trip – there were still things to be organized. But his thoughts kept returning to the girl in the empty street – her full-lipped mouth and smiling eyes, the cloth of the jersey stretched over her breasts, the provocative curve of her hips and thighs.

'*Vous couchez seul, monsieur?*'

In Zagreb Zlata met them at the station and escorted them to her modest two bedroom flat on the top floor of an apartment block not far from the centre. The view from the sitting room window was of an inner courtyard. Here and there clothes hung drying from improvised lines outside the windows. Pots of flowers and herbs stood on window ledges.

After two days spent seeing the sites and walking in the impressive local parks, they prepared to set off for the Dalmatian coast. Tickets were bought for the short train journey to Split. From there they would take a ferry out to their holiday apartment on the island.

For Jack the Dalmatian coast introduced into his life a kind of exotic beauty he had not experienced before. The ancient city of Split itself, with the remnants of Emperor Diocletian's palace absorbed so entrancingly into the sprawl of its centuries old buildings and narrow passageways, was charming and delightful. The weather now was warm and the skies clear, and together the three friends sat in the great central square over coffees and revelled in the evocative quaintness of the place.

Awaiting the sailing of their ferry in the late afternoon, sitting on benches along the edge of the stone pier, Jack marvelled at the shimmering pearlescent light that glowed over the clear blue water of the Adriatic – a light that he'd seen only once before, he remembered, captured on film in Bertolucci's *Death In Venice,* shining over the canals and arcaded facades of that ethereal city. The light seemed almost palpable, and Jack felt enthralled by it, losing himself in daydreams and memories – only barely aware of the casual murmuring of the two women at his side, who talked so easily together.

The island of Šolta (pronounced Sholta), situated in the central Dalmatian archipelago an hour's boat ride from Split harbour, is a rocky promontory that rises from the water like a hump-backed serpent, its pine forested hills giving it a coat of puffy green scales. The town of Maslinica at its north-western edge curves tightly around a small harbour, the pier again wrought in close-fitted white stone. There are few shops, just narrow streets of terraced houses, angling away from the harbour up the adjacent hills and along the short valley beyond.

Every morning after their arrival Zlata and Peggy would walk down to the small harbour to examine the night catches brought back by the local fishermen. Together with the village women they would pick over the daily selection and haggle over prices – carrying their purchases off in raffia baskets to be cooked for lunch or dinner. It was a way of living that hadn't changed for centuries. Jack and Peggy found it an entrancing place.

The first several days (they were to spend a full ten days on the island before returning to Zagreb to take the train back home) they spent doing what all holiday-makers do – they swam, they sunned themselves at the water's edge, or on the small terrace outside their rooms where they took their meals and which overlooked the harbour. Or they sat contentedly reading the holiday novels they had brought along with them, or conversing quietly over glasses of local wine as the roseate evenings drew into dark starry nights. As meat was pretty much unobtainable on the island, they took occasional trips by ferry in to the market stalls of Split – returning a couple of hours later with hampers filled with joints of pork and lamb, fresh fruit, salad vegetables and peppers, or chicken for the grill. But for obvious reasons they mostly ate seafood, and there was a large selection for them to choose from – including local lobsters so renowned for their quality that the harbour was often visited by Italian boats that had crossed from their own coastline to plunder the Croatians' catch to fill their ice chests and fridges.

During these days Jack and Peggy basked in the warmth of the Adriatic sun, browned their bodies, and felt the anxieties of the previous months dwindle away. They wrote postcards to Peggy's father and to their friends, and, holding hands like newlyweds, walked together along the pathway that skirted the island's edge, talking about the baby that was growing in her womb, and enjoying the explosions of cloud colour in the evening sky as the sun settled into the western sea.

It was a good time for them and they felt rested, rejuvenated, and filled with renewed affection for one another.

A few days into their stay visitors arrived. Zlata had a brother, Reiko, who was a young architect in Zagreb that they had met briefly during their first days there. Reiko had a thick head of dark hair, rugged good looks and a boyish charm that was obviously a hit with the ladies, for the stories Zlata told of his chequered love life were endless and entertaining. One of his former amours, a young lady named Tanja, Zlata had kept as a friend, and it was this lady who now appeared on the island, together with a companion named Sophia. The latter, it transpired, had just undergone an acrimonious divorce, and had been persuaded by Tanja to get away from it all with a few days' break at the seaside. Tanja herself, in her late twenties, was still a student, though of what had not been made clear – something to do with social work or business, Jack thought. They had met her briefly when she had dropped by Zlata's Zagreb flat, and had found her pleasant enough, though somewhat withdrawn. While she spoke hardly any English, she did speak fluent French, and as both Jack and Peggy were Francophiles, they were able to converse with her quite easily. They were pleased to discover that behind her reticence she was intelligent and well-read, and had a keen interest in culture and current events.

It has also to be said that Jack found Tanja attractive. At five foot eight or nine, with short dark hair, alluring brown eyes, and a figure that – though not fulsome in the way of the Paris working girl – was very pleasantly rounded, Tanja offered Jack ample material for his libidinous daydreams and musings.

For a few days the group shared excursions – to the beach, to Split on the ferry for shopping, or on walks around the island – and the atmosphere amongst them was relaxed and cordial. Sophia seemed to forget the pain of her ruptured marriage. Even Tanja smiled with greater frequency, Jack noticed. He also noticed that she tended to smile more often with him than with the others, and he wondered about that.

There came an evening when, after they had enjoyed a meal under the ancient flowering tree on the terrace and were sitting chatting together around the table, Zlata and Peggy had left them for a few moments while they went to Zlata's room to find some passage in a book they'd been discussing. The light from the few candles stuck in wine bottles on the table was low and flickering, and Jack was leaning forward, his arms folded in front of him on the table, his eyes fixed upon Tanja as she told him about a recent film she had seen, when something unexpected happened that rocked him soundly.

Tanja was sitting across from Jack. At her side, Sophia had her head turned away, watching the light reflections dancing on the water down by the harbour's edge.

Finishing her comments about the film, Tanja took a final pull on her cigarette and reached across the table to grind it out in the ashtray beside Jack's hand. Then, impetuously, glancing to the side to confirm that Sophia was still not looking, she locked her eyes on Jack's, placed her hand over his and gave it a squeeze – smiling coyly, wetting her lips with her tongue. Jack's mouth dropped open. But before he could respond Zlata and Peggy returned, the hand was hastily withdrawn, and the conversation picked up where it had left off.

For the rest of the evening, Tanja paid scant attention to Jack. By the time they said their goodnights he had even begun to wonder if he had imagined the entire episode.

A few hundred yards along the coastline from the village, nestled in a clump of pines, was an open air disco – a circular cemented dance floor positioned under a string of vari-coloured Chinese lanterns suspended from cables strung from the surrounding trees. At the back of the dance floor, a small hut housed the bar counter and also sheltered the turntables and amplifiers. Hung in the trees at the edge of the cement slab, speakers pumped out a string of the latest international dance favourites selected by the barman/disc jockey for the couples to move to each evening until midnight. Around the dance floor, under the trees, tables and chairs were placed for those not dancing.

One evening a few days after the visitors' arrival the group of holidaying friends happened to pass the place during their postprandial promenade and – entranced by the play of coloured lights cast by the lanterns over the swaying couples on the floor – decided to stop to enjoy a drink or two and people watch. As it was late there were few couples on the floor and the music had been turned down to a reasonable level. Jack liked the place, enjoyed watching the dancers moving together under the soft coloured lighting. The others found it amusing, too, and the next night the visit was repeated.

On the third night they again stopped at the disco for a drink but, it having been a rather busy day, Peggy and Zlata soon showed signs of flagging. Jack, however, seemed to have found a second wind, and was deep in a spirited three-way conversation with Tanja and Sophia about the political future of Yugoslavia after Tito's eventual demise when Peggy tugged at his sleeve.

'Darling, I'm really tired. I'm going back with Zlata.'

'Already? But we've only just got here.'

'I know. But I...' she put her hand on her abdomen, '...we, are too tired to sit up anymore.'

Jack's brow crinkled with disappointment.

'Oh.'

'But you don't have to come back yet, silly, if you'd rather not. I'm a big girl. I'll be fine with Zlata.'

Zlata put her arm around Peggy's shoulder. 'Of course you will. Let Jack stay here and bore himself talking politics. Like you, I'm for bed.'

'I will stay, if you don't mind,' Jack said to them.

Peggy got up and, giving her husband a quick kiss on the lips, linked arms with Zlata and disappeared with her down the pathway towards the village.

The evening progressed and time wound on, Jack buying two more rounds for the girls as their conversation shifted directions several times from politics to films to life in general.

But eventually Sophia – whose French was limited and whose knowledge of English even worse than Tanja's – having had enough of fighting to keep up with the others, suddenly stood, putting her hand on Tanja's shoulders and smiling across at Jack.

'Je vais me coucher, mes chers. Mais continuez, vous deux, je vous en prie. Vous avez des choses à discuter, évidemment. Mais moi, je n'en peux plus. Je suis trop fatigué.' She ran her hand through Tanja's short dark hair. *'Á demain, Coco.'*

And with a wave she turned away and vanished along the dark pathway.

For some moments Jack and Tanja sat in silence, smoking and listening to the music. There was only one couple left dancing now, and the rest of the tables were empty. Behind the bar the disc jockey – a young German who wore his baseball hat back to front – was putting vinyl records back into sleeves, obviously packing up for the night.

'Last dance,' he called out to the floor at large, in accented English. A moment later, Frank Sinatra's voice erupted from the speakers intoning 'Strangers in the Night' – a suitable slow dance for the evening's close.

Jack looked up at Tanja. *'Vous voulez danser?'*

She shrugged. *'Pourquoi pas?'*

They rose and moved onto the floor. Jack opened his arms and she stepped into them, grasping his outstretched hand with her right as he slid his other hand around her back.

By this time they'd both drunk quite a lot, and their movements were slow and heavy as they shuffled gently together over the gritty concrete. The other couple had gone. They had the floor to themselves now.

Jack closed his eyes, pulling the girl closer to him. Her cheek was on his shoulder, her hair by his mouth. She smelled of something French … Chanel? He wasn't sure. But the scent was effective. It reminded him of the working girl in Paris. He felt his senses quicken, felt the warmth of Tanja's breasts as she leaned against him. He squeezed her hand while caressing her back with his fingertips. And she responded, moaning slightly.

When the music ended Jack slipped his arm around her and drew her towards the pathway.

'*Vous voulez vous promener un peu?*'

'*Oui. Mais tu dois me tutoyer*, Jack.'

'*D'accord.*' Then, after a moment, '*Merci.*'

Turning down the path away from the village they walked together for a time under the shadowy trees beside the lapping water. Above them, a star-spangled heaven stretched to the horizon, where, through fingers of high cirrus clouds, a sliver of moon cast a faint glow over everything, leaving a shimmering trail of silver across the barely rippled surface of the sea. Around them cicadas chirped in the shadows. As they walked Jack's hand slid over Tanja's waist and hip, caressing with his fingertips. Lifting her elbow she put her hand over his.

Suddenly he stopped and stepped apart, shaking his head and frowning.

'This is wrong.'

She looked at him. '*Quoi? Qu'y a- t-il, Jack?*'

'*Ce n'est pas bien, ce que nous faisons. Ce n'est pas juste. Je suis marié, comme tu sais.*'

She stepped towards him, reaching out to stroke his bare arms with her fingertips.

'*Pourquoi pas? Personne ne saura jamais. C'est quelque chose unique pour nous deux – ce moment-ci. Et pour cette nuit seulement. Demain nous reprendrons nos chemins séparés, comme avant.*' She drew one of his hands up, flattened his palm over her breast, holding it there with her hand. '*Tu ne le veux pas?*'

'Tanja...'

'*Dis-moi.*' Her dark eyes looked up into his in the faint moonlight. '*Tu ne le veux pas, vraiment*, Jack?'

Capturing her hand in his, he drew it to his mouth and kissed it. *'Oui, je le veux. Bien sûr, je le veux.'*

Drawing her toward him, he kissed her upturned lips, then led her down a slope to a sandy flat under stunted trees near the lapping water's edge. The spot was naturally shielded from the pathway. It was private enough. Only from the sea could they have been seen. Stooping to brush aside the few sticks and pebbles, Jack knelt and pulled her down beside him. On their knees, they held each other as Jack's mouth came down on hers again, searching, demanding. His hands reached for the buttons of her blouse.

It was a night he would always remember – this indulgent dalliance by the side of a moonlit sea. The silky smoothness of her warm skin, the taste of her mouth, the scent of her French perfume. The delicious perfection of their lovemaking on his spread shirt, the exquisite sweetness of their caresses, the slow building rhythm of their coupling. The sudden flash of her climax as she shuddered under him, crying out with little gasps of pleasure, clutching at him with trembling fingers. Then his following shortly after, its arrival voiced in a muted moan of ecstasy as the waves of pleasure rolled over him. Finally then, lying over her, catching his breath. The tenderness of her embrace as she pulled him tight against her with both arms, willing him to stay inside her, to hold the moment for as long as it could be held.

'Reste comme ça,' she whispered in his ear. *'Ne bouge pas. Reste comme ça!'*

When the first inklings of dawn appeared in the east they rose from the sand and brushed themselves down and dressed. They did not touch as they walked back along the path towards town. Nor did they speak. The time for such intimacy had passed. Now it was simply time to go home.

At the edge of the village she turned and touched his arm.

'Je vais te quitter ici. Il faut que personne ne nous voie ensemble à cette heure. Tu comprends?'

He nodded. And watched as she turned up a side street, away from the stone pier, towards the parallel track that led through the upper village to the little apartment she shared with Sophia. Before she turned the corner she turned back to give him a little wave. Then she was gone.

Hands in pockets Jack walked alone along the stone pier towards his own accommodation. And saw, as the first rays of the morning sun caught the tips of the trees on the hills above the harbour, the lone figure of his pregnant wife plodding along the quay in search of him, clutching the sleeves of a sweater wrapped loosely over her shoulders against the morning coolness. Quickening his step he moved towards her, formulating his cover story as he went.

She believed him, of course. Actors are such romantics, aren't they? How fitting he should fall asleep beside the sea with the moonlight dancing on the water before him, lapping gently at his feet.

She was such a trusting soul, was Peggy.

But for the rest of his life – though he would always remember the exotic excitement of the illicit lovemaking by the sea – he would equally never forget the guilt he'd felt for having let himself go so easily. For having betrayed his young and trusting wife even while she was carrying his first and only child.

(London, 2009)

I'm Sorry to Announce…

'Excuse me. Can I talk to you?'

It was late and I was bein' quiet as a mouse, mopping the floor of the corridor in half-darkness – the strings of Christmas lights blinking on and off here and there along the walls – when I heard this voice behind me, a kind of faint whisper.

'You have a nice face. Can you spare me a minute or two? Please?'

I turned around and there's this lady lying on her side in her hospital bed, gazing out the door at me. She must've been watching me work. Beyond her, the curtain had been pulled between her and the patient in the next bed. The room was dark, except for the low-wattage night light in the ceiling.

I'd never seen the woman before. I don't usually work this corridor, but my boss had called in sick earlier and I was having to do his corridor as well as my own. We have to mop all floors at least once each shift, you see, because of the MRSA virus – something that's been causing a lot of trouble in hospitals all over the country.

Anyway it was near one o'clock in the morning, and the halls were empty. Most of the patients were fast asleep. I'd just come off my break and was half finished with the corridor when she spoke to me.

I didn't know what to do at first. We usually don't talk to patients. I looked round, but the night nurse was nowhere in sight. She was probably at her station round the corner at the far end, working on her patient notes. Anyway I was alone in the corridor.

I stepped closer to the door, leaning on my mop handle.

'Do you want me to get the nurse? Do you need anything?'

She shook her head. 'No. I just need to talk to someone. You came along just in time. Can you spare me a few minutes? Please?'

She pulled a hand from the bedclothes and wiped at her eyes with a tissue she had bunched up in her fist. When I got closer I could see she'd been crying, her eyes were all puffy and red against her pale skin. Her head was covered with a pinned scarf, the way women do who're on chemo, to cover their hairless scalps. I took one last look down the empty hall, then pulled my bucket into the room and leaned the mop against the doorjamb. There was a chair beside her bed. I pulled it up and sat down on it.

'Okay. I can spare a few minutes. What's the matter, can't you sleep?'

She shook her head. 'I like your accent,' she said, smiling. 'Where're you from?'

'Barbados. But I been here since I was little. My name's Bert.'

'Bert,' she repeated. 'Nice. How long have you worked at the hospital?'

'Two years. I was at the Royal Free before, but the commuting was too much so I was glad when a position came up here. It's not a wonderful job, but I'm happy.'

'Are you married?' she asked.

I shook my head. 'No. Got a girlfriend, though. We bin together five years.'

'Any children?'

'No. My girlfriend has two, though. Little boy, and a girl of 12. They're trouble enough without bringing any more kids into the world.'

'You must still have family in Barbados. Don't you miss them?'

'Oh, I go back every couple years to see 'em. Got two sisters there, married, with big families. Fact is I'll see them at Christmas in two weeks time. Flying out on the 21st.' I sat back in my chair. 'What about you? You from 'round here, a Londoner?'

She shook her head. 'No. Originally I came from Germany. But I've lived in England for years.' She smiled. 'That's what my accent is, German. But it's not so strong now.'

I shook my head. 'I wouldn't recognize it anyway, even if it was stronger. I's terrible at figuring out where folks is from. Always have been.'

'Well, I understand. There's so many accents to keep track of. It's hard enough to recognise them even when you've been born here.'

I leaned forward again, resting my elbows on my knees. We were only inches apart, whispering so as not to disturb the patient beyond the curtain.

'What's your name?' I asked.

'Hanna,' she told me. 'Hanna Weitz. I'm fifty-five years old, and I work…' she hesitated, '…*worked* … as a librarian for Lambeth Council, in Brixton.'

'Librarian, huh? You married?'

She shook her head. 'I was married once, a long time ago. I have a daughter, living in Manchester. But we're not very close. She doesn't get in touch very often anymore. Sometimes I lose all track of her for months at a time.'

'Any grandkids?'

'No. My daughter doesn't want children. She's a businesswoman. Always travelling around the world. She has no time for children.'

'Hm. That's a shame. So you're not married now?'

'No. I live alone. Don't even have a cat. I like to travel on my holidays, you see? It's been my passion – ever since my divorce. I used to have a cat. Before. But I gave it away. I don't think it's fair to an animal to have to keep making arrangements for it to be looked after whenever you're away.'

There was a pause then. Finally she bit her lip and frowned, looking up at me from lowered eyes, like she was ashamed.

'Can I ask you something, Bert? A favour?'

'Surely.'

'Would you … would you be kind enough to hold my hand? Please?' She reached her right hand out over the side of the bed. 'Would you mind?'

''Course not.' I took her hand with both of mine and held it. I was shocked at how cool and bony it felt. 'There. Now what was it you wanted to say to me, Hanna?'

For a moment she just looked at me. Then her face crumpled and I could see she was fighting hard to keep from crying again. But she couldn't stop the sobs. They were so strong when they came they shook the whole bed. Finally she blinked two or three times and managed to get control of herself. When she did, she spoke again.

'I'm dying, Bert,' she said, her voice so quiet this time I could hardly hear her. 'The doctors told me today. There's nothing more they can do. I needed…' She stopped while another shudder shook her, then went on. 'I just needed to tell someone. That's all.'

I squeezed her hand, nodding slowly. 'I understand. I'm so sorry…'

'No, Bert. I don't want your sympathy. I just need you to listen. Telling someone else makes it somehow more acceptable, you see? That's strange, but it's true. We all have to die sometime after all, and though I'm a lot younger than I expected to be when … when I 'popped my clogs' as the English say … I'm not too bothered by it. In a way, it doesn't matter. I have nothing really left to do in my life, you see? And no one will miss me when I'm gone.'

Well, when she said that I was right shocked. I mean, for her to say such a thing surely meant she had led a very sad life indeed.

'What about your daughter?' I asked. 'Why isn't she here?'

'The hospital's trying to find her. And they might. The question is, will it be in time? Anyway April was always much closer to her father than to me. She's very like him – very self-centred. Very … insensitive. But a stickler for form. She'll come if they do track her down. And she'll go through the motions of caring for me. But it'll be a chore for her – something I'm sure she'd rather avoid. She thinks I'm rather silly and weak, you see? I don't think she really likes me.'

'That's a terrible thing, Hanna. If it's true. It's hard to believe any daughter could be so uncaring about her mother at such a time.'

She smiled ruefully. 'It's the truth, Bert. Oh, I learned that about her over the years as she grew up. She's thirty now. I don't think she'll change at this late date.' She smiled again. 'Leopards and spots, you know.'

She didn't say anything for a while. After a minute she began rubbing my fingers with her thumb as I held her hand. I had the feeling she was thinking how the warmth of a human touch can have its own healing qualities, and was hoping to draw that healing balm from me, a sympathetic stranger. Maybe something good was happening for her, maybe I helped? I don't know.

'She wasn't always like that, of course,' she said finally. 'April, I mean. When she was little, in the years before my husband left me, we had a normal relationship as mother and daughter. She was a lovely child, very affectionate. It was four years after the divorce, when she decided she wanted to leave me to live with her father and his glamorous new wife that the change came. My ex-husband is a rich man. Very arrogant and outspoken. Once that appealed to me. I found it attractive. Exciting. If I told you his name you'd probably recognize it. He could give her the kind of life I never could, with my modest librarian's salary. And she wanted that – she preferred being wealthy, having the freedom to buy whatever she wanted whenever she wanted it, to do whatever took her fancy.' She sighed. 'We're very different, my daughter and I. I have always required very little to be content with my life, and I've always earned my own way. It's a point of pride with me.'

'But she's still your daughter,' I reminded her. 'She must love you as her mother. It'd be awful not to.'

'For what it's worth, I suppose that's true. I'm sure she does love me, in her way. To a certain extent. For appearance sake. Blood-love, and all that.'

'And if the hospital finds her? When they find her? What then?'

She shook her head. 'They'll send me home with her to die – if she agrees to look after me. To my tiny flat, not hers. She wouldn't want me dying in her space, I'm sure.'

'Must you leave the hospital?'

'They'd like me out of here, the doctors. There's no reason to keep me here anymore. And they need this bed. It's only a matter of time, now, anyway, and anyone can give me the medication I need to control the pain.'

'How much time do you have?'

'One month. Three months. It's hard for them to know. As far as I'm concerned, now that I know there's no possible cure, the sooner I go the better.' She sighed, deeply. 'Let there be an end.'

The way she just accepted that moved me, right down to my soul.

'How can they be so sure?' I asked her. 'Maybe they made a mistake, got your files mixed up with someone else? Maybe they're just plain wrong.' I squeezed her hand. 'You can't give up hope like that, Hanna. You gotta believe the Lord will listen to your prayers and heal you. You do go to church, don't you?'

She shook her head.

'Haven't been for years. I don't really think I'm a believer anymore, truth to tell. I wish I was, though. It'd give me something to hang on to, a thread of hope.'

'You should try prayin' anyway.'

'Oh, I do.' She smiled at me. 'There's nothing to be lost by trying.' She sighed again. 'But it's hard to find reason to hope anymore, and that's the truth. A month ago, when the cancer came back, they put me on what they said was an exciting new medication – so far only experimental – said it might slow up the spread of my cancer. At first I was optimistic, believed it would work, that the cancer would be turned around. No one wants to believe the worst. But it was wishful thinking, and over the last weeks I've been getting weaker, not stronger. I finally had to give up work, check myself into hospital. They did more tests, took more x-rays. Nothing had improved. Instead the tumours were larger, and the cancer had moved all round my body. There's no stopping it now. It's galloping through me.'

For a moment she was quiet. Then a sudden grimace of pain wrinkled her brow and she shifted slightly on the bed, moaning and gripping my hand more tightly.

'You all right?' I asked, alarmed. 'Should I get the nurse?'

'No. It's only a spasm. It'll pass in a moment. They come and go. I'm due for another injection soon anyway. No, please, just sit with me awhile, Bert. I'm sorry if I've embarrassed you. I know it must be awkward – a strange white lady clutching your hand and rambling on about her troubles. But I had to tell someone, you see? And there really is no one else.'

She went on holding my hand for a long time, like she was afraid to let go for fear she might slip away forever if she did, disappear down a great gaping hole in the earth. Which was what was going to happen to her, I guess, come to think of it.

'I'm glad you spoke to me, Hanna,' I told her, meaning it. 'I feel honoured you've shared this terrible news with me – though of course I wish it wasn't so. We may be strangers, but I do care about you, even though I only just met you. That's God's truth. And I surely wish you didn't have to face … what it is you have to face … alone.'

She was getting weaker now, I could tell. Sleepier. For a time, she closed her eyes and said nothing. Her breathing became deeper. But I knew she wasn't asleep 'cause her thumb was still stroking my fingers.

'That's the worst of it,' she said eventually – a whisper. 'Dying doesn't frighten me, Bert. Honestly. But I do hate having to go through it alone. without anyone beside me. Family, I mean. A loved one. Slipping away in an empty room with no one nearby. Knowing no one really cares about my passing. It's awful to feel at the end that your life has amounted to nothing at all. That you've left nothing behind you that matters, no one that really loves you, no cherished memories. That's the greatest pain of all.'

I stayed with her another quarter hour, but we didn't speak. We just held hands, feeling in those minutes of touching a lifetime's worth of closeness flowing from one to the other.

Eventually her thumb stopped moving over my fingers. I waited a bit longer, till I felt her muscles relax in sleep. Then I laid her hand on the blanket and left her, drawing my mop and bucket back into the corridor as quiet as I could so as not to wake her.

When I finished my shift at six in the morning I looked into her room again on my way out of the building. She was fast asleep, lying on her back, her mouth open, her drawn face crinkled in a frown. That was the last time I saw her. When I came back to work after the weekend she was gone.

That morning, after I'd left her room at the hospital, I was standing in the grey dawn light on the platform at the station, waitin' for the train that would take me to my little studio flat and a well-deserved rest. The snow the weather folks had promised had finally arrived, and was falling thick around me in large fluffy flakes. Already it'd covered the tracks and everything else an inch or two deep. As I watched it drift down in the morning quiet I thought about Hanna's whispered words, and of her loneliness in these last days.

Over my head, an announcement blared suddenly from the tannoy speaker.

'I'm sorry to announce...' the lady's recorded voice began, and went on to tell me that my train had been cancelled due to the snow and to please await further announcements. 'We're very sorry for the delay to your journey,' she said.

That was bad news for me, certainly – a wait of another half hour at least till the next train was due. But I had the presence of mind to think, just the same, how really small my inconvenience would be because of this announcement. It was nothing, really. All of us on that platform, drawing our scarves closer round our necks in the freezing cold, we were all lucky. At least we'd get to our destinations eventually. We'd get home to the comforting warmth of friends and family. That was a sure thing.

For poor Hanna Weitz, on the other hand, the announcement made to her by the doctors the previous day – made I'm sure with deep sadness in their voices and in their hearts – brought with it much greater inconvenience, and far heavier consequences. Her journey was one she would've loved to have delayed. For her destination was one none of us on that snow-swept platform would likely have to visit for many years to come.

(London, 2012)

A Christmas Story

Christmas Eve in Munich, Germany, in 1964, was perhaps no different for the inhabitants of that fair city from all the other Christmases they had enjoyed since the commencement of the post-war boom of the late fifties. But for the young American trudging along the near-empty streets through ankle-deep snow it was all very new and exotic. And decidedly sad – despite the clusters of brilliantly coloured Christmas lights festooning the street lamps, and the cheeriness expressed in the ruddy faces of the people he passed as they called the greetings of the season to one another in a language he still only barely understood.

With his gloved hands thrust deep into the pockets of his pea jacket, a black woollen cap pulled down over his ears and a thick scarf wound tightly around his throat, Boyd Carson trudged, head down, along the broad avenues and across the snow-covered squares. On the wide pavement before the *Alte Rathaus* a thirty-foot tall Christmas tree sparkled with flickering, candle-like white lights. In the shop windows of the great department stores on the *Maximilianstrasse* boughs of evergreens framed cornucopias of wonderful things to eat and drink, gleaming arrays of white goods, televisions and hi-fi sets in shiny hardwood cabinets, and elegant winter clothes in kaleidoscopic hues gracing the forms of haughty mannequins that stared out through the plate glass windows with chiselled coldness.

He had just come from the *Frauenkirche*, the great 15th century cathedral near the *Marienplatz*, where he had sat for some minutes in the cavernous, white-walled nave, chaffing his freezing hands and watching the devout kneeling in the shadowy light to bid their Saviour *guten abend* on this, His birth night. But their unabashed piety made him nervous. Boyd was no longer truly a Christian, and in truth he felt an outsider here. So eventually, and in spite of the attraction of the deep-throated organ piping a medley of carols through the soaring columns, he had slipped out and back to the street.

Pulling back the cuff of his coat Boyd looked at his watch. 6:30. Soon he would have to return to his lodging house just off the *Sendlinger Tor Platz* for the Christmas Eve dinner he'd been promised by Liesl, the pension's live-in maid.

Though the pension's owner, Frau Graf, had gone away to her son's family in Dortmund for the holidays, the middle-aged Liesl would be staying on in the flat she shared with her widow employer at the top of the building – partly because it was necessary for someone to remain 'in charge' over the break, and partly – as Liesl had told him herself – because she had nowhere else to go. Seemingly all the other tenants had gone away as well – joining their families in various corners of the country – so that only Liesl and Boyd would be remaining in the pension.

Liesl had smiled and touched his arm. '*Es machts nichts*,' she had said. 'We shall make the evening something special for ourselves anyway. I shall prepare for us a feast, and we will have our own Christmas party, *ge*? *Veleicht* I can my friend Hanna invite. She speaks very good English – much better than me. That would be jolly, *nicht var*?'

Boyd was grateful for her generous offer. He had wondered how he'd spend Christmas Eve alone in this foreign city, thousands of miles from home. This would be his first Christmas away from his family, and the thought of not being with them at this special time was painful to him. At least now he had a dinner to look forward to and some company to share it with.

He shifted the paper bag he was carrying to his other hand and set off down the street again. Desultory pedestrians hurried past him – last minute shoppers making for streetcars and car parks. Few cars passed by. Most people were already at home, doing whatever German families did together on Christmas Eve.

Boyd had been living in Munich for two months now, having taken a year off from his university studies in California to see Europe. He'd arrived in Munich in late October (missing the Oktoberfest, which in fact takes place mostly in September). He'd spent several weeks touring England – until his limited funds ran out and he had been forced to seek a job. As he learned from fellow travellers in the youth hostels, Germany was the only country in Europe where a foreigner could legally find employment. So he'd set off for Munich by train.

Within three days he was fixed up – had found himself accommodation, had passed his required medical examination as a *gast arbeiter*, picked up his work permit from the central Munich Police headquarters, and had secured a job as a warehouseman in a factory making hot water heaters on the city outskirts. If he remained in employment for six months, he was assured, the German government would refund all the taxes collected from him during that period, thereby enabling him to pay his return airfare to the states. It was a very attractive offer, made by a government desperate for foreign workers to handle the increased labour demand brought about by the economic boom, and as Boyd had no other option available to raise the money he had settled in for the German winter.

Every morning he left the pension at 8:15 to take the *strassenbahn* for the forty-minute journey into the suburbs to the gates of the Dr. Stiebel Werke factory. After clocking in his days there were spent doing the usual things warehousemen did – offloading materiel from rail boxcars (flat packs of corrugated cardboard boxing or galvanized water heater tanks stacked in the cars like cordwood), or spending tedious hours inventorying basket loads of various water heater

168

components. Most of his fellow *lager arbeiters* were *auslanders* like himself – mainly Turkish, or Italian. There was even one Brit, who had come to Germany as a soldier, met a girl, married her and stayed. Everyone was good-natured, and though Boyd was the only American in the group he got on well with them all.

Over the previous weeks, he'd made friends with one or two of the younger Germans at the plant, and had even visited their family homes in the surrounding countryside – travelling by train through picture postcard villages held in snowy suspension, reminding him of the little bottle he'd had as a boy that, when shaken, would swirl flakes of snow over the tiny buildings nestled at its bottom. But as the days drew on towards Christmas it was clear that no invitation was going to be forthcoming to share someone else's year-end family celebrations, so he was pleased that the pleasant but plain Liesl had provided a solution to his dilemma.

Turning down his street he saw the lights of the Texas Bar ahead of him, where he often stopped after work for a glass or two of good Bavarian beer. It was a modern place – all mirrors and tubular steel and black leather, with shiny black marble tabletops and bargirls who wore tight-fitting, short-sleeved white blouses and black miniskirts over legs in fishnet tights, and who offered table service. Boyd had enjoyed his evenings spent there, growing mellow as the drinks came and went, listening to Diana Ross and The Supremes crooning their yearning lament that seemed to speak to him of his own loneliness:

'*Baby Love, my Baby Love, I need your love, Oh how I need your love...*'

He would cross his arms over the little table and sip his lukewarm beer, and watch the girls as they carried trays of glasses to and from the tables, or – at paying-up time – as they whipped up their skirt fronts to access the change belts they wore beneath (an action he found deliciously erotic). Boyd liked the place, and knew one or two of the girls by name. But he was too shy ever to draw them into a real conversation let alone to ask them for a date.

He had been without the comfort of female company for several months now – ever since he'd broken off with his college sweetheart the summer before. Having only just turned twenty-one two months earlier – celebrating the occasion by getting mildly drunk in a pub in England – he was feeling the lack of feminine companionship fiercely now as the weeks went by in this unfamiliar foreign city.

There was Christine, the teenage work experience student who came once a week to work in the office of the warehouse boss, Herr Mai – a round-faced little man with a pot belly and soft voice, who, Boyd understood, had been an SS Captain during the war. Christine had short black hair cut in a pageboy that framed her delicate, pretty face like a picture, and a slender girlish body that was rounded in all the right places. Working in the yard Boyd would see her passing from time to time, heading from an outside office into the main building carrying a handful of invoices or order sheets, and for a moment he would stand transfixed, savouring the swinging action of her walk, the curve of her shoulders, the bobbing of her black hair around her ears, her pale neck and slender arms. At night, sipping his beer in the Texas Bar, he would imagine how amazing it would be to be loved by such a creature – to hold her in his arms, to nuzzle that slender neck and clean dark hair, to kiss her perfect eyes and crimson rosebud of a mouth. Sometimes it was hard for him to get to sleep at night, thinking of her. But it was hopeless. Though Christine did sometimes throw a smile in his direction – making his heart stop momentarily, and butterflies to flutter up in his chest – she was far too young for him really, only sixteen or so. She probably didn't even speak English. So Christine came to represent for him simply the image of the feminine that he so much craved, and from whom in this foreign city he felt so completely cut off.

In the evenings the clientele of the Texas Bar was mostly made up of young people, and Boyd was embarrassed by his inability to step forward to introduce himself in an effort to make friends. But his knowledge of the language was rudimentary, and they seemed so dauntingly brash and self-confident, these young German city-types, in their smart suits and woollen overcoats and scarves. Their sophistication made him feel even more acutely the scruffy, naïve, northern California boy that he was.

At weekends the Texas Bar was often crowded with gaggles of American G.I.s from Munich Post, and when they arrived with their loud voices and exaggerated back-slapping macho bonhomie Boyd would withdraw within himself, finish his beer, and creep quietly away to the sanctuary of his room – to read or to write, or to switch on his tiny transistor radio to listen to music on AFN (the European American Forces Radio Network). All his life he'd felt alienated from such groups of loud men, as if they were a race apart, and these young soldiers, behaving with what he saw as an occupying conqueror's swaggering arrogance, made him feel – in spite of himself – ashamed of his nationality.

But tonight there was no inclination for Boyd to pass into the warmth of the Texas Bar for a jar or two of Lowenbrau and a tempting glimpse of female thigh, and he walked on by, aiming for the doorway toward the end of the street surmounted by the simple neon sign announcing 'Pension Graf'.

Letting himself into the entry hall with his key, he climbed the narrow stairs to the second floor and unlocked the door to his room.

Inside, a large double-glazed casement window overlooked the snow-covered street and the windows of the apartment block opposite. Beside the window was a table and chair. A narrow bed stretched along one wall. On the table was a lamp, several notebooks, yesterday's edition of the *Herald Tribune*, and his transistor radio. In another corner of the room a small sink offered him facilities for washing and cleaning his teeth. Arranged down the wall opposite his bed was a chest of drawers and a dark mahogany wardrobe with a full-length mirror in one door.

Removing his cap, coat and scarf, he hung them over the back of his chair and pulled the curtains closed over the window. Then he switched on the lamp and turned on the radio. Immediately the drawling voice of an American services newsreader filled the room. A new consignment of US Special Forces personnel had been sent to southeast Asia to continue their training and advising activities, part of President Johnson's commitment to help the South Vietnamese Army contain the incursions of their communist northern neighbours.

Boyd frowned as he sat on the bed to pull off his wet boots. He'd been following this business for the last few weeks, and though the announcers made efforts to describe the American involvement as 'limited' and 'modest' it was obvious to anyone paying attention that the number of Ho Chi Minh's North Vietnamese Army sorties into the south was increasing not diminishing, and that the American 'help' was not going to be nearly enough to stem the tide. The whole area was a potential quagmire, with communist rebels hidden amidst the indigenous population, threatening the feeble stability of the corrupt southern government more with each passing day. It could come soon to outright war, Boyd knew – just as it had for the French scant years before. And if it did his own ass could be on the line. There was no certainty he'd be able to maintain student deferments indefinitely, and given his loathing of sharing time and space with groups of boisterous men how would he cope if he was drafted? Or was it simply cowardice on his part? He wasn't sure. What he was sure of was that he didn't want to have to test himself under such circumstances – in a war that seemed so entirely unnecessary, given the conflict in no way directly threatened American interests. Boyd had no time for the 'domino theory' of creeping communism. All he wanted was for the whole thing to just go away.

He stood up, pulled off his shirt and undershirt, filled the sink with steaming hot water and washed himself with the washcloth, thinking as he scrubbed how the whole damned world had gone to hell over the last couple of years. Kennedy assassinated in '63, Johnson taking over and immediately escalating America's involvement in South Vietnam. What happened to all that euphoria generated when the handsome Kennedy had been elected and had brought his young wife and family into the White House? The Bay of Pigs, the Cuban Missile Crisis and Lee Harvey Oswald's bullets had put an end to all that. Now it was a wary world, a world on tenterhooks, waiting for the next disaster to strike. It wouldn't have to wait long, Boyd reckoned.

By 7:30 he'd finished his ablutions, had dressed in clean underwear and jeans and a smart plaid Pendleton shirt, and now stood before the wardrobe mirror combing his hair. Giving himself a final check he popped the comb into his back pocket, grabbed the paper bag from the bed and switched off his radio and lamp. Letting himself out into the hall, he locked his door and headed upstairs.

Standing at the cooker in the kitchen of the apartment at the top of the building, Liesl heard his light rapping and smiled.

'Ja! *Com herein*! Come in!' she called, reaching for a cloth to wipe her hands.

'*Grüß Gott!*' she chimed when Boyd appeared smiling in the hall doorway with the paper bag. She stepped towards him and touched her cheeks to both of his. 'What have you there?

He produced a bottle and a rectangular box.

'Courvoisier and chocolates. I know you told me not to bring anything, but I thought these wouldn't be amiss. Okay?'

He put the items on the counter and crumpled the bag into a ball. Turning toward the cooker, he sniffed, raising his eyebrows and smiling.

'Wonderful cooking smells in here. Where can I put this?'

He held out the crumpled bag. Liesl pointed to a bin.

'Put it there. Brandy and chocolates? These are always welcome! *Vielen dank*, Boyd. You are too kind. And the goot smells are of the *schweinebraten* – roasted pork – which is nearly ready. The traditional *Deutsche* Christmas dinner is goose, but we are not enough for a goose. So I thought pork would do.'

'You're right. Pork will do nicely.' He winked at her. 'Now I know why you asked if I was Jewish.'

She blushed and nodded. 'Ja. I didn't want to make bad mistake, *ge*?'

'So this is your lonely American, Liesl?'

The new voice came from the doorway to the back of the apartment, where a dark-eyed woman in her forties stood leaning against the doorjamb, her arms crossed. She was of medium height, with dark hair that hung just above her shoulders, and a pleasant, slightly plump figure. She wore a wine-coloured sweater over black trousers and she was smiling.

'Ah! Hanna!' Liesl made the introductions. 'Boyd Carson, this is my goot friend, Hanna Beck. Hanna, this is Boyd.'

They shook hands.

'Hanna has opened a bottle of Riesling. Would you like a glass, Boyd? Then you two can sit in the other room and chat till the dinner is ready.' She gestured towards the sitting room.

'Riesling sounds good.'

Hanna poured a second glass which she handed to Boyd and the two of them slipped out of the kitchen and into the living room, leaving Liesl to her culinary preparations.

Slipping off her slippers Hanna settled herself on the sofa, curling her legs beneath her. Boyd sat in an armchair opposite, near the window. On a table in the corner a metre-high Christmas tree blazed with tiny white lights, its decorations of tinsel and coloured balls glittering. Beneath the tree were a few wrapped presents. On a sideboard surrounded by standing Christmas cards and family photographs the dial of an old cabinet radio glowed and soft Christmas music sighed from its speaker. For a moment they sat sipping their wine and listened to the carols.

'So, Mr. Boyd American, why are you in Germany?'

'I've taken a year off college to see Europe. But I ran out of money, so I came here to find a job.'

'Ahhh. And when do you go back?'

'In the spring, after I've worked six months.'

'What kind of work is it, your job?'

'I'm a *lagar arbeiter* at Dr. Steibel Werke. Not very exciting.' He sipped his wine. 'What do you do, Hanna? For work, I mean.'

She made a face. 'Boring job. Secretary and personal assistant to the manager of a painting and decorating business. Not very glamorous. But it pays the bills.' She sipped her wine. 'How do you spend your time when you're not working?'

Boyd explained that he was trying to write, that his evenings were mostly spent sitting at his little table, framing sentences in his notebooks, creating stories from ideas that had occurred to him during his weeks in Germany.

'You want to be a writer, eh?'

'Yes. I want to try.'

'Good for you. Then you need to get experience of life, no? How old are you now?'

'Twenty-one.'

'Have you a girlfriend?'

'Not anymore. I broke off with her during the summer.'

'And you've not met anyone here?'

'No.' Boyd smiled ruefully. 'I should've listened to the doctor who did my medical examination. If I'd taken his advice I could've solved two problems at once.'

Hanna cocked her head. 'How do you mean? What did he say?'

'He told me to find a *schlaf lexicon*. That way I could both have a girlfriend, and learn German at the same time.'

She laughed. '*Schlaf lexicon*. I like that. And you have not found one yet?'

He shrugged. 'I'm too shy, I guess. I find it hard to meet new people. Especially in another language.'

Hanna pushed out her bottom lip. 'Too bad. Poor lonely boy.' She sipped her wine again and smiled. 'But never mind. Maybe in the new year you will find your sleeping dictionary and all will be well.'

Boyd nodded. 'That'd be nice. What about you? No husband or boyfriend?'

Hanna made another face. 'I have had enough of men. I was married once but it didn't last. Now I live alone and like it.'

A few minutes later Liesl called them to the kitchen where the small table was set for three places. In the centre sprigs of holly framed the main platter. At each end of the table thick red candles had been lit. Liesl directed Boyd to the head of the table and the two women sat opposite one another at the sides, tucking serviettes onto their laps. Smiling, Liesl raised her wineglass.

'To our American guest. *Wilkommen und fröhliche Weihnachten*! *Und zum neuen Jahr Gesundheit, Glück und viel Erfolg!*'

Boyd looked to Hanna. 'Translate, *bitte*.'

'She welcomes you and wishes you a Merry Christmas, with health, happiness and much success in the new year. I second her wishes.'

Hanna raised her glass and the three of them touched glasses and drank. Then Boyd raised his glass again.

'One more toast. Merry Christmas also to you lovely ladies. And thank you for having me as your guest this snowy Christmas Eve. It means a lot to me, it really does. It would've been a pretty lonely night for me otherwise.'

They drank again and placed their glasses on the tabletop. Then they addressed the spread that had been prepared: roast pork with applesauce, steaming green vegetables, red cabbage, potatoes, dumplings, and gravy.

As they served themselves and ate Hanna questioned Boyd about his family in California. What would they be doing on Christmas Eve? He described for them a typical American Christmas.

'Do you have a big family?' Hanna asked, when he'd finished.

'One brother and one sister, both younger.' He sipped his wine.

Then he lifted the wine bottle from its ice-filled bucket and topped up everyone's glass. 'What happens here at Christmas? Is there a traditional routine?'

'Oh, yes,' Liesl replied. 'On the morning of Christmas Eve the father of the house decorates the tree by himself. Then the room is closed to the family so that the *Christkind* can brings the gifts during the afternoon, while everyone is away at church. In the evening, after the evening meal, the room is opened again, the Christmas tree lights are lit for the first time and the children are allowed to open their gifts. After that everyone sings carols together and reads passages from the Bible.'

'Sounds pretty religious,' Boyd commented, half-smiling.

Liesl nodded. 'We are very religious in Germany.'

'What happens on Christmas Day?'

Hanna answered this time. 'Much the same. The family goes to church together in the morning – again – and comes home afterwards to eat their Christmas dinner, which they often share with friends or extended family.'

'But you have no families to go to?'

'My parents were killed in the war,' Liesl told him. 'In an air raid. They were hiding under the stairs of their house in Berlin. It was a direct hit.'

Boyd frowned. 'I'm so sorry.'

Liesl smiled. 'No need. It wasn't your fault. It was war. These things happen. Anyway when they died you were only a baby.'

Boyd nodded. 'That's true. Where were you when they died? Weren't you with them?'

'No. When the bombing started my parents sent me out of Berlin. I was here, in a village just outside München, with an aunt. After my parents died she was the only relative left. Last June she died of cancer. Now there is no one.'

'No brothers or sisters? Other aunts or uncles?'

'No.'

He turned to Hanna. 'What about you? Where's your family?'

She smiled wryly. 'Like many Germans my family is cut off from me, on the other side of the wall in East Germany. I hardly have contact with them.'

'That must be hard. Especially at a time like this.'

'It is all the same to me. I learned long ago I was alone in the world and that I had to look after myself. It is a habit I have become accustomed to.'

When the main course was finished it was followed by the traditional Christmas sweets – *lebkuchen* and vanilla *kipferln* – which had been baked by Liesl that morning. When the meal was complete, Liesl served them all cups of strong black coffee and small glasses of Boyd's brandy, while Hanna opened the box of chocolates and offered them around.

Once everyone was settled again Hanna raised her brandy glass, smiling at Boyd.

'*Prost*, American!'

'*Prost*,' he echoed, and they all three touched glasses again.

They drank and sat back, enjoying a choral version of *Stille Nacht, Heilige Nacht* that wafted through from the sitting room radio.

Finally Boyd broke their silence.

'I'm curious. How long have you two known each other? Where did you meet?'

The women exchanged a glance. Liesl raised an eyebrow and, after a moment, Hanna shrugged.

'We met in Berlin. In 1947,' Liesl said finally. 'I was working as a waitress in a small restaurant. One evening on my way home I saw Hanna sitting alone on a park bench. She was crying, obviously upset. There were few people about so I sat with her, tried to find out what was wrong.'

Hanna reached out to grasp Liesl's hand on the tabletop.

'She was my guardian angel. That was one of the worst days of my life. She ... listened to my troubles, helped me to make things better. Since then she's been my closest friend. No one means more to me than Liesl.'

The American frowned. 'What happened? Can you tell me?'

Hanna patted her friend's hand and withdrew it, collecting her brandy glass and emptying it before answering.

'Let's just say it was the worst thing that can happen to a young woman. I was prepared to end it all. If Liesl hadn't appeared when she did I probably would not be here tonight. Truly, she is my guardian angel.' She clapped her hands. 'But enough of this nonsense from the past. This is Christmas Eve! We must be merry! Pour us another brandy, American, and tell us about your work at the factory.'

And so the night rolled on, with one topic of conversation segueing neatly into another as the three revelers laughed and conversed and the brandy was consumed and the candles burned down towards their saucer bases. When the brandy bottle had been emptied and the chocolate box half-depleted a stillness fell over the three. It was nearly midnight.

Liesl sighed and sat back, crumpling her serviette and laying it on the tabletop before her.

'*Wunderbar*! What an evening! But now, my friends, I am tired and I must go to my bed. It has been a long day.' She rose slowly to her feet and pushed her chair in to the table. 'But don't let me stop you. No one has to work tomorrow and the night is still young.'

Hanna raised her glass to her friend and blew her a kiss. '*Gute nacht, liebling*. I'll see you later.'

After clearing their brandy glasses and coffee cups to the sink, Liesl moved to rest her hands for a moment on Hanna's shoulders from behind, bending to plant a kiss on the top of her head. When she squeezed Boyd's shoulder in transit towards the door he reached up to grasp her hand.

179

'Sweet dreams, Liesl. You've given me a night I shall never forget. Thank you.'

With a weary smile and a wave Liesl disappeared towards her bedroom, shutting off the radio on her way, leaving the dark apartment heavy with silence.

For a moment the two left at the table said nothing, lost in their thoughts. Then suddenly Hanna rose to her feet.

'Wait. We have not finished yet. I have something special to share with you.'

She stepped into the sitting room and returned a moment later with her shoulder bag, removing from it a virgin bottle of Jack Daniels Tennessee mash whiskey, which she placed on the tabletop. Switching off the overhead light she produced a tray of ice cubes from the refrigerator, then grabbed two small tumblers from a shelf and returned with the lot to the table where she sat, arranging the objects before her. Amused, Boyd watched her in the flickering candle light. Cracking loose the ice cubes in the tray, Hanna dropped two in each tumbler, opened the whiskey bottle, poured a generous amount into each glass, then passed one to him.

'You're amazing!' He lifted his tumbler towards the candle flame, enjoying the dark colour as he swirled it around the ice cubes. 'You sure you want to do this? It is pretty late.'

She picked up her tumbler and sipped.

'Don't you want to, American?'

He sipped his own drink and sat forward, cradling the glass between his hands on the tabletop and smiling across at her. 'Sure. Why not? After all, it's Christmas Eve.' He nodded towards the bottle. 'Jack Daniels is not the usual drink for a German, I think.'

She smirked. 'No. But I like it. I like Americans. I have been drinking whiskey since the war.' She lifted her glass and drank again, then replaced it on the tabletop. 'I've spent rather a lot of time with your countrymen, you see?'

'That explains why your English is so good. What were you doing that you spent so much time with Yanks?'

She sat back, rubbing one forearm with her other hand. 'I worked for a time as a typist with the American Air Force. In Berlin. A long time ago.'

Picking up her drink, she drained it, then poured another. Boyd watched her.

'What'd happened when Liesl found you that day on the bench? Why were you so unhappy?'

Swirling her fresh drink, she sipped at it, then sat back, holding her glass in one hand and smiling at him.

'Ah, little American. You wish to know all of my secrets, eh? You want old Hanna to entertain you with the story of her miserable life so that you can write it up as a tale with which to amuse others?' She looked down into the glass, rattled her ice cubes. 'Well, you would be disappointed, I think. It's not much of a story. Rather boring, really. Anyway, it's all ancient history.'

'No. I'm interested, Hanna. What happened? Was it to do with the Americans? Were you involved with one of them?'

She lifted the glass and sipped again. Then she sighed, and placed the glass carefully on the table.

'When the war ended I was in Potsdam – training to be a typist and secretary. When the Allies occupied the country there were lots of jobs for young Germans who could type well and who spoke reasonable English. I had studied English since *hochshule* and was crazy about jazz and American movies. I managed to get to Berlin and found a job with the American Air Force, in the typing pool. After a year I was promoted – given special assignments in the offices of senior officers. I did well.' She smiled, and glanced at him. 'In those days I was very attractive, if I do say so myself – pretty hair, nice figure. I looked after myself, you know? The Americans got me stockings and lipsticks. It was a good life and I enjoyed the work.'

Boyd reached across to prise two ice cubes from the tray and refill his drink from the bottle.

'Were you involved with anyone?'

She smiled. 'Not at the beginning. I dated a few G.I.s, but I always found them a bit … simple, you know? They only ever had one thing in mind. When I learned that I stayed away from them, kept to myself.'

Boyd took a long sip and sat back in his chair. 'So what happened?'

'In 1947 the Russians blocked off Berlin from the rest of Germany. The Americans had to set up an airlift to supply the city through a narrow corridor to the west. I was very much involved when it was being organized, typing out and copying the details of schedules and arrangements.'

She stood suddenly and moved to the kitchen counter, turning to lean back against it, crossing her ankles and cradling her drink in her folded arms.

'In October of '47 General Curtis Lemay was made Commander of the US Air Forces in Europe. Have you heard of him?'

Boyd nodded. 'I think so. Wasn't he later Commander of SAC, the Strategic Air Command?'

'Yes, he was. He's an exceptional man. It was he who organized the Berlin airlift, who made it work. He was ruthless and he always got what he wanted. Many people thought he was a monster. But not me.' She sipped from her glass. 'Two weeks after the Russians imposed the blockade I was called to his office. He sat behind his desk, glowering at me, chomping on an unlit cigar. I was terrified. I knew his reputation, knew he could be a demon to anyone he found wanting. He asked me who I had worked for before, asked if I liked my work, if I'd gotten on with my bosses? I told him what he wanted to know. Then he leaned forward and asked me if I would work for him as his primary typist, attached to his office. Of course, I said yes.'

She smirked again, remembering.

'In those days I was very impressed by uniformed men in powerful positions. He told me that he'd heard about me from the other officers, had heard that I was a hard worker, that I always delivered what was asked of me on time. He asked if I could take dictation in English as well as type. I told him I could. I'd had a lot of experience by that time. He said that organizing the airlift was going to be a monumental job, with many things to be arranged and details to be dovetailed together, that I would be on call at all hours of the day and night. He asked me if I wanted to be a part of it. Of course I did, and I told him so. So I was moved to his office, and from that time on we spent most of every day together – sometimes nights too.'

She moved to the table again, refreshed her glass with ice and whiskey and sat back in her chair. Boyd waited patiently for her to continue.

'General Lemay was married,' she said at length, 'and he had a teenage daughter. There was a picture of the wife and daughter on his desk. I saw it every day. I even met his wife once, when she came for a visit and was shown around by a junior officer. She had a nice smile.' Reaching into her bag she produced a packet of filtered 'Hah-Bay' cigarettes and shook one out.

'You don't mind if I smoke?'

Boyd shook his head.

'Liesl doesn't like it,' Hanna said. 'I only do it when she's not around.'

She leaned forward to light the cigarette from the candle flame. Then she went on.

'One night – it was close to Christmas, actually – we were alone, finalizing a report which was to be sent to President Truman about how effective the airlift had been in supplying the needs of the city up to that point. It was a detailed document and we worked together at it for several hours, sitting side by side. By that time we knew each other well. He would often put his arm around me as we sat together, or would touch my shoulder in passing as I typed. I knew he was fond of me, that he found me attractive. When the document was finished he phoned for a courier to take it to the radio room to be wired to the states. When we were alone again I gathered my things and was preparing to leave when he suddenly stood in front of the door.

'"Don't go," he said. "I have a bottle of whiskey in my desk drawer. You did a lot of hard work tonight. Let's have a drink together to celebrate."'

Hanna leant forward to tap her cigarette ash into the candle's saucer. Then she took another pull on the cigarette, exhaled, and shuddered slightly before continuing.

'Well, we had one drink together. Then another. And another. And then he moved close to me, pulled me into his arms and kissed me. I was surprised, of course, and a little afraid. But I was also attracted to him – attracted by his power, by the scent of his American aftershave. He was not a bad looking man. So I kissed him back. And when he put his hands on me, murmuring about how much he wanted me, I responded.

'There was a little room beside his office with a bed where the General sometimes catnapped or even spent the night if he'd been working late. That night there was no one else on the floor. Everyone had gone away for the holiday, except for the guards on the main door downstairs. We were completely alone. He drew me in there, into that room, in the darkness. And he undressed me – very slowly and tenderly. Then we made love. That was the first time. The beginning.'

She drank from her glass, took a final pull on the cigarette and snuffed it out in the saucer. Then she sat back, her hands clasped in her lap, almost primly. Boyd watched her closely in the candlelight, his arms crossed over his chest.

'The affair went on for some months,' she continued. 'Mostly we made love in that little room beside his office. Sometimes he was able to take me with him on trips – to Paris or Vienna – and he would arrange to meet me in my room late at night. But that was risky for him, and he hated the thought of being discovered. Then one month my period failed to come. I waited one week, two weeks. Then I went to my doctor. He told me I was pregnant. I didn't know what to think – whether to be happy about it, or horrified. I knew Curtis was married, knew he would never divorce his wife and ruin his family life so that he could marry me. If I was honest with myself I knew exactly what I was to him – a *Kraut* mistress to keep him amused while he was away from his wife. His *fräulein* whore. But I still believed the baby might change things, that he might care enough for me to make things all right somehow. I knew he was powerful enough to make anything happen that he wished to happen.'

Boyd leaned forward.

'Did you love him?'

She smiled, a hard, cynical smile.

'Did I love him?' She shook her head. 'Little American, you are so young. How could you possibly know what it was like in those days? The war was only two years over. My family were all in the Soviet section, soon to be locked away forever behind an iron curtain. There was no room in Berlin in 1947 for love. There was only room for what was practical and useful, for what guaranteed you food to eat and a roof over your head. Did I love him? He was fifteen years older than me. He was no Clark Gable, but he had treated me well, had given me gifts. He'd looked after me. No, I didn't love him. But I was fonder of him than I've ever been of any man – my own father included.'

'What did he say when you told him about the baby? What did he do?'

'He went crazy. I waited until we were alone in the office and would not be disturbed. Then I let it pour out, about the baby, about my worries. He told me I was a fool for not having taken precautions. The baby must not live, he said. I had to have an abortion. He lit a cigar and paced the room, scowling and ranting. I sat in my chair, my head down. There was nothing more I could say to him. Then he offered me money, told me to leave Berlin – to go to Munich or Stuttgart and find a doctor who would terminate the pregnancy. When I pleaded with him to let me have it – I was raised a Catholic, after all, and abortion is a mortal sin – he yelled at me not to be stupid. The baby had to go, he said. There could be no risk of his reputation being tainted by this unwanted life, no chance that his family should suffer the shame of it being exposed to the world. Finally he shoved a roll of dollars into my hand and told me to go and not to return. He would square things with the authorities, invent a reason for my disappearance, something they would accept – a sudden family bereavement, an illness. I was just to go and he would sort everything out so that it would appear is if I'd never existed – for him – that I had never shared a moment of his life.'

Boyd watched as she seemed to shrink within herself, becoming smaller, tighter, more constricted – reliving her torment.

'What happened then?'

He reached across to shake a cigarette from her pack and lit it with the candle, sitting back in his chair as he drew his first puff.

Hanna sighed.

'I grabbed my things and left the building. I wandered the streets for hours in a daze. I didn't know where to go. Finally I found myself on a park bench with darkness falling around me. I had decided I would do away with myself – hurl myself beneath the wheels of a streetcar or under a train. It was then that Liesl turned up from nowhere – like an angel. Somehow she made me trust her. I told her what'd happened. She stroked my hand, comforted me, told me she had an aunt in a village near Munich. She said she could arrange for me to stay with her. And that was that.'

She spread her hands wide, signifying the end of her story.

'You stayed with Liesl's aunt until the baby was born?'

'Yes.'

'Did Liesl move here to stay with you?'

'Eventually, yes, she did. She gave up her job in Berlin and came to Munich. She's worked at various jobs here since then. She's been with Frau Graf for the last eight years.'

Boyd nodded. 'You told me you were married once.'

'Ha! That was a joke, a stupid mistake. A man I met at Oktoberfest. It lasted two months.'

'And the baby? What happened to your baby?'

'That was the greatest tragedy.' Hanna sighed again, deeply this time. 'I wanted him so much, you see? This child created from our hopeless love. Or non love. But the baby was stillborn. Something went wrong in the last days. There was nothing anyone could do.'

She bent forward, her hands on her knees, dropping her head. Boyd leaned across to put a hand on her shoulder.

'I'm sorry. So very sorry.'

After a time Hanna sighed, shuddered and sat up, forcing a tight smile.

'Thank you. It was very hard at the time to lose him. The baby, I mean. It was a boy, you see? The baby was a boy. But perhaps it was for the best. In any case it brought me Liesl, so the experience was not without some good.' She reached for the bottle and poured herself a finger more of whiskey, then held it towards Boyd's glass. 'A final shot?'

'Why not?'

She poured his measure and together they lifted their glasses, staring across at one another in the now guttering candlelight.

'To life,' Hanna intoned, 'and to all the wonderful tragedies and comedies it brings us.'

'To you, Hanna Beck,' Boyd returned, 'and to the strength you showed in rising above such a terrible experience.'

They touched glasses and drank, draining them in one gulp.

Then they rose together and carried the glasses to the sink, put away the ice tray and set aside on the counter the half-empty whiskey bottle. Boyd pinched out one of the candles and Hanna the other. Through the kitchen window a pale amber light reflected off the ceiling from the streetlights below.

Boyd stepped toward the hallway. Hanna followed.

'Where are you going, American?'

He turned.

'To my bed downstairs.'

She reached out to touch his arm.

'Can I see your room?'

He looked at her, then nodded.

'If you want.'

They made their way silently down the hall, leaving the door ajar for Hanna's later return.

Sometime toward morning Boyd woke in the darkness to the sound of his door snapping shut. For a moment, he was disoriented. Then in the dim light he recognized the chair beside his bed and the table before it. Felt the warmth of the sheets where Hanna had lain close against him.

She wanted just to be held, she'd said. She'd only stay a few minutes. They had nestled together under the duvet in their clothes, Todd gathering her into the cradle of his arms. When she'd fallen asleep he'd listened for some time to her breathing. Her light nasal flutter struck him as slightly comic. In the dim light she had looked older, and he realized suddenly she was only a bit younger than his mother. But what did that matter? Finally he'd bent forward to plant a kiss on her forehead, and allowed himself to drift off to sleep.

Now he lay in the darkness, listening to the creaks as Hanna climbed the stairs to rejoin Liesl. Tomorrow they would both be gone early, to spend the day with friends in Schwabing.

Through the slit of the curtain Boyd could see snow falling again in the amber light – great fluffy flakes that would bury the empty streets once more in a blanket of sound-numbing cotton.

Boyd considered getting up to remove his clothes, then abandoned the idea. He pulled the thick duvet close around him like a cocoon, smelling with pleasure the residue of Hanna's scent on the pillow.

Within moments sleep had returned to claim him, drawing him down into cosy darkness, his last thoughts a wry reflection on the whimsical nature of fate, delivering as it had to him such an incredible Christmas Eve. This night would be fixed in his memory forever, he knew. Every Christmas for the rest of his life he would recall these two remarkable ladies, and remember with gratitude the dinner he'd shared with them in Frau Graf's pension apartment just off *Sendlinger Tor Platz*, where in 1964 he'd been privileged – however briefly – to come to know, and to shelter in his arms for a time, the discarded former mistress of General Curtis Lemay.

(London, 2009)

Vanda

Old Arthur died today. The first death we've had for almost a month.

It was me that found him, at just after five this afternoon – a few minutes after my tea break. I'd popped into his room to leave some clean bedding and towels in his cupboard when I suddenly realized the room was silent. There was no longer the protracted, rasping intakes of breath that had echoed out into the hallway for the last twenty-four hours. He'd been on half-hourly watches. He must've slipped away just after the nurse's last visit.

I put the laundry down and moved to the bed. Arthur's eyes were opaque slits and his mouth was open. Placing two fingers on his neck I felt for a pulse, but there was nothing. He was definitely gone. Gently, I closed his mouth and pulled his eyelids down. Then I went downstairs to fetch the sister.

It was unfortunate, really, that he was alone when he died. Only an hour or so earlier he'd been visited by his daughter and son-in-law. I'd seen them before I'd taken my break – two middle-aged people in coats and scarves and hats. I asked if they'd like some tea, and when I brought back the tray with two cups and a few biscuits I stayed with them for a few minutes.

The daughter had taken off her outdoor things and was swabbing Arthur's mouth with a sponge on a stick, trying to clear the thick mucus that had collected inside. The husband was on a chair on the other side of the bed, leaning forward with his hands in his lap, staring at Arthur's face. He looked upset, too.

Over the last months I had often seen the two of them when they'd made their visits – especially in the late summer and early autumn when the days were warm enough to take him outside. Arthur had always lit up like a Christmas tree when he saw her, throwing up his hands in pure delight. Ninety-two he was, and deaf as a post. Most of the time he just sat in his wheelchair and stared into space. Hardly ever spoke, unless spoken to by some staff member. Numb, I guess. Lost in his past. But when the daughter turned up he'd wake up again.

'My darling!' he'd cry. 'How wonderful to see you!' And then, as they wheeled him away from the others, out of the lounge and along the corridor towards the outside door, 'It's always the unexpected pleasures that are the best,' he'd add, happily, clutching her hand.

It was obvious that this daughter was special to him. He was more animated and cheerful with her than he was even with his own wife – the daughter's stepmother – who visited twice a week. She came dutifully and drank her cup of tea, staying always until the minute hand on the clock by his bed had made a full circle. One hour exactly twice a week, that was her gift to him. She sat and worked at her knitting, with Arthur sitting in the wing chair beside her – neither one speaking, both watching a sub-titled television programme on the big set by the window. Arthur's gaze, however, always seemed to pass beyond the television screen and out the adjacent window, as if his mind was miles away in another sphere.

Arthur seemed almost to ignore her, and I got the impression he was pretty upset with her for having put him in the Manor in the first place, rather than arranging for him to be cared for at home. He clearly had money enough. For Arthur it represented a kind of betrayal, I guess, and he never forgave her for it – remaining sombre and tight-lipped throughout her visits, and growling irritably at the slightest gesture she made towards making him more comfortable. Sad, really, that their twenty-odd shared years should end like that.

I had brought the daughter another packet of sponge swabs and some lemon water with the tea tray and for a moment I stood beside her as she patiently worked away at his mouth. At one point I put my arm around her and squeezed, and she turned to give me a smile.

'You're very kind,' she said. 'I'm Eunice and that's Greg. What's your name?'

'I am Vanda,' I told her.

'How do you spell that?' she asked, looking confused.

'It's Polish. V – A – N – D – A.'

'Oh,' she smiled. 'I understand. Wanda with a V. Vanda.'

'That's right.'

We both looked down at Arthur, listening for a moment to his harsh breathing.

'It won't be long now, will it?' she asked quietly.

'No,' I told her. 'Not long. Maybe tonight, maybe tomorrow. But soon.'

She nodded, caressing the old man's pale, thin hand.

'We can't stay much longer. We have an engagement. I don't think he knows we're here anyway. But we'll be back in the late afternoon. And we'll stay then to the end.'

'That will be good. Who knows, maybe he can tell that you're here. It might mean a lot to him.'

'I hope so,' she murmured, and tears welled in her eyes.

Giving her another squeeze I'd left them to it.

Nice people. They'd visited him every week since he'd been admitted to Sylvan Manor six months before. Just an ordinary couple, but nice. They'll be so sorry they missed his passing.

It's always hard for me to see the visitors that come to spend time with their loved ones who are slowly slipping away. Husbands and wives, brothers and sisters, sons and daughters. The dying aren't the sad ones. We all have to die after all, and usually they come here having spent long and productive lives. And we do try to make their last days as comfortable as possible. No, it's the relatives I pity most. For us the dead will be forgotten within hours, their pain and discomfort a thing of the past. But for the relatives the pain will go on and on and on. It's hard to forget that.

When the final stage arrives, the last hours, there's never any way to know exactly when death will come. Some people fight it longer than others. Or their bodies do. Weeks sometimes. Funny, you'd think the body would just want to give up. But it doesn't. Not always. Like with Ania. Sometimes it can go on and on. The business of dying can be so … tedious.

The funny thing is that today is my birthday. I'm fifty-seven today, and no one knows that but me. Not here, anyway.

Maybe that's why old Arthur's passing has affected me so much.

At eight o'clock in the evening I finish work, climb wearily into my little Fiat and set off for home. When I stop the car in the darkness in front of my building I sit for a few moments, thinking. What can I do to celebrate? It's my special day. I need some picking up after the events of the afternoon. I need to spoil myself a little. I'll go to the Chinese up the street, I decide. Order a takeaway. Then I'll bring it home and enjoy it in front of the television. After that I'll soak in a hot bath in candlelight and listen to some Liszt or Chopin – with a glass or two of the sparkling wine I bought yesterday that is chilling in the refrigerator. Then maybe I'll be able to sleep soundly, with no dreams of Ania and the terrible thing that happened to her.

I shake myself. 'Vanda Kacziński,' I tell myself, 'stop this brooding! Do you want to get bad again? Get out of the car and walk. You are fifty-seven years old now. You can do it – just as you've done it every day for the last eighteen months.'

And I get out of my car and lock it, and I walk up the road toward the takeaway, clutching my handbag as I go.

When I get the food home I put the bag on the counter while I take off my coat and scarf and put them away in the hall closet. Taking the bottle of wine from the fridge, I open it and pour myself a glass of the straw-tinted bubbly. Then I prepare my set meal for one, my favourite – crispy duck, sweet and sour chicken, Chinese mixed vegetables and special fried rice. When I pop the lids from the plastic containers delicious smells rise with the steam. Sipping my wine I begin to feel better.

I serve myself a portion of each dish over a bed of the rice and retire to the sitting room, flicking on the television as I settle into my favourite armchair, balancing the plate on my lap.

The nine-o'clock news is on – more sad stories of British soldiers killed in Afghanistan by roadside bombs. I think of their poor families. Such a waste of young lives. It's so sad when the young are taken from us unnecessarily.

I'm half way through my dinner when the phone rings. I pick up the handset from its cradle, switching the television to mute with the remote.

'Yes? Hello?'

'Vanda, it's Edek.'

I close my eyes. I should've known he would call.

'Hello, Edek. Thank you for calling. I got your letter yesterday.'

It's hard for me to speak Polish now, it's been so long. There is a sigh down the phone from the other end.

'It's good to hear your voice again, Vanda. I wanted to wish you Happy Birthday in person. I miss you, darling. I'm sitting here in this empty house – our house – and I'm thinking of you. I wanted you to know that.'

'Thank you, Edek. It's kind of you.'

Edek is my husband. We've been married nearly twenty-five years, now. But since Ania's death we've mostly been apart. For some months even in the same house, before I moved away completely.

'Vanda,' he goes on, 'you talk to me as if I was a stranger. You're my wife. I love you. I want you home. You've been in England eight months now. I need you here. We must start over again.'

I rub my forehead with my fingers. My food is growing cold on the plate before me.

'I'm not sure I can do that yet, Edek. I still need time. I'm sorry.'

'Vanda, I miss her, too. You know that. And it would be so much easier to deal with this grief if we were together.'

'But you drove her away!' I want to shout. *'If she hadn't left us she might still be alive!'*

But I say nothing. What is the point?

This is the problem with us, the way Edek turned against Ania when she became a teenager, always complaining about this or that. She could never do anything right. Then she came home one night with her hair cut short and bleached, with greenish streaks here and there. It stuck out from her head in crazy tufts, the way the young people like their hair nowadays. I thought it was quite charming. Funny even. But Edek went berserk, shouted at her. 'What have you done to yourself?' he cried, waving his arms. 'Why do you want to be such a clown? You look ridiculous! You look terrible! How can I hold up my head in the street with such a crazy for a daughter!'

A few weeks later she came in with a tattoo on her arm and a silver stud pierced through her eyebrow. Edek went ballistic again, shouting and screaming. I tried to stop him but he just waved me away, declaring I was too soft with her.

Finally Ania moved out. Just after her eighteenth birthday. She came to tell me one afternoon at the hospital where I worked.

'I love him, mamma,' she said, 'but I can't take his disapproval anymore.' And she hugged me, hard. 'One of my friends has offered me a room in her flat. I'm sorry, but I must take it.'

For a long time I just held her. I didn't want to let her go.

It was a month or two after that that it happened, the horrible thing.

'Vanda?' Edek asks down the phone. 'Are you still there?'

'Yes, I'm here.'

'Well, what do you think? I'm right, yes? Isn't it time you came home?'

'I don't know, Edek. I'm not sure…'

His voice rises in intensity.

'Well *I* am sure! I *know*! Being apart like this is helping no one! It's destroying us! I go to the shipyard every day, I do what I must do to make a living. And every night I come home to this silent, empty house, to rooms full of memories – of you and of Ania and of our life together. It is killing me, Vanda. Is that what you want? For me to be dead, too?'

'Of course not, Edek. I'm sorry…'

'Sorry is not enough. Not anymore. I can't live this way. It's been eight months since I've seen you. We aren't husband and wife now, we're becoming strangers. If you don't come back soon I'll divorce you! I might as well find a new life if our old one is truly finished.'

He is crying now. I can hear it in his voice.

'Edek, I'm sorry if you feel you must do that,' I tell him. 'And I'm sorry to cause you such pain, but …'

I can't go on. There is silence as I listen to his sobs down the phone line. Finally, he collects himself and speaks again.

'Have a Happy Birthday, Vanda. Your mother sends love. I need you, darling. Please reconsider. I don't want a divorce. I just want you home again. Think about it, please. Call me!'

The line goes dead.

On the screen across the room flickering images document the heavy snowfall disrupting travel in the north. There have been fatalities – vehicles in accidents, fallen trees. I lift the remote and switch off the television.

The food on my plate is cold. I have no appetite left. Rising, I carry the tray back to the kitchen.

Ania was raped and murdered two years ago by a boy she knew at university – a student of microbiology, as she had been.

I was employed then at the hospital as a senior nurse in obstetrics. I loved my work – helping to bring new life into the world, making young mothers as comfortable as possible before, during and after their ordeal.

One night in the middle of my shift two plainclothes police officers turned up – a man and woman, both wearing dark anoraks. Sombre-faced, they showed me their badges, asking if they could speak with me alone.

'What is it?' I asked, panicking. 'Did something happen to Edek?'

My husband works around heavy equipment at the shipyard. I was always afraid something would happen to him. But the officers wouldn't say anything more till we were in the little consulting room beside the nurses' station.

They closed the door, pulled out a chair and made me sit down. Then they sat opposite me.

'Mrs. Kacziński,' the man said, 'I'm sorry to have to tell you that your daughter Ania…'

Gasping, I rose to my feet.

'What has happened to my baby? Is she…?'

The woman stood and gently pushed me down again.

'Sit down, ma'am,' she cooed. 'Please.'

When I sat again the man carried on.

'Your daughter is gravely ill, Mrs. Kacziński,' he said, his hands clasped in front of him. 'She's been raped and beaten. It happened at the edge of a park, as she was walking home from a party, apparently. She must've been followed. A passer-by disturbed the man and he ran off. But the witness phoned us immediately on his mobile and was able to give us a good description. We caught the rapist a few streets away. Your daughter is in the hospital here now.'

I stood again, icy fingers clutching my heart.

'Then I must go to her.'

This time they both rose to their feet.

'Mrs. Kacziński ...' The woman laid a hand on my arm. 'Contact your husband first. Then you can face this together.' She sighed. 'I have to tell you that ... she is not expected to live.'

I fainted then.

Minutes later I woke up in a bed, with the concerned faces of colleagues I have known for years hovering over me.

That was the beginning.

When I was finally able to see Ania later that evening her head was swathed in bandages. All I could see was her nose and slightly open mouth, with tubes trailing from it. Drip stands surrounded the bed, and her breathing was being assisted mechanically. She was in a coma. The doctors said it was probably best that way. She'd been struck about the head repeatedly with something heavy, severely damaging her brain. Even if she woke up she would never be my lovely Ania again.

For two weeks it went on like this. Two weeks of daily attendance at her bedside, listening to her mechanical breathing, watching her vital signs on the displays. At the end of that time my old friend Dr. Koslovski came to me as I was sitting with her, pulled a chair up beside me and took my hand. He told me there was no longer any hope for her, that it was clear she could now only endure as a vegetable, her life prolonged artificially by the feeding tubes and the breathing machine. He sighed, and squeezed my hand.

'Vanda, it would be best to let her go. To turn off the machines and let things take their course. You have to face it, dear. Ania is not coming back to you.'

At first I couldn't even consider such a thing. But later on, after Edek came and Dr. Koslovski spoke to both of us at length in his office, Edek took his part and pleaded with me to let her die. Finally I agreed.

Two days later Edek and I sat holding her hands while the drips and tubes were removed and the machines turned off. Within minutes she was gone.

The next weeks are a blank to me. I don't even remember the funeral. Nor do I remember the arraignment and trial of her murderer. For weeks I wasn't aware from moment to moment where I was or what I was doing. They put me to bed and sedated me. Edek tried to comfort me, but I couldn't stand him touching me. I'd push him away. I couldn't help feeling that if he hadn't taken against her as he'd done she wouldn't have left home and this would not have happened. She'd still be alive. Indirectly, Ania's death was his fault, as I saw it. I couldn't sleep in the marriage bed with him any longer – the bed we'd shared for so many years – and I begged him to go. So he made up a bed in the guest room, and there he stayed from then on. But he continued to look after me every day. To feed me and bathe me, and to make sure I drank enough liquids. I was in catatonic shock and couldn't move. My mother, I later discovered, came to cook the meals and look after him. It was not fair of me to leave him in the lurch like that, but I couldn't help myself. I was a broken thing, off my head.

After some weeks I began to recover. Finally I sat up in bed, was able to feed myself, even rose and walked about the house. Eventually my mother went back home and I began to cook and keep house again and to look after Edek, who had finally resumed his work. But I couldn't face returning to the hospital. No more pregnant mothers-to-be. No more babies. That was finished for me. And I couldn't feel for Edek again what I'd felt before Ania's death. That, too, seemed finished. Collateral damage. He went on sleeping in the guest room. I was sorry for him, but I could do nothing. Finally I left him and went to stay with a nurse friend. Edek would come to visit, but it was awkward. We didn't have much to say. I knew he was hurting, but I couldn't do anything to help.

I decided to leave Poland, to find employment in another country, far away from the trauma I had suffered in Gdansk. A nurse colleague suggested England, told me it'd be easy to find work there. I spoke a little English so I made enquiries, found some addresses, wrote letters. Eventually I was hired long distance by the manager of Sylvan Manor in London's western suburbs on the strength of my Polish credentials. But only as a carer, not as a nurse. My Polish qualifications were not recognized there. Still, the salary was reasonable, and there was the provision of good accommodation nearby. So I left Gdansk. Left Edek, who stood at the airport watching me pass into the departure area like a man witnessing an execution.

It took eight months to recover some semblance of normality in my life. But I wasn't ready yet to return to Poland, to face Edek and the memories. The loss.

Not yet.

Perhaps I never would be.

I put the Chinese leftovers in the fridge in their closed containers, pour myself another glass of sparkling wine and go to the bathroom to draw a hot bath. Maybe that will lift my spirits again.

For special occasions I keep a box of candles in a cupboard, which I now open – spreading the little coloured tea-lights all around the room and along the edge of the bath. I light the candles with a taper, turn off the overhead light. In my bedroom, I unbutton my carer's uniform. In a moment I stand naked before the wardrobe's full length mirror, staring at the stranger in the glass.

Finally I slip on my towelling robe, turn to the bedside table to insert a CD into the radio-music box and to switch it on.

Beside it lies Edek's folded letter where I left it the night before. He had enclosed a picture that was taken at our wedding at the small country church so many years ago. The picture lies on top of the letter, the smiling figures beaming up at me from the past – so young, so full of hope. We were so happy then, clutching one another as though we couldn't stand to be not touching, even for a moment. Life held such promise then.

Settling into the steaming, scented bath, I let myself sink under the bubbles, feeling the heat of the water spreading into my muscles, relaxing them. Lizst's *Liebestraum* plays through the half-open door from across the hallway, and I feel his wonderful music working its magic, soothing me, calming the tension. The lights of the tiny candles flicker, casting shadow patterns over the walls and ceiling.

In the drawer of my bedside table is a photograph of Ania taken when she was five years old, climbing onto her first bicycle. Her face is radiant with joy as she glances towards the camera. I took that picture. It's the only one of Ania I have here, the only photo of her I can bear to look at now. Today before I left for work I pulled it out again and held it in my hand, succumbing once more to tears as I remembered the girl behind that joyful face and the pitifully few years we were given to share together. I suppose it was Edek's letter that prompted me to look at it again. But it hurt. It always hurts.

Now, cradling my chilled wineglass in the cocoon of the hot bath, feeling the tension of the day dissipating with the heat and the numbing of the alcohol, I lay my head back on the tub rim and stare at the dancing shadows on the ceiling, lose myself thinking of the newly-weds in the photograph starting their journey together. Remembering their joy when the girl-baby had been born to them, the little bundle that had filled their lives with such happiness.

Remembering the horror when she was taken so brutally away.

And – strangely, for I have seen so much of death in the last eight months – remembering the still, stroke-ravaged face and pale, thin hands of old Mr. Arthur in his bed. And the loving daughter who at this moment must be suffering so terribly, too.

Today is my birthday.

Tomorrow decisions must be made. Life must go on.

But tonight is for remembering. For weeping for those who have gone. And for the happy times that passed away with them.

Sipping the chilled wine, I release myself to the tears that stream down my cheeks and drip into the lavender-scented bathwater.

(London, 2010)

A Policeman's Lot

This all began three and a half months ago, back at the end of September.

I'd been on night duty all week. About ten o'clock one evening we got a call at the Springwood Station from a lady up in Faulconbridge (our station covers all the towns from Glenbrook up to Katoomba in the Blue Mountains). For the previous half hour she'd been listening to the sounds of a violent row coming from her neighbours' house – screaming and shouting and things being smashed up. She said it sounded like they were out of their minds with drink and she was afraid someone was going to get hurt, maybe badly. When she told the Sergeant her address we jumped to it, for her neighbour was well known to us.

My name's Barry Palmer and I'm twenty-four years old. Two years ago I finished training and earned my ranking as a Constable in the New South Wales Police force. It was a hard slog for me, for I was used to lazing around and going for the easy option all through my school years. I wasn't really a bludger, just not very self-motivated, I reckon. It's a wonder I finished with reasonable marks. Maybe I'm a late developer or something. Anyway, I don't know what made me go in for law enforcement as a career. Police work is demanding, and it took me a while to get used to the new discipline enforced upon my life. But I made it. I had good teachers and good mates in the Force. And I love the work, so it's turned out all right.

I was surprised, when I joined the Springwood Station, at how many domestic violence cases turn up here every week. Almost every night there'll be a call from some poor woman on her mobile, locked in her car or her bathroom, begging us to come out to deal with her drunken, drug-addled partner/lover/husband, who's threatening to beat the living daylights out of her once he gets his hands on her. Or we get calls from the neighbours who hear the screams and the shouting. And we go out. We have to. It's our job. But it's our least favourite callout. We never know what we're going to walk into. Often times – it's common knowledge – the battered woman herself will turn on us while we're trying to restrain her attacker. In my first two months with the Force I had to physically prevent two bruised and bleeding ladies from attacking the officers who were taking away the very men that had just given them their hidings. And sometimes – would you believe it? – it's the *men* we have to protect from their violent *female* partners! I tell you, the world is going crazy. People are weird and getting weirder. Especially people who're supposed to care for one another. And most especially people whose common sense is knocked off kilter by drugs or booze or a lethal combination of both.

But I'm rambling.

The person who lived at the address in Faulconbridge we were racing to was a no-hoper named Davie Seick, who had grown up locally but had left home early on and drifted down into the seamy backstreets of Blacktown and Sydney. There he quickly became involved with one of the major drug-dealing bikie gangs, the Comancheros. In his early twenties he'd been busted by the Sydney Drug Squad for dealing, and had served three years in Long Bay Prison. When he got out he apparently kept his distance from his old mates – as he was bound to do by the terms of his probation – but he still roared round New South Wales on his Harley Davidson causing trouble wherever he went. He might even have kept on dealing after his release, but no one was ever able to nail him for it. It was rumoured that he still worked for his old mob as a standover man – a hard-arse who collects their unpaid debts through violent intimidation – for a percentage of the recovered money. Davie was a prime candidate for such a job, being built like a brick shit house and fit as a Mallee bull, with loads of tattoos and piercings and muscles overlaying his muscles. But he never stayed long enough in one place for the Force to get a chance to collar him. For the last several years he'd been dividing his time between weeks spent in his old haunts in Sydney followed by – when his homesickness for the home ground got the best of him – periods up here in the mountain towns, where he regularly created havoc for himself, his neighbours, and for us. Whenever he was on drugs or on the piss – which was almost constantly – he became violent, picking fights with anyone who happened to be available. In a pub that was usually some unwitting bloke that glanced at him the wrong way. If he was at home then the victim was whatever sheila he'd brought up to be his current squeeze – they seemed to come and go like the days of the week.

Anyway, we'd been called out to his various addresses (he changed residence fairly frequently for obvious reasons) several times over the last couple of years, and as he was so big and strong the Captain sent two units to cover the callout rather than one. So when both cars converged on the quiet Faulconbridge street and parked in front of Davie's run-down rental there were four of us at the door when he opened to our knock.

'What the fuck do you hoons want?' he growled, glaring out at us.

Davie was clearly mad as a cut snake. When we told him we were responding to a call about possible domestic violence and asked to see his lady partner he refused at first, shouting at us to 'rack off back to your bloody fucking station'.

Then suddenly this girl appeared behind him, nursing a bleeding nose and a nasty cut lip. She was giving him a mouthful – screaming that he was 'a fucking brute' and 'a vicious bloody animal' and demanding that we take him away and charge him with assault. When Davie went for her again we jumped inside and wrestled him to the ground – though it took all four of us to hold him down and get the cuffs on him.

When all the shouting was over and Davie had quieted down the Sarge instructed me to remain with the girl to take her statement, while he and the others took Davie to the station to charge him with assault and battery and resisting arrest. He was so dangerous they reckoned it would take three men to hold him if he started up again.

As I watched them haul him down the porch steps and back to the car, little did I know what I was in for staying behind.

When the others had gone I got out my notebook and pen, sat down on the tattered sofa and asked the woman to sit in the armchair opposite so I could take down her account of what'd happened.

Her name, she told me, was Miranda Byers. She was in her late twenties and was clearly part Abo, with short curly dark hair. While she dabbed at her bloody nose and lip with a tissue, she told me she'd been living with Davie for the last couple of weeks, and that before then she'd had a room near King's Cross in Sydney – though she came originally from a small town in the Northern Territory up near Katherine. She'd left home at seventeen and had been working since then at various jobs – waitress, cocktail hostess, cashier – in the restaurants and casinos of Adelaide, Melbourne and Sydney. She'd even worked for a time as a pole dancer, she told me.

She was obviously drunk, and probably drugged to the teeth as well. I asked her if that was the case – if she was high – and she told me they'd spent all afternoon downing tinnies. She didn't mention drugs. When I asked her specifically whether she had taken any that day she said that earlier on Davie'd given her a pill which he'd said would 'make everything rosy', and that shortly after she'd taken it she felt frightened because it wasn't like any other high she'd ever experienced. When she'd asked Davie what it was he'd lost his temper, told her she was 'a gutless cunt with no sense of adventure' and began to slap her around.

It was the usual sordid story of substance related violence.

As I sat scribbling down her statement she suddenly stood up.

'Fancy a brew?' she asked me.

'Thanks,' I told her. 'But I never drink on duty.'

'Well, I'm having one,' she said. 'I'm parched.'

She went off and came back soon after swigging from a longneck. She'd obviously stopped off at the bathroom on her way, rinsed off the blood and given her hair a comb. Apart from the cut on her lip, her face was now clean and presentable. For the first time I realized the girl was actually quite attractive, with dark, sensuous eyes and a generous mouth. She also had a nice figure – something which was now more apparent as she'd taken off her jeans and sweater and was now wearing a thigh-length white towelling robe tied at the waist.

I have to admit Miranda was starting to get to me, to give me ideas, awaken desires that caused my heartbeat to race and my forehead to bead up with sweat.

I'm still single, you see, though I do have a girlfriend I met a couple years ago through my church. Donna's quite pretty, short with dark hair and a nice figure. She's a year younger than me and a bit withdrawn by nature, but she's very loving and attentive. She spends two or three evenings a week with me in my Springwood apartment, but she still lives at home with her parents. We talk about getting married later on, but for right now we're happy to carry on as we are, holding down our separate jobs (Donna's a librarian at the Springwood library) and saving money for the future. The fact is, though, owing to her strict church upbringing, Donna doesn't have much imagination when it comes to sex. She always leaves it to me to initiate things, and isn't interested in anything other than getting it over with as soon as possible in the missionary position. For a 24-year old bloke with a keen sexual imagination that's a bit hard to take.

To make matters worse, Miranda had now curled herself languidly on the sofa beside me, tucking her bare feet underneath her – all of which made me extremely nervous. I tried to concentrate on writing up the statement. I wanted out of there asap.

'Haven't you finished with that yet?' she purred, taking a pull on her bottle and reaching to place it on the coffee table before of us. Then she settled back and turned towards me, running an arm along the sofa back behind my head. As she did that her robe fell open, revealing a fair amount of her left breast. She was clearly not wearing anything underneath.

I moved away from her.

'Miss Byers,' I said, trying to focus, 'I need you to read this over and sign at the bottom if you're happy with it.'

'Come on, Officer,' she murmured, running her finger down my arm and grinning like a shot fox. 'Why don't you put that notebook down and pay some attention to me? What are you, a block of wood?'

She dropped her hand to my bare knee, ran her hand higher along the inside of my thigh. I pushed it away but she just giggled.

'Come on, handsome. Don't you like it?' she cooed, putting her hand right back on my thigh. 'I know you do, whatever you say.'

Well, she was right. I did like it. I knew it was wrong, that if I was caught carrying on with her I'd lose my job. But somehow her nearness was like a drug to me, suggesting the promise of all the unknown illicit pleasures I'd been dreaming about but had been denied with Donna. And Miranda was a very attractive girl.

By now she was rubbing my crotch.

'There now, Constable,' she said, smiling wickedly. 'You see? There's clearly life rising in the old fella so you can't pretend you don't like it.' She leaned towards me. 'You know, I've always wanted to shag a policeman, and this seems the right time to do it. What d'ya say? You going to be the lucky copper tonight, pretty boy? Or are you gonna be a gutless wonder?'

Opening her robe, she grabbed my hand and flattened it against her naked breast – and I lost it altogether.

The next thing I knew she was straddling my thighs, the dressing gown now completely open. Grasping my face with both hands, she pushed me back against the sofa, pressing her mouth against mine, forcing my lips open.

'No, please...' I tried to push her away. 'This is wrong! Stop!'

But she paid no attention, just pressed forward against me and kissed me again, jamming her tongue deep in my mouth.

I raised my hands to resist, but there was no strength in them anymore, no will behind the action. Meanwhile her fingers were undoing my shirt buttons. When her hands reached down to undo the belt of my shorts I gave up all pretence of struggling. Swept on in a tsunami of raw emotion, I allowed myself to lie back and be carried away by it. The wicked pleasure of it all was just too amazing.

I won't go into detail about what happened over the next half hour. Suffice it to say that by the time I got back to the station I was feeling drained, and mighty guilty.

I won't pretend I didn't enjoy what'd happened, but I knew it was wrong. And I felt ashamed I'd given way to it so easily.

The first thing I did after I'd handed in Miranda's signed statement was to head for the men's room, where I locked the door and gave myself a thorough wash. I felt like I had her scent all over me, and I scrubbed and scrubbed. The thought of what I'd just done – the risk I'd taken – made me almost physically sick, and there was a moment when I thought I was going to lose my dinner. But it passed, and a few minutes later I was able to go out and take up my duties again.

Half an hour afterwards I realized I'd left my ballpoint pen on Davie's sofa. Or in it. I was sorry about that. It'd been a Christmas present from Donna. But I wasn't about to go back to ask for it.

I had three days off at the end of that week of nights. When I turned up for work again – on day shift again now – I asked what'd happened about Davie. The Sarge told me the girl had dropped the assault charge. She'd come in the morning after Davie's arrest and pleaded with the duty officer to let him go, yammering on that she loved him and needed him and that the previous night's blue was just the result of a little misunderstanding, that it wouldn't happen again. Well, without her testimony there could be no assault charge. And since there wasn't enough evidence to carry on with the charge of resisting arrest Davie'd been let go a couple of hours later. Apparently Miranda was there to meet him.

I shook my head in disbelief, wondering what'd happened when he'd got her back to his shack in Faulconbridge? He must've given her a right going over.

What was Miranda feeling now, I wondered? Was she still with him? I worried about that, for I knew that that wouldn't be the last time he'd work her over, and it might be even worse next time, depending on how out of it he was. It's a shame to see an attractive girl throwing herself away on a dunny rat like Davie, but maybe that's the only kind of man she'd ever known.

Apparently she'd also asked about me at the station … that 'nice bloke' who had taken her statement, she'd said. She had something for me, she told them, but she wouldn't let on what it was. I got a lot of ribbing about that, and I was glad I hadn't been there when she came by. I assumed it was my pen she was on about.

One evening a few days after that I passed by Davie's house when I was up in Faulconbridge doing some shopping. Pulling my car to the curb, I glanced up at the sitting room window. The Harley was parked in the carport, but I couldn't see anyone and I was about to drive away when Davie appeared in the window and glared down at me, frowning, his tattooed arms crossed over his bare chest. He must've recognized me, even though I wasn't in uniform. Anyway, I immediately slipped the car into gear and drove on – disappointed that I hadn't seen Miranda.

Over the following days and weeks I was either too busy with peacekeeping duties or too exhausted from a heavy social schedule with Donna to think any more about Miranda or what was happening with her. When I did remember her I was immensely relieved to find the whole event slipping quietly into the distant past. I had jeopardized my whole career that night, and had barely managed to hide the transgression from my colleagues. Never again, I said to myself. I had learned my lesson.

The last thing I heard about Miranda was that she'd been picked up a few weeks later by one of our patrols, wandering alone around the streets of Faulconbridge in a bewildered state – obviously drugged to her eyeballs. My mates took her back to Davie's place and made sure she was all right. When they asked her what'd happened she'd apparently just broken into sobs, muttering about some bad news she'd had and that she didn't know what she was going to do about it. The boys said there was no sign of the Harley. Davie must've pissed off back to Sydney for a while.

It was two months after that that the second bad thing happened.

It was January. Thursday the 13th was a free day for me, so when I finished work on the 12th I said 'yes' to an invitation from some of my shift mates to head out for a meal with them and their wives and girlfriends. Donna joined us and we spent a long and enjoyable evening in a chink restaurant, laughing and talking, and I got her home around midnight. I hit my bed looking forward to a relaxed day spent mostly sleeping and watching telly.

A phone call at 9:30 the next morning changed all that.

'We've got a jumper,' the Sarge's deep voice told me. 'Up at Katoomba. Happened a couple hours ago. Couple ladies out walking their dogs saw this girl take a dive from the rocks beside the Three Sisters. They couldn't see where she landed, but they were sure she wouldn't survive a fall from that height, so one of 'em pulled out her mobile and dialled 000. Alan and Scott turned up in their unit five minutes later. They crawled around till they had a view down to the jumper's body. It's a girl all right, and she's certainly very dead. More to the point, there's no possible way of reaching her from below. The bush is too thick, and she's apparently landed on a little shelf of rock some metres up. It's going to have to be a stretcher extraction by helicopter. You'll have to go down to prepare her for lifting. You got that Palmer?'

'Sir,' was all I could muster, groggy from having only just woken up.

'You've got forty minutes to get yourself up here. Bring your gear. The other team members will be waiting for you.'

As soon as he hung up I swung myself out of bed and started dressing.

A year earlier I had been selected by my superiors to undertake a six-week course in abseiling. They needed a replacement for a member of the Force's mountain rescue team who had moved on to some other posting. It's not surprising there have to be officers at Springwood trained in climbing and abseiling techniques. After all, we live on a ridge of mountains that offers an almost continuous line of sheer cliffs, near-vertical drops of hundreds of metres down to the bush below. It's not uncommon for us to be called out to help some poor devil who has tried to climb down some rock face and found himself unable to carry on either upward or downward. Or they might have slipped and injured themselves and can't get out without help. When that happens either they or their climbing partners phone for us and we'll suit up and abseil down and haul them out.

There's also, of course, the odd occasion when – either accidentally or deliberately – some pour soul ends up dropping to his or her death from one of those cliffs. I'd not been called out to one of those yet. Without question they're the worst, because you never really know what you're going to find till you get down there.

Ten minutes after I arrived at the station the back of the Police van was loaded with our equipment and we headed up to Katoomba.

When we arrived at the Three Sisters car park we could see the crowds pressed up against the rails at the lookout point, peering downwards. There was nothing to see, but the very idea of a girl's body lying somewhere down there, smashed over the rocks like a dropped egg, was enough to draw the ghouls and the thrill-seekers from all directions. Our job, of course, is to make sure they never get to see what they're hoping to see, that everything's carefully wrapped up and hauled away quickly and discreetly without anyone's sensitivities – or perverted appetites – being excited in the slightest degree. Just a quick drop, an investigation of the site, and a neat extraction of the damaged goods – in this instance by helicopter winch.

Within a couple of minutes we had unloaded the van, pulled on our equipment backpacks and made our way to the girl's jump-off point – one of the other constables carrying the aluminium stretcher that would carry the body up to the chopper. All along the cliff edge uniformed colleagues were posted to keep the public away from the scene. There's always some dickhead who'll try to get close enough to take a picture of the bloody remains with his phone if he can, to show his mates back at the pub (sick bastard). Obviously we can't let that happen.

My partners in the team were Brad Fellowes and Con Mitchell, both years older than me and both seasoned mountaineers. Con, in addition, is a trained paramedic, and carried a small but well-equipped medical kit with him in his shoulder pack.

Brad set the fixing points for our ropes, we strapped on our helmets, and the two of us – Con and I – one after another with me in the lead, hooked up and dropped over the edge, slipping lower and lower over the bush-carpeted valley below. Brad stayed up top, keeping watch on our lines and on call if we needed anything.

It took a minute or two to descend low enough to clear the outward jutting cliff face so we had a view down to the girl's landing point. When we did, even from a hundred metres up the sight was pretty awful. She had somehow managed to land on her back on a rock shelf beside a boulder. Her dress was bunched up over her thighs and abdomen. One bare leg was angled up over the boulder, the other splayed to the side. Even from that height I could see blood.

Slowly, we dropped lower. I could see that one of the girl's arms was twisted unnaturally behind her. The other lay across her face, partly obscuring it, as if she'd deliberately placed it there to shield her eyes from the sun.

I was the first to hit the ground, and when I unclipped myself and turned to walk the five or six metres to where the body lay my throat suddenly seized up and I felt a wave of nausea wash over me. Now I could see the girl's face. Even partly obscured by her draped arm there was no mistaking who she was.

The short curly hair. The full lips. The dusky skin.

Davie's Miranda.

As that realization hit me I felt my body lock down and my mouth drop open in shock.

A moment later Con grabbed my arm.

'Hey, sport! You all right? You look a bit crook. Better sit a minute.'

He eased me onto a nearby boulder. I couldn't take my eyes from Miranda's face, that bit of it I could see. On the temple nearest to me was a large, blue-green bruise, and her eye was blackened. These were not wounds she'd incurred in the jump. These were clearly from an earlier beating – almost certainly carried out by Davie, her psychotic lover.

The rest of her body seemed unmarked – except for the back of her head where the rocks had smashed into her brain.

'Here, take a whiff of this,' Con said, breaking a vial of sal ammoniac and passing it before my nose. I breathed it in, felt the sharp chemical scent hitting my senses like a freezing Antarctic wind.

Then Con stepped away to Miranda's body. Kneeling, he gently pulled the awkwardly bent arm from behind her back and arranged it at her side. Then he lifted the other arm from her face, letting it gently down to the ground beside her.

Now I could see her clearly. Her open, opaque eyes. Her lips slightly parted, as if about to speak.

With the delicacy of a surgeon Con closed her eyes, holding his fingers there till the eyes stay shut. Then he stepped away to retrieve the aluminium stretcher that we'd lowered down before our descent.

I knew the form. The body would now be slipped into a plastic body bag, then laid within the concave contours of the stretcher. Then it would be strapped down. When all was ready, the hovering helicopter would lower a cable and the line would be fixed to the stretcher's three lifting chains. Then it would be hoisted into the sky, to be transported in the helicopter's bay to someplace nearby where it could be shifted into an ambulance and taken down to the morgue in Penrith.

I knew exactly what had to be done, what was expected of me. But for the moment I couldn't do it. I couldn't move. Instead, I sat there, frozen, letting Con do all the work.

He laid the stretcher out on a level piece of ground and undid the straps. Then he approached me again.

'You okay, cobber? You still look a bit green at the gills.'

'I'm fine,' I croaked. 'It's just...'

I stopped, too choked up to continue.

'Here,' he said, producing his water bottle and passing it to me. 'Take a swig of this. It'll help.'

I did so, twisting off the cap and swallowing down several desperate gulps.

'This your first jumper, then?'

I nodded. 'But that's not the problem, Con.' I looked him in the eye. 'I know this girl.'

He stiffened.

'Strewth! Sorry, mate. What, a friend of yours was she?'

'No. Not a friend.'

I explained that she was the victim of a domestic violence callout we'd attended a couple of months back and described the details – including the fact that she was Davie Seick's latest squeeze.

'That bastard,' Con growled, and spat.

'Yeah,' I told him. 'Her name's Miranda. She was going to charge him with assault but later changed her mind.' I shuddered. 'Now she's topped herself. Must've had enough of Davie and his drugs and his abuse.'

Con moved to the stretcher and stood waiting for me to join him.

Fighting waves of nausea, I pulled myself up and walked over to help him. Together we lifted the broken body and laid it flat beside the stretcher, bending the broken limbs into alignment.

While Con unrolled the black body bag I reached down and pulled the skirt of Miranda's dress over her bare legs. Con laid the bag out ready, then stood up, staring down at her with a frown.

'Jesus. Look at that, mate.'

I looked down. 'What?'

'Can't you see? This girl's preggers.' He shook his head. 'Poor cow.'

Where the dress had been bunched at her waist before, a slight swelling could now be clearly seen on her lower abdomen. She was pregnant, all right.

I rose to my feet and stepped back.

Con was fitting the body bag now, working the black plastic around and under Miranda's corpse. When he'd finished he motioned to me and I stepped forward to help him lift the body into the stretcher. She wasn't very heavy. Then he tied the straps across it, securing them for the lift. Through the ringing in my ears I could hear the chopper, circling a couple of hundred metres up. I still couldn't take my eyes from the plastic shrouded body. Finally Con stood and reached a hand to my shoulder.

'Take it easy, mate. You've had a shock. I'll take care of the rest. You just concentrate on getting your strength back so you can haul yourself out of here. I don't want to have to carry you up, sport!'

He laughed and stepped away, looking up to wave at the bloke leaning out of the chopper's bay above us. He waved back and moments later the unspooled cable dropped down towards us.

The rest I viewed in slow motion, like I was in some kind of dream. The line was attached and the stretcher, with Miranda's plastic-wrapped body strapped into it, was winched up and away. Seconds later it was pulled aboard the chopper, the engine revs increased, and the pilot eased the great booming bird away to the southeast.

Con turned back towards the abseiling lines to prepare for the ascent. I was about to join him when I noticed a reflected glint off to one side, not far from the landing point of the body. I stepped over to investigate.

Lying between two rocks, the silver casing of my ballpoint pen caught the noonday sun.

I looked behind me. Con was busy clipping himself into his gear. Quickly I stooped down, retrieved the pen and pocketed it. Then I turned to join him at the cliff face.

As we drove off in the van half an hour later, the throng of people still crowded the Three Sisters viewing point. Even though the chopper and the body were long gone they couldn't prise themselves away from the tragic scene.

Back at the Station the Sarge took one look at me and ordered me home. Once he'd learned the identity of the jumper he understood my reaction. Sympathetic, he told me to take a couple of days off, adding that there was counselling available if I wanted it; I just needed to let him know. I nodded and thanked him and made my way out to my car.

For several minutes I just sat there, staring at the steering wheel. The image of Miranda's face filled my mind – her dark hair against the bloodied rock, the bruising, her open, unseeing eyes, her lips parted like she was about to speak.

And that bulge at her abdomen. The foetus, its life brutally snuffed out in the first weeks of its growth. Whose baby?

Davie's?

Or mine?

Finally I shook myself free of the dreadful image, the morbid thoughts. Switching on the ignition, I started the car, focused on driving home to my apartment, on parking the car and locking it, on getting myself inside and closing the door.

Several hours have passed since then. I must've slept for some of them because I woke up an hour or two ago face down on the bed, as groggy as if I'd slept fifteen hours straight.

I got up, splashed water on my face in the bathroom, made myself a cup of tea. Now I'm feeling better. A bit more philosophical about the day and what it means.

I'm out on the little balcony now, sprawled on my plastic chair, clicking the button of my recovered ballpoint in and out as I stare at the distant mountains. Strange to think that the last person to touch the pen before me was Miranda.

Donna's come over and is inside rustling up something to eat. I can hear pans rattling, cutlery being laid out.

When I told her what'd happened she was horrified. She could understand my shocked condition. She's a good person. I'm lucky.

And so glad she'll never know the truth.

I've got a cold Tooheys in my hand and the sunset has painted the sky a brilliantly streaked pattern of reds and yellows to entertain me. Just another evening in paradise.

I'll get through this, I know. And I won't ever let myself slip up again like I did with Miranda. I've learned my lesson. From now on I'll be a good copper and play everything strictly by the book.

I'm sorry Miranda had to go like that. I reckon she just felt there was no other option left for her, that she'd tried them all and found only dead ends.

Still, though it shames me to confess it, there's part of me that finds something comforting about Miranda's death. At least now I won't have to worry she might spill the beans to someone one day about …

what happened between us that night. That secret is safe now.
    I do wonder, though, what that baby would've been like.
    If it was mine, that is.

(London, 2010)

The Hole

In Memorium
Jackie Warren
1965-2011

They started digging in late July, just as a freak heat wave tormented London and the south with temperatures climbing into the mid-thirties Celsius. But that didn't bother the boys.

The hole was Sal's idea.

'Remember that underground passage that's supposed to lead from the old convent to somewhere near the park?' he asked his brothers one afternoon as they sprawled over the back lawn after a vigorous roughhouse session. 'I've got an idea it might pass right under our garden, near the back wall and the fig tree. Why don't we dig a hole and find out?'

Adam looked across at his fourteen-year-old middle brother and smirked. 'What makes you think that? Why should it be there?'

Sal thrust his chin forward. 'Why shouldn't it be? It's worth a try, isn't it? All we have to do is dig. If it's there and we go deep enough we're bound to run into it.' He glanced towards the house, looking for and finding his mother's bandana-wrapped head moving beyond the kitchen window. 'Remember, that's how those nuns escaped carrying all their gold plate and candlesticks. Maybe they stashed some of it in the passageway? If they did and we found it we'd be rich! We could get Mum the best doctors then, and all the best treatments. Who knows? I think it's worth a try.'

Sal was referring to a local legend that grew out of an event that occurred near their south London home during the reign of Henry VIII. A convent had stood at the edge of the green at the top of their street. As the self-appointed head of the new Church of England, Henry had insisted that all Papist convents and monasteries within his realm be closed, and all their assets confiscated by the Crown. Accordingly he had sent soldiers to force their closure and to collect the plate and treasures kept by them.

When the soldiers arrived at the convent, however, their commanding officer was allegedly held up at the front door for some minutes by the plucky Mother Superior, who refused them entry and harangued them bitterly on the iniquity of their mission. After repeated demands the officer finally lost patience and forced his way past her – only to discover that the convent was empty. The nuns had in the meantime all fled via a secret subterranean passageway which brought them out into the safety of a wood some distance away. More importantly, they'd taken with them all the convent's treasures, leaving their chapel, cells and refectory walls bare of any valuable utensils, crosses or adornments whatsoever.

Enraged, the officer had ordered the immediate execution of the Mother Superior, whereupon her head was summarily struck off and stuck upon the point of a halberd. This grim standard was left fixed in the ground of the village green for days afterwards – a warning to all of the dangers of defying royal decrees.

'Well, what do you think?' Sal asked, glancing at his older brother.

Adam lay back on the grass, draping an arm across his forehead and squinting up into the sun.

'Go ahead if you want. You might be right. But you'd better ask Mum first. It's her garden, after all.'

Sal asked his mother that night. As they cleared the dinner dishes together he proposed his plan to dig a hole at the garden's back corner and explained why. Would she mind?

'How big of a hole?'

Sal knitted his brow, considering.

'Big enough to climb down into. Big enough so's I can dig in it.'

'I don't know, Sal. It might be dangerous. It could cave in on you while you're working.'

'Oh, Mum! You needn't worry about that. The earth's mostly clay, and clay should stay solid. Anyway, we wouldn't be working in wet weather.' He stopped to look at her, swiping a strand of blonde hair from his forehead. 'It'd be a pretty important discovery, wouldn't it, Mum? If we found that passage. A piece of history, right here in our back garden.'

His mother sighed.

'Oh, Sal. Why can't you just keep snails, like Jared? It's far less disruptive.'

'I don't have any interest in snails, Mum. Sorry.'

'Well, to speak truth, neither do I.' She sighed again. 'How deep would you have to dig?'

Sal frowned. 'I don't know. A couple metres, at least.' He watched her rinsing plates in the sink. 'I'll keep the earth piled all on the back side, away from the lawn, I promise. And I'll make it quite a big hole so there's no chance of it caving in.'

She paused and smiled at him, shaking her head.

'All right. As long as you promise to fill it back in when you've finished. But be careful!'

By the time Adam returned home the following afternoon after playing football with his friends he was surprised to see how deep Sal had managed to dig in just a few hours. Now the tow-headed boy was up to his waist in the pit, and the mound of earth piled against the fence was growing higher by the minute.

At the front edge of the hole, staring down tight-lipped at the activity below with his hands stuck deep into his pockets, was Jared – the third and youngest brother. At eleven he was not quite old enough to share completely in the plots and exploits of his older siblings, but he was always accepted by them no matter what they were engaged in as a silent partner and welcome spectator. Now, as he sensed Adam approaching, Jared turned to him, shaking his head.

'He's been at it ever since lunch. If he keeps on like this he'll hit Australia soon.'

Sal tossed another shovel-load of earth onto the pile and turned, leaning on the shovel handle to catch his breath.

'Want to help?'

'Where's Mum?' Adam asked, standing beside Jared at the lip. 'She's not downstairs.'

'Lying down,' said Sal, wiping a strand of hair from his eyes with the back of his hand. 'She had another session at the hospital this morning and it made her sick. She says she'll be fine after a bit. She'll come down soon to make the tea.' He glanced again up at Adam, shielding his eyes from the sun. 'You want to have a go? I need a pee.'

'Sure,' said Adam.

Sal climbed up out of the hole, accepting a helping hand from his brother. Then Adam hopped down in his place. As Adam seized the shovel and threw himself into prising up clods of clay Sal turned away and strode towards the house. Frowning, Jared took a step or two after him.

'Sal?'

The sweating boy stopped and turned.

'Yeah?'

'Is Mum really going to be okay?'

Sal stood silent for a moment, then took a step back towards him.

'Sure. She'll be fine. It's just that the treatment is sometimes pretty hard on her. You remember what Dad said.'

The boy stared morosely at the ground, scuffing the grass with his toe.

'She doesn't seem to be getting any better, though, does she? I mean, she's all right for a few days, then she gets bad again. Is it always going to be like that? Will she ever get completely well again? And have her hair back?'

Sal reached out to ruffle his brother's dark mop.

'You just have to believe she'll get better, Jared. She has to get better. That's all there is to it.'

With a squeeze of Jared's shoulder, he went inside.

Sadly, Sal's assessment of his mother's condition was really more wishful thinking than known hard fact.

Ellen Wright had been diagnosed two years earlier with cancer, and had been immediately operated upon to remove the malignant lump in her breast as well as the adjacent lymph glands the doctors feared had already been contaminated by the destructive cells. Then came weeks of intensive radiation and chemo treatment. Ellen had lost her hair, had suffered days of nausea and discomfort. Finally, however, the doctors had declared her clear of the wicked disease and for a time her life, and her family's, had returned to normal.

Ellen was a teacher's aid, spending several hours each day at a nearby school working with children from deprived backgrounds. A natural with youngsters, her work was highly valued by pupils and teachers alike, and since she'd begun her volunteer efforts several young people had made remarkable leaps of progress as a result of the time she had spent with them.

Ellen's hair grew back – a fine chestnut fuzz that she proudly showed off to her neighbours as a victory trophy. And she had thrown herself back into her work with the same enthusiasm as before, glorying in her recovery and unwilling to consider the marginal possibility that the cancer could return at some later date. Neighbours along their street could smile again as they watched her striding healthily along the pavement, shepherding Jared to and from school in the mornings and afternoons. For months her positive attitude, and her health, held, and the family's relief manifested itself in weeks of boisterous good spirits and peals of laughter.

Then a routine check-up at the hospital brought news that plunged the household once again into a slough of despair. The cancer was back, this time in the liver. Back Ellen went for tests, and thereafter endured weekly infusions of industrial strength chemicals – cocktails designed to slow the cancer's spread. Her hair – so recently and so proudly regenerated – went again. For weeks Ellen swung from days of remission, when she felt almost normal, to days of pain and sickness when all she could do was to lie on the sofa or on the bed in her darkened bedroom, curled into a ball and fighting back the nausea. And as the good days came less and less often Ellen began to despair of ever being healthy again.

One night while the boys slept Ellen and Stuart – her civil servant husband – had discussed what they had been told by Ellen's oncologist that morning. The chemicals weren't reducing the cancer. Not only that, there were signs that it might be moving into her bone marrow. There was only one last defence the doctors could offer and that was a doubtful one – trying out various recently-developed and as yet uncertified drugs which the pharmaceutical companies hoped would provide a breakthrough for cancer patients. Ellen had come away with a bagful of plastic bottles and a determination to believe that something in that load of goodies would do the trick. It had to. The boys needed her. And anyway, there were still so many things she wanted to do with her life.

Nonetheless the grim alternative had to be faced and discussed, if only as a distant possibility. Gripping one another's hands tightly, and speaking in low voices, Ellen and Stuart agreed to keep this latest news from their boys until something more certain was known. Hopefully one of the new capsules would miraculously shrink the cancers and turn Ellen's health around. If that was the case, there'd be no need to cause the boys more upset by preparing them for a scenario that would likely be avoided.

For a month things seemed to carry on without any noticeable deterioration. But then the bad days came again and Ellen was gradually worn down by the strain. Try though she might to pretend otherwise she knew she was losing the battle. Every day she felt closer to having to admit that fact both to herself and to her family.

Now, clenching her teeth against the pain and clutching her abdomen with both hands, she shuffled to the kitchen sink to draw a glass of water. Glancing out the back window, she could see her boys hard at work at their project. In spite of the pain and the nausea that threatened to engulf her, she had to smile at them and their enthusiasm. Her blessed boys. And their hole.

By the weekend the hole had been so deeply dug that, seen from the kitchen window, Sal completely disappeared from view when he climbed down the ladder into it to work. Adam stood at the upper lip, passing down a bucket on a rope to be filled, then hauling it up and dumping it onto the ever-growing pile of earth pressed against the back fence.

'Don't you think we're deep enough to have found it if it's there?' asked Jared, standing as usual with his hands in his pockets at the hole's rim.

Sal stopped long enough to scowl up at him.

'Oh, go tend your snails! Don't be a spoilsport, Jared. Who knows how deep the passageway might be? We just have to keep going and hope we're in the right place. I'm not giving up yet.' He glanced up at Adam holding the rope above him, squinting into the bright sunlight. 'Don't you think I'm right, Adam? It's worth pressing on, isn't it?'

Adam, who was – to be honest – only marginally interested in the endeavour, shrugged. 'It's your project, Sal. You're the one to decide.'

Sal frowned, pressing his lips together.

'Well, I say we carry on. Okay?'

'As I said,' Adam returned, 'it's your decision. I've got to go soon, anyway. I'm meeting Nigel.'

'It's nearly lunchtime,' put in Jared, glancing back towards the house. 'Mum hasn't come down all morning.' He looked back at his brothers. 'Do you think she's all right?'

Adam put an arm around his youngest brother's shoulders.

'She's fine. She's just having one of her bad days, that's all.'

'She's been having a lot of those lately,' mumbled Jared. 'I don't think she's ever going to be better again.'

Sal threw the shovel aside and glared up at his brother.

'Don't say that, Jared! It's just the new medicines, that's all. They're hard on her. Dad said she might get worse before she gets better, didn't he?'

'Yeah,' murmured Adam, 'but that was weeks ago. She hasn't gotten any better yet.'

'Well, she will!' growled Sal through his teeth, climbing abruptly up the ladder and huffing off past them towards the house. 'You just wait and see, both of you!'

Adam watched him go, his arm still around Jared's shoulders.

'I hope he's right. That's all I can say.'

'Ditto,' said Jared, and leant his head against his brother's shoulder for a moment.

'Come on,' said Adam, dropping the rope. 'I'll make some sandwiches and soup. We'll leave Mum to rest, shall we?'

After lunch, when Ellen had still not appeared, Jared waited till Adam had departed for his rendezvous and Sal had headed back out to the hole. Then he made a cup of tea, collected a couple of biscuits on a plate and put the whole lot on a tray. Carrying it upstairs, he knocked gently at his parents' closed bedroom door.

'Mum?'

'Yes?'

'It's me, Mum,' he said quietly. 'Can I come in?'

'Of course, my angel.'

Balancing the tray on one arm, Jared turned the knob and stepped inside, closing the door behind him. Ellen was lying on her side on the bed under the coverlet, clutching a handkerchief in one hand. The drapes were drawn, leaving the room in deep shadow. Jared approached the bed.

'I've brought you some tea and biscuits.'

Ellen raised herself onto an elbow, smiling at her son.

'How lovely! Just set the tray on the dressing table, darling. I'm afraid I have no appetite at the moment, though.'

Jared did as he was told, then turned towards her, frowning.

'Are you all right, Mum? You haven't been downstairs all day.'

'I'm fine, Jared. Just a little weak and sick, that's all.'

He stepped closer and looked down at her, noticing now the redness of her eyes.

'You've been crying, Mum. Why? What's wrong?'

'It's nothing, sweetie. I had a bad dream, that's all.' She reached a hand towards him. 'Come here, my big boy. Lie down with me and give your mum a cuddle. I could use a cuddle right now.'

Kicking off his shoes Jared slid into bed beside her, clutching her tightly as she tucked the cover around them both. Then she kissed his head where it lay against her breast.

'There now. That's better. I feel better having you here.'

'Me, too,' he murmured.

Ellen stroked his long hair.

'My sweet Jared. I'm so sorry.'

'That's all right, Mum. Just get better, okay? We miss you downstairs.'

'I'll do my best, honey. I promise. I'll do my very best.'

Three days later Ellen had to be taken into hospital. The pain and sickness had become too much for her. When the ambulance arrived at teatime, Stuart – who'd taken a couple of days off from work to look after his wife – helped her into the ambulance with his arm around her while the boys stood awkwardly on the pavement, looking on. Then the ambulance drove off, with their mother and father inside it.

Adam being sixteen, Stuart had left the younger boys in his care.

In their parents' absence the boys did their best to carry on as normal – Adam warming up the casserole their father had prepared the night before, and fixing a green salad to have with it. Sal laid the table, while Jared fetched glasses of squash.

They ate without speaking, none of them eager to discuss this new and alarming development. When they'd finished, the three brothers did the dishes together, after which they went into the sitting room to watch television.

It was after nine o'clock when their father got home, looking tired and drawn.

'How is she?' asked Adam, rising from the computer in the corner of the sitting room where he had been working. Jared and Sal were both sprawled on the sofa, watching television.

'She's fine,' Stuart said. 'She's sleeping.'

He stood for a moment staring vacantly at the telly screen. Then he sighed.

'Sal, do you think we could turn that off? There's something I need to tell you.'

Sitting on the sofa with his boys, his arm around the youngest, Stuart told them everything he knew about their mother's condition, warning them about the likelihood of her imminent death. Then he answered all their questions, and was surprised at how well they all took it.

Jerad and Sal were a bit teary, but not one of the boys had dissolved into floods. Afterwards Stuart made them all a cup of tea. Then they'd all gone dispirited to bed.

Ellen was home again two days later, better than she'd been but still weak and nauseous. Over the next couple of weeks, when she felt up to it, she dragged herself along the street to the school to spend a little time with her young charges. But those occasions became fewer and fewer, and now the neighbours, when they caught sight of her making her way back through the late autumn afternoon, frowned to see her obvious pain, sensing her increasing despondency as she shuffled weakly along the pavement.

When the Christmas season arrived Stuart did his best to brighten up the house with the usual preparations. Having taken extended leave from his job, he now spent his days looking after the needs of his sons, and of his ailing wife.

Digging out the boxes of Christmas things from the cupboard under the stairs he and the boys shared the work of putting them up – decorating the small tree in the corner, hanging Christmas cards on strings across the chimneybreast, sticking sprigs of holly and evergreen onto the mantle behind the candlesticks. While they worked Ellen lay on the sofa, curled in a blanket, watching them with a pained half-smile of encouragement. Sensing her discomfort, the boys struggled to remain bright and upbeat. Knowing this was probably the last Christmas they would spend with her, they tried with all their might to put a cheery face on things – though in their hearts the ache of what they knew was coming ate at their spirits like a curse.

People came and went, family and friends, bringing cards and presents and gifts of prepared food, trying to inject at least the superficial vestiges of holiday cheer. When she could Ellen sat up with them, smiling tightly but saying almost nothing. Until finally she couldn't bring herself even to do that, and stared dully at the floor when visitors came, or turned away, pulling the blanket over her face.

God knows how they got through those holiday weeks – the husband and his boys sensing their beloved wife and mother's end was close, the wife knowing that each new day now was a gift and that there might not be another. Neighbours passing the house in the freezing night could only shudder in their wraps as they guessed at the torments being endured beyond the curtained windows.

On New Year's Eve the neighbours across the street were glued to their televisions and failed to notice the flashing lights of an ambulance as it pulled to a stop outside the Wrights' house. Moments later the racked figure of Ellen Wright in her dressing gown, flanked by her husband and a paramedic, shuffled miserably along the pathway towards it from the front door. She climbed inside, the ambulance doors closed and it drove off into the night.

She never came home again.

Ellen Wright passed away on the second day of the New Year, peacefully, in hospital, surrounded by her family. Although exhausted by her struggle, she'd been awake and aware until close to the end, and had been able to clock them all, and to smile farewells to each in turn, before her eyes slowly closed and she slipped away into drug-induced oblivion. Three hours later she was gone.

In the days between her dying and the funeral the Wright house stood silent and empty – the boys having been sent away to stay with friends with children their own age to help distract them from their grief, Stuart making the rounds to attend to all the grim logistics involved in putting a beloved family member away below ground. During the hours he was alone at home – to keep himself busy – he carefully took down and stored again the Christmas decorations, and carried the tree out to await collection beside the wheelie bins in the front garden. When that was done, and the house was returned once again to its brooding, neutral state, there was nothing for him to do but to sit disconsolately on the sofa, empty and drained, staring at the walls, feeling tears trickling down his cheeks in an unstoppable stream.

The funeral was both tasteful and touching, with live music played by a trio of musical friends. At the front of the church, above the large congregation, a blown up projection of Ellen's face smiled out from a screen. Bunches of flowers in vases flanked the modest coffin on its trestles at the top of the central aisle.

Ellen would have been pleased at the tearful eulogy read haltingly by her teacher colleague, the reassuring Lord's Prayer intoned by the vicar, and at the careful selection of her favourite hymns and secular songs that spoke of peace and love, and of the value of hope in a contentious and uncertain world.

The vicar – a pleasant-spoken but quietly authoritative man – managed quite brilliantly with his simple sermon to address both the need in his audience for sombre reflection and the joyful celebration of a life well-lived that had directly touched a great number of them in positive and truly memorable ways.

And then it was over. The pallbearers carried the coffin out to the hearse followed by Stuart and his sons, and the congregation filed silently out after them into the thin winter sunshine – a timely break from the bleak rain of previous days.

Half an hour later most of the mourners reassembled in the nearby churchyard, staring numbly at the flower-strewn casket, and beyond it toward the rectangle of shadow that was to be Ellen's final resting place. At the head of the grave stood Stuart with his boys, the four of them holding hands.

The vicar led the short service of interment, at the end of which a black-coated member of the funeral cortege stepped forward with a white dove, which he'd taken from a portable cage. Bending down, he placed the bird in Jared's nervous hands, whispering to him words of encouragement. Then he stepped back. Lifting the bird, Jared gently kissed the back of its neck, then lifted his arms and opened his hands. In an explosion of sound the freed dove flapped up and away, circling the silent crowd once or twice as it gained altitude. Then, having got its bearings, it angled off over the trees and was soon lost from view.

There was a reception, of course – an informal affair held in the function room of the local pub, with a good number of the mourners gathered around tables, munching sandwiches and cakes and drinking from wineglasses and pint pots. The atmosphere was lively, a sense of release pervading everyone. Stuart and his boys now talked animatedly with their friends, even occasionally laughing – finding in the convivial gathering a normality that had been lost to them during the preceding days.

Returning to the house a couple of hours later, however, Stuart and his sons felt again the emptiness that resonated through it now. He had been careful to remove any traces of Ellen's last tortured days there, and had put a framed copy of the church picture of her on the mantle in a position of prominence. Apart from that, the house was as it always had been, as Ellen had created it – and that in a sense was the most difficult thing of all for them to accept, that her creation could continue to exist without her being part of it.

Stuart made a pot of tea and the four sat at the table for a time, discussing the day's events. It'd been a good send off for her, all agreed. There had been lots of love expressed, and positive feelings, even in the face of the grief felt by all. Ellen would've been pleased.

Later, as Stuart sat on the sitting room sofa leafing numbly through the many cards and letters of condolence they'd received, the boys left the house for the back garden, standing together in a silent circle in their Sunday suits, hands in pockets, awkward and uneasy.

'I'm glad it's over,' said Sal finally, glancing defensively towards Adam. 'It was hard seeing her in so much pain.'

'Yes. So am I. It was an awful Christmas.' Adam turned to his youngest brother, who stood beside him staring at the ground. 'You okay, Jared?'

Jared wiped a tear from one eye.

'Yeah. I'm okay. I guess.' He scuffed his toe in the grass. 'I'm going to miss her, though.'

Adam laid a hand on his shoulder.

'We all will. That can't be helped. We'll just have to get on without her somehow.'

'Pretty much like we've been doing for the last couple of months,' Sal murmured.

'Exactly.'

Silence returned. Then Jared seemed to come to some kind of decision and nodded. Raising his head, he turned to his brothers.

'She was a pretty good mum, though, wasn't she? When she was well.'

Adam and Sal glanced at one another.

'The best,' said the eldest.

And without a word the three boys moved together, clasping one another tightly in their arms.

Rousing himself from a reverie of memories, Stuart Wright shook himself, pushed the cards and letters to one side and got to his feet.

He fancied a drink of water to moisten his dry throat, and wondered where his boys were.

Moving into the kitchen, he selected a tumbler from the shelf and stepped to the sink to fill it.

Outside the back window the afternoon was waning, but he could still see them at the bottom of the garden. They'd taken off their suit jackets and ties, which were piled carefully on a garden lounger, and stood together beside the hole they had dug in happier days.

Stuart drank, watching them.

With their white shirt sleeves rolled up, each one took a turn with the shovel to bite deeply into the pile of soggy clay and to fling the load down into the cavity below. Their fruitless dream of discovering the secret passageway was long dead now. Anyway there was no longer any need for treasure. It was time to put things back the way they'd been, to restore their mother's garden to its normal state.

As she had wished.

First Adam wielded the shovel, then Sal, then Jared – one after another, methodically, formally, determinedly, completing their own ritual of restitution and regeneration.

From behind the kitchen window Stuart Wright watched his boys in the gathering darkness, and felt at one with them, as they all four – each in his own way, and together – began the long and painful process of filling in the hole.

(London, 2011)

Antonio's Treat

When he reached Malaga Tim Barton collected the hire car from the office outside the terminal and set off immediately east along the coast highway, hurrying to get beyond Nerja, to leave behind the timeshare condos and beachfront hotels and fish and chip stands that had erupted like a rash along the sea, turning the Costa del Sol in the years since the sixties into a tawdry Spanish theme park.

After the miserable cold of London, the warmth of the Spanish autumn afternoon was welcome.

Driving along with his window open, Tim surveyed the small towns along the way, picking out amidst the myriad new buildings occasional clusters of original whitewashed and tile-roofed houses that spoke of the old days, when the Spanish south coast had been sleepy and forgotten and largely unpopulated, except for fisher families and dirt farmers scraping meagre livings out of parched clay fields.

It'd been a while since he was last here, something over two years now, and Tim's friend Dominic had been concerned about what Tim would find when he reached the old *cortijo* that was Dom's holiday bolthole on the coast south of Granada. Though they spoke of it often, the two friends had been unable over recent months to find a time when they were both free to make the trip down together. Dom still loved the crumbling old farmhouse on its hill overlooking the sea – a house which had seen generations of Spaniards born and bred within its walls over two centuries. In Tim Dom had discovered someone who loved the old place as much as he did; who could appreciate fully its lack of amenities, savouring instead the rough, primitive, unselfconscious environment it offered, where a man could simply be himself, enjoying the basics of life – sun and sea and local food and wine – without having to project an image to anyone, or conform to one.

Over the preceding quarter century the two friends had periodically travelled down from London together, and had spent a week or ten days in the thick-walled house, spending their afternoons swimming in coves along the coast, taking daytrips to the quaint mountain villages of the Alpujarra (the next range to the north), or making exploratory sorties up to Granada and Cordoba, or along the coastal highway towards Almería. But these shared trips to Spain had dwindled in frequency over the previous decade, trickling down to one every eighteen months or so, as the two friends entered their sixties and the pull of Spain was less often and less strongly felt, though never entirely forgotten.

Tim glanced at his watch. Antonio would be expecting him around 3 PM. Tim would drop by his house in the village first. Cristina would have the keys if Antonio was away.

Antonio de Vega was the farmer whose land surrounded the hill the *cortijo* sat upon. A thick-set, affable Spaniard in his forties, he was a shrewd agrarian businessman, with a head of dark, curly hair and a pleasant manner and smile. It had been arranged years before that Antonio would keep the keys to the *cortijo* so that he could make periodic visits to the house in their absence to check for rats, or wind and rain damage. His wife Cristina, who touched up the interior whitewash when required, was a timid soul who kept largely to herself, and who, it was rumoured, suffered from regular bouts of depression.

Dom and Tim had often in the past enjoyed evenings with the de Vegas, their aging parents and their teenage sons, sharing glasses of red wine and *tapas* with them in the large kitchen/dining room of their house on the seafront.

Antonio's agricultural success was clearly evident from the terraces of the *cortijo*. The fields below the old house were covered with translucent plastic sheeting stretched taut over pole and cable frames – forming vast greenhouses, or *invernaderos*, that gave Antonio and the other local farmers three or four crop yields a year with careful management – a practice widespread along the southern Spanish coast. In most years Antonio and his colleagues in the narrow valley, or *rambla,* that led up from the coast made sizeable profits, and with Spanish membership in the European Union this demand for out of season vegetables would surely continue for years to come. Visiting British friends usually found the acres of milky plastic sheeting below the cortijo disturbing or ugly, but neither Dom nor Tim did. During the days one could hear from the *cortijo*'s terraces the murmur of the workers' voices nattering on beneath the plastic, or the tinkle of music from their transistor radios, as they weeded the beds or trailed tomatoes and beans up climbing strings, or hauled out the dying vines when the harvest was complete for the local goat herd to gobble down to mere shreds. At night, when the workers went home to their houses in the seafront village, the valley was completely silent under the star-spangled heavens – save for the singing of the cicadas, and the occasional shriek of a fox foraging further up the *rambla* at the base of the *Contraviesa*, the coast range.

'What's the word on Cristina?' Tim had asked Dom before he left. 'She doing any better?'

'Carlos tells me she's taken up the lease on a shop in the village – a kind of general odds and ends store.'

Dom's friend Carlos Marín had a half interest in the *cortijo*, though he seldom went there. As he was half-Spanish/half-English it was left to Carlos with his fluency in the language to make periodic telephone calls to Antonio to check on the state of things.

'Cristina's been working there during the weekdays, now that the boys are grown,' Dom went on. 'Apparently she's happier than she's been for a long time. Probably because she has a bit of independence again.'

'I shouldn't wonder,' Tim had murmured. 'Can't imagine her life has been a bed of roses over the last years, what with three men in the house to look after and her husband's mother and father only a house or two away.'

After an hour, when Tim reached the turnoff to the village, its buildings arrayed along a frontage road beside the sea, he swung the car off the highway onto it. At his right, gentle breakers lapped a sandy shore between stone piers. Tim slowed the car before a house front midway along and stopped.

'¡Hola, Tim!' Cristina greeted him as she opened the door to his knock. 'Antonio no está. ¿Quieres las llaves, no?'

'Sí, Cristina. Por favor.'

Seconds later he was striding back to the car, clutching the ring of heavy, medieval-looking keys. Starting up again, he drove along the frontage road to the *supermercado* at its end, where he halted long enough to buy several bottles of chilled drinking water, wine, bread, olives, cheese and *chorizo* as nibbles. Then he turned the car back along the front and crossed over the coastal highway to take the deeply rutted gravel road up the *rambla* toward the *cortijo* – locally known as *La Casa de los Ingleses* (the house of the English) – standing prominently on its crown of hill in the near distance.

The first day or two at the *cortijo* were always spent the same way – dusting and sweeping out the rooms of the two-storied house, rooms that had been locked away in darkness for months behind wooden shutters and iron grills, vacant of life save for the ubiquitous *lagartitos*, the tiny lizards that stole in through cracks and under eaves and turned the house into their own private sanctuary from summer heat and winter chill. Then the area flanking the house had to be cleared of the waist-high grass and brush that had grown up in the intervening months, sometimes completely obliterating the pathway to the front door. This was achieved the hard way, using a hand-scythe, a traditional broad-bladed *hoz* (hoe), a rake and an ancient wooden fork (the forked branch of a tree limb, barkless and strong as steel) – hacking it all down and collecting the lot into a pile on the wide terrace above the house, awaiting the cooler, winter weather for burning. It was always hard work, this initial preparation, but it was work Dom and Tim had both always enjoyed. Now, alone and shirtless in the warmth of the afternoon, Tim threw himself into it with the pleasure of a boy renovating his neglected clubhouse.

Immediately after his arrival, Tim had unpacked from their store the candles and gas lamps that would provide the night lighting. After that came the connecting up of the bottled Calor gas to the two-ringed cooking hob, and to the refrigerator that would preserve the food and cool the drinks during his stay. Then he checked to see that the water supply was adequate in the cement holding tank, or *aljibe*, on the slope above the house. When all that was settled, it was time to head outdoors.

Now, stripped to the waist and wearing old trainers and a pair of well-worn shorts, Tim attacked the brush surrounding the house, feeling almost immediately the sweat dripping down his face, back and chest as he bent to his work under the late afternoon sun.

It was slow work, what with the constant ache in his side, and he took frequent rests – which was only fitting for a man of his years – collapsing onto a deckchair set out on the southern terrace overlooking the distant sea with a mug of tea clutched in his fist. As he sat there, the sun's warmth burnishing his body and soothing his soul, he thought of his good friend Dom, sorry he was not here as well. Their years-old friendship had always been at its best, he mused, away from the pressures of their London lives, the lives shared with others.

But Dom had been busy, and that was that, so Tim would have to savour the sun and sea and silence on his own – something he had frequently done before, and enjoyably.

After his break, when the pain had eased and he had regained his breath, Tim rinsed his cup in the kitchen sink indoors, then threw himself back into his clearing efforts. By 6:30 the pathway from the car to the *cortijo*'s front door had been cleared, the downstairs rooms swept and mopped, and the trappings of comfort and utility opened out and readied for use. There were candles in sconces placed randomly around every downstairs room, and gas lanterns hung from hooks on the ceilings. There was running water from the kitchen tap, a chemical toilet set up in a back room and a fridge that was becoming colder by the minute.

Returning from carrying the last fork load of brush up to the mounting pile on the upper terrace, Tim wiped his hands on his shorts and surveyed his work.

'I reckon that's enough for today,' he pronounced. 'Now, old man. How about a wash and a nice glass of *vino* before heading down to the village for dinner?'

So the tools were laid aside for the moment, and the dust and sweat was washed away in the kitchen sink. When he had dried himself Tim slipped on a fresh shirt and a pair of clean trousers, poured himself a glass of red from the bottle he'd opened earlier (to breathe during the afternoon), and stepped around to the terrace overlooking the sea, where he sat watching the late October sun sink behind the mountains to the west – the *rambla* taking on a darker, cooler ambiance in the shadows of early evening.

This had always been a special time for them both, this ritual of taking a glass or two of wine before dinner, feeling the heat of the day dissipate as the sun sank from sight. Now, in the silence of the empty valley, Tim could just hear the breaking of the waves on the village beach a mile away. From somewhere behind him came the tinkling of bells as the village goats made their way down the slopes from their daily foraging expeditions to the hills above, moving slowly like a mottled hand over the earth, caressing it, the goatherd and his dog a trailing afterthought.

Out on the wedge of sea held within the V formed by the mountains flanking the *rambla* a fishing boat chugged slowly westward, the sound of its engine thrumming in the distance.

It was nearly eight when – dressed now in chinos and a patterned short-sleeved shirt – he locked the *cortijo*'s front door with the great key and made his way up the slope behind the house to the rented SEAT. As he reached the car, a white van came around the corner of the rutted track and pulled to a stop beside it. A moment later the driver's door opened and Antonio appeared, grinning down at him.

'*¡Hombre! Siento mucho que no estaba cuando habeis llegado,*' he said, apologizing for having missed his arrival. '*¿Que tal? ¿Que noticias tienes? Dime.*'

Tim moved to shake Antonio's hand, responding to the man's greeting in his unpracticed Spanish. Both he and Dom had taken lessons at the *Instituto de España* in London years before, and could understand well enough the lazy *andaluz* accent of the south coast, but it took a day or two before Tim's ear was attuned to the language and for the first hours it required intense concentration.

Antonio climbed out and the two men stood chatting together amiably for a few minutes, Antonio leaning against the white van, his arms crossed.

Had Tim found everything as expected? There had been no surprises?

No, no surprises. All was as it was when they were last here.

No *ratitas*?

No sign of them.

Cristina and the boys had whitewashed the inside walls a month before. Had he noticed that?

Yes. Everything looked wonderful. Thanks for that.

No problem. Plenty of water?

Yes. The *aljibe* was still half full.

Bueno.

They spoke then about Dom, Tim relating his latest news. Then Tim asked after Antonio's family – the boys, the aged parents, Cristina's new job at the shop on the front. Antonio confirmed that everything was good. Cristina's new venture was doing well. She was happier than she'd been in years, and earning a bit of money for herself besides.

'You must come down before you go back and take something with us,' he told Tim. 'When do you go?'

Tim shrugged apologetically.

'I'm only here till Thursday.' He turned to look down the valley, towards the distant sea. 'I have work to get back to, unfortunately.'

Antonio made a little moue with his mouth.

'No matter. It is a very short time, but work is important. We have to earn to live, no?' He reached out to clap Tim on the shoulder. 'Listen, I have something I want to share with you. I thought of it when Carlos said you were coming. A treat. Are you free Wednesday night?'

Tim smiled. 'Of course.'

'Excellent. I will come to collect you around eight o'clock. *A eso de las ocho.* I want to drive you to a place along the coast – a place I think you will find very interesting. It will please me to share it with you.'

Tim raised an eyebrow.

'Mysterious. I look forward to it,' he allowed. 'Do I need to dress up?'

The Spaniard shook his head, grinning.

'No, no. Dress just as you are. Casual but smart.'

'*De acuerdo.* See you at eight Wednesday night then.'

The following two days were spent completing the maintenance chores on the house and land and relaxing often with a drink and a book in the deckchair overlooking the *rambla* and the sea. The ache in his side had eased somewhat since he'd ceased his heavy exertions, and for long periods he forgot about it altogether.

The second afternoon Tim drove westwards along the coast to Motril, the nearest large town, to purchase odds and ends for the house – cleaning materials, a new bottle of Calor gas, and several bottles of linseed oil that he would, over the next days, daub over the house's ancient exterior doors and shutters, to preserve them from the ravages of the burning sun and the wet winters.

After the first evening, when he'd taken his dinner at the seafront restaurant he and Dom usually frequented in the village, Tim fell into their normal routine of eating out only occasionally. The rest of the time he prepared his meals himself in the *cortijo*'s kitchen: breakfasts of fruits and yogurt; lunches of salads or thick soups, accompanied by helpings of *jamón Serrano,* cheese from La Mancha and chunks of bread from the village baker. For his dinners he barbecued meats on the outside grill, or made stews of white beans with onion and garlic, tomatoes and spicy chorizo; or boiled up pasta which he covered in a rich sauce garnished with chunks of Spanish sausage – all of it washed down with glasses of the sharp but delicious local wine. For both Tim and Dom, a large measure of the joy they'd always felt in being in Spain had come from eating well, and now Tim pursued this indulgence on his own.

Despite the lateness of the autumn, on the third afternoon Tim drove along the coast to their favourite beach, nestled in a bay hidden from the road, to try the water. Gritting his teeth, he threw himself into the surf, spent five minutes swimming stiffly in the clear sea, then staggered out – ruefully acknowledging as he towelled himself down that the water now really was just that little bit too cold for comfort.

Each evening – after the sun was truly down and the dishes (if any) had been washed and put away – Tim sat at the dark oak table in the front room, poring over a book under the light of the candles and the overhead gas lantern until 10:30 or 11:00. Then the book would be closed, the nightly ablutions performed over the sink in the kitchen, his pills taken, and he would ascend the stairs to his bedroom, candle in hand. Opening for fresh air the single screened window that overlooked the sea, Tim would then crawl between the sheets. As always, he slept like a log in the silent house, with the soothing buzz of cicadas and the soughing of the distant surf resonating through his dreams.

Late Tuesday afternoon a bank of clouds appeared over the mountains and swallowed the sun two or three hours before it was due to disappear, plunging the *rambla* into brooding shadow. By Wednesday morning, when Tim awakened to the voices of the workers in the fields below, it had still not rained. But it threatened to do so all the rest of the day.

In the unnatural gloom of Wednesday evening, Tim ate a light meal of omelette and salad and sat outside afterwards, finishing a glass of wine. Above him the clouds loured, heavy and menacing, and the air was still – not a breath stirred the grass, or the leaves of the jojoba trees beneath him on the lower slopes. Had he been a superstitious man, Tim might have taken the sombre weather as an omen for the evening to come, but as he knew nothing of what Antonio had in mind or where he intended to take him there was no way of judging how apt or not such a sign might be.

Promptly at eight o'clock there was a sharp honk and Antonio's white van appeared on the road above the house. Dressed and ready, Tim grabbed a sweater, locked the house door and climbed the slope to the van, sliding onto the front passenger seat beside Antonio.

As they wound down the hill through the *rambla*, a light drizzle began to fall. By the time they reached the coast highway, rain was falling in good earnest.

In spite of the weather, Antonio seemed in particularly good spirits, seemingly eager to get to their destination. At the highway he turned east, towards Almería.

For the first few minutes the two men made desultory small talk – Tim raising questions about the quality of the year's harvests, asking how much rainfall the coast had had over the winter. The harvests – as Dom had been told by Carlos – had been excellent, and the rainfall since August had been regular and abundant. There was no water shortage in the *rambla* this year as had happened occasionally in the past, which was good news.

'So, this place you're taking me,' Tim said, when their conversation had dwindled to a stop. 'What is it?'

Antonio turned to give him a toothy smile.

'You'll see. Don't worry, it won't be long now. I think you'll not be disappointed.'

The van raced on along the wet two-lane road, past ancient Adra, then along the coast through the suburban sprawl surrounding Almería, by which time the grim evening light had began to fade. By the time they passed the turning to Mojacar night had fallen completely. For the next half hour Tim sat silently in the darkness, listening to the swish-swish of the wipers, watching the lights of houses and villages sweep by through the rain-streaked windows, wondering when this trip would end.

It was close to 9:30 when they reached the outskirts of a large town. Almost immediately Antonio turned left into what seemed an extensive industrial estate with large warehouse-like buildings ranged over a grid of new streets. From the flashing neon signs above some of the entrances, however, it was soon clear that the estate housed not only industrial units, but a complex of bars and nightclubs as well, outside several of which groups of men stood smoking under the lights, hugging the walls to avoid the rain.

Pulling the van to a stop between two parked cars, Antonio switched off the engine and turned to him, grinning.

'*Aqui estamos*. Here we are. *Venga, amigo*. I'm going to show you a part of Spain you've never seen before.'

The two men stepped down from the van and hustled across the street through the rain towards the clutch of men standing beside a doorway. Above the door a sign proclaimed the establishment as '*La Laguna Azul*', the Blue Lagoon. Flashing neon images beside the name depicted a stemmed cocktail glass and an arcing palm tree, below which a well proportioned grass-skirted dancing girl provocatively switched her ample bottom from side to side with a wicked grin on her face.

Moving through the men, Antonio led the way inside. Despite the group at the door, the place was surprisingly empty. The shadowy room was decorated in a half-hearted tropical mode, with false palm trees angling up to splay long drooping paper fronds over an oblong dance floor. The space was quite large, with a bar and stools along one side and archways leading from the main room into smaller rooms at the back and sides. Beside the dance floor three or four tables and chairs were placed. A few men sat on stools at the bar, chatting quietly with young ladies in abbreviated skirts and sleeveless blouses, deeply open at the neck. At one of the tables, five or six more girls sat together, similarly dressed. When the newcomers entered, the girls turned to watch them, interested.

'What do you want to drink?' Antonio asked, bellying up to the bar. Behind it, a middle-aged man stood waiting.

'I'll have a *cerveza*,' Tim replied. 'A San Miguel.'

Slapping his hands together, Antonio ordered and the bartender stepped away to collect two bottles from a cooler, which he opened and placed on the counter before them, together with two tall glasses. Antonio paid him, and the two men poured their beers, each taking a long sip when they'd finished.

'*Gracias*, Antonio,' Tim said, raising his glass in a salute. 'So, what're we here for? What's special about this place?'

The Spaniard grinned.

'Watch and wait.'

At the table across the room two of the girls stood up and made their way leisurely towards them. Antonio's grin widened.

'You see?'

Tim turned to the women.

There was a brunette and a blonde, both in their early twenties, both attractive. Like their colleagues at the table, they wore low-cut, tight-fitting tops, skimpy hot pants or short skirts over bare legs, and high heels. And they both arrived at the bar sporting practiced 'come-hither' smiles. The blonde was obviously known to Antonio, who embraced her quickly, giving kisses on both cheeks. Slipping his arm around her, he turned to Tim.

'*Señor* Tim, this is Karla. You'll find all of the girls here friendly, *amigo*, and very willing. See you later.' He winked. 'Have fun.'

Turning, he moved off with the blonde to the far end of the bar, where he stopped to order her a drink.

Tim turned to the brunette, who smiled up at him, invitingly. Her dark hair was long, and trailed down over her breasts. Tim was reminded of the sultry East London singer, Amy Winehouse.

'You want to dance?' she asked, in heavily accented Spanish.

'No thanks. But we can sit and talk for a while, if you like.'

She shrugged.

'Okay. But you have to buy me a drink.'

'What do you want?'

'We always drink champagne.'

'I see. Okay.'

Tim nodded to the bartender, who picked up a champagne bottle from an ice-filled bucket and poured a stream of amber liquid into a fluted glass.

Lemonade, Tim reckoned, at a grossly inflated price.

He paid the man, passed the glass to the girl, and followed her across the floor through an archway into an empty side room, sitting beside her when she settled onto a velvet-covered bench against one wall. Across the room, a floor to ceiling mirror reflected their images back at them in the dim, red-tinted lighting. Beyond the arch, Tim could see Antonio and the blonde dancing close together to the music thumping from speakers positioned in every corner of the room. Antonio was smiling and murmuring to the girl and she was smiling back at him – a smile that hinted at more than just a casual acquaintance.

'So,' Tim began, in English, taking a sip of his beer and turning to look at the girl beside him. 'Where're you from really, and what're you doing here?'

She smiled. 'My Spanish is terrible, no?' Her English was not much better. 'I'm from Russia. I'm just work here for three months. Then I go home.'

'Working where precisely?'

She looked around her. 'Here. This bar. I'm a hostess. Like the others. We're paid to keep the customers happy.'

'By dancing with them?'

She shrugged.

'Yes. That, and ... other things.'

She held his eyes and smiled coquettishly.

'Ahh. Of course. I should've known.'

In the other room, Antonio and the girl were still dancing. As Tim watched, Antonio suddenly stepped back and, grasping the blonde's hand, pulled her away through a beaded curtain at the back of the room, beyond which Tim caught a glimpse of a stairway leading upstairs. So much for Catholic fidelity, he mused, remembering the long-suffering Cristina and her bouts of depression. He took another swallow of his beer.

'Do you want to dance now?' the girl asked again. 'Or anything else?'

'No. I just want to talk. Is that allowed?'

She shrugged again.

'Whatever you want. But you'll have to buy me drinks or the boss will get mad.'

'I can do that. What's your name?'

'Lara.'

'I'm Tim. Visiting from London.'

They talked and the evening rolled on. Tim learned that all of the girls in the bar were Russian, that they'd been working in the Blue Lagoon since August, and that they'd been hired in a batch from Vladivostok from ads placed in newspapers – told they were going to work as barmaids and hostesses in luxury hotels and restaurants on the Costa del Sol. Nothing had been said about becoming sex workers. But once they'd arrived, if they refused their bosses demands they were beaten, then sent back home. Unless they changed their tune, which most did. Hearing that, Tim frowned.

'That's terrible. Do you want help? Do you want me to go to the authorities?'

She grabbed his arm.

'No, please. You mustn't do that. They will hurt my family. They have contacts in my country. No, I'm in no real danger working here, and it will soon be over. In the meantime I am earning good money – even saving a little.' She smiled at him. And winked. 'Anyway, I enjoy my work.'

Tim stared at her, feeling protective paternal urges that conflicted sharply with his natural attraction to the girl. Not that those feelings mattered much anymore.

'What did you do in Vladivostok?' he asked at last.

She brushed her hair away from her face. 'I am student. I am study to be nurse. I have two years left.'

Her dark-rimmed eyes looked up, suddenly apprehensive. Tim followed her glance to the open archway, where a man stood looking in at them with a disapproving frown. Laughing, Lara turned and grabbed Tim's arm.

'Come on, let's dance!' she said loudly in her crude Spanish. Pulling him to his feet, she thrust her body tight against him.

Reading the situation perfectly, Tim put his arms around her, holding her close, becoming for a moment the attentive 'john' the girl had wished him to counterfeit. And felt some honest enjoyment in the effort – a frisson of remembered passion that made his skin tingle. After a minute or two, when the man had moved out of view, Lara pulled back from him and looked up.

'Sorry about that. It was the manager. I hope you didn't mind.'

'Not at all.' He touched her shoulder. 'Come on, let's refresh these drinks. That'll keep them off you for a while.'

Sometime later, when they'd become even more relaxed together, and after they'd danced again several times to the slower pieces, Lara suddenly reached across to run her finger along the line of Tim's jaw.

'You're very handsome,' she murmured. 'Are you sure you don't want to make love to me? I'm good.'

'I'm sure you are.' Tim glanced around. 'Where would we go?'

'There are rooms upstairs.' She smiled. 'With showers.'

As if that would make all the difference.

He shook his head.

'No, sweetheart. It's a lovely idea, but it won't work, sadly. Not with me.'

She pursed her mouth.

'Mm. A pity. It would be easy with you. Such a nice man.'

He shook his head. 'No. Not nice. Just a realist.' He reached out to squeeze her hand. 'And faithful. I'm married, you see?' he lied.

'What does that matter?' she asked, running her hand along his leg. 'Your wife is not here, is she?'

'No,' he returned. 'She's not.'

Nor could she be, having died four years before.

Tim grasped Lara's hand, stopping the caress, and squeezed.

'But it won't work all the same, lovely. Sorry.'

Shaking her head with a pout, Lara freed her hand and sat back, reaching for her drink.

After another half hour, when the ache in Tim's side had flared up to an annoyingly persistent throb and he had just about exhausted his store of small talk, Antonio appeared in the archway, alone.

'Well, *amigo*? I hope you've been enjoying yourself?'

'Of course, Antonio. Lara has looked after me well.'

Antonio smiled, showing his teeth.

'Good. Then I think we should go. It's getting late.'

Tim stood up. Slipping the fifty euro note he'd been clutching into Lara's hand, he bent forward to kiss her cheek.

'I've enjoyed being with you, lovely,' he told her, straightening. 'Look after yourself. And good luck with the nursing.'

Then the two men walked away, leaving her on the bench.

With a wave to the bartender, Antonio crossed the room to the entrance and walked out into the night, with Tim at his heels. Rain was still falling, though more lightly now.

'Well,' said Antonio, when they were back in the van. 'What did you think? Nice girls, eh? You wouldn't have found that in Franco's *España*, would you? No?'

Laughing, he reached over to slap Tim boisterously on the knee. As he turned to start the engine, Tim glanced out his window, raising his eyebrows and rolling his eyes.

Two hours later Tim stood in the open doorway of the *cortijo* looking out at the night, a glass of quality Rioja in his hand. Behind him on the table, next to the open book, a candle spluttered in its holder, casting dancing shadows over the walls. Tim looked up. The rain had stopped now, and the last clouds were sailing off to the north, revealing a starstrewn firmament. To the east, a waxing half moon floated in a clear sky. The air was fresh and clean smelling after the rain. Stepping out, Tim moved around the house to the terrace overlooking the sea. The grass under his feet was already almost dry.

What an evening, he thought. What a night!

Staring down at the moonlight reflected off the water, Tim realized with a jolt that this might well be the last time he'd ever stand like this on this terrace. After all these years of knowing the old *cortijo,* of loving the place and this view, this night could be the last.

Even his old friend Dom knew nothing of the dark spot in Tim's liver that presaged an early demise. No one did, save he and the doctors. In two days' time, after his return to London, he would enter King's Hospital to begin the last-ditch chemo treatments. But he held little faith they would make any difference. His father had died of the big C, after all. His, too, had been in the liver. No, there was little hope.

Which was why these days in Spain had been so important to him.

How fitting, Tim mused, that Antonio should have chosen this visit to give him his special treat. Almost as if he had known it would be his last. It hadn't panned out as Antonio had expected, perhaps, as far as Tim was concerned anyway, but it had been an exceptional evening all the same. Unforgettable in its way.

Tim thought of Lara again, of her elfin good looks, her long dark hair and tanned flesh, the feel of her body pressed against his on the dance floor. The longing it had raised in him, without hope of issue.

If only he was younger. And healthy.

He smiled.

The thought would have to suffice. And the memories.

Raising his glass to her against the starry sky, Tim drank the last of the wine.

And headed inside.

(July, 2010)

Little Infidelities

The whole thing happened so unexpectedly.

Julia had dropped Evan at school and was driving along the street in a haze of preoccupation, thinking of how she had to stop to do some shopping for tonight's dinner, and to pick up some dry cleaning for her television producer husband, when all of a sudden there was this van standing stationary in front of her that she hadn't noticed before. She slammed on the brakes but it was too late, and as she skidded into the van's rear bumper she felt the crunch in the pit of her stomach. Fortunately she hadn't been going fast, and the braking had slowed her almost enough. But there was damage, she was sure of that. What would Harvey say? He was always griping about her driving as it was. What would he say about this? There'd be more shouting at the least.

Apprehensive, Julia stepped out into the grey morning and shut her car door. A tall blond man in workman's clothes was getting out of the van, his face sombre. Julia hoped he didn't have a temper like her husband's.

'Travelling a bit too fast, were we?' the man asked with the hint of a smile, as they met at the collision point.

There was not much to be seen on the van – a scratch or two on the heavy, black metal bumper. The van's towing tongue, however, had crushed the centre of the wrap-around front bumper on Julia's

Toyota. But from what she could see that appeared to be the extent of the damage, thank heaven.

'I'm terribly sorry,' Julia stammered. 'My mind was miles away. I didn't notice you in time.' She leaned over to inspect the crumpled bumper more closely. 'Oh, dear. My husband will kill me for this. He's always after me about my driving.'

'Don't worry about it, Mrs. These things happen. It could happen to anybody. It'll cost a few hundred to get that bumper replaced, but there shouldn't be any other problems.'

'I sincerely hope so.' She glanced up at him. 'You're American?'

'Canadian, actually,' he confessed, smiling. 'But near enough. Sorry about that.'

'No, no,' Julia spluttered, embarrassed. 'I didn't mean anything bad, honestly.'

'It's not a problem. Anyway I've lived here ten years, so that must count for something.' He looked back at the two or three cars that were waiting at idle behind them. 'Look, let's pull around the corner and park. Then we won't be holding people up. We can exchange details then.'

'All right.'

A moment or two later, the two vehicles had been repositioned along the curb on the adjacent street. Watching the white van turn the corner, Julia had seen the advertisement on its side – a picture of an excavator with the words 'Reynolds Landscaping' and a telephone number.

Leaning across, Julia withdrew from the glove compartment the clear plastic envelope that held the insurance details and climbed out again. The man – who appeared to be her age or a little younger – was kneeling, carefully inspecting his bumper.

'Find anything else?' Julia asked as she joined him.

'Nope. Only the surface scratches. No other damage.'

'I have my insurance details here if you want them.'

The man stood and turned to her. 'That won't be necessary. But I will take your name and contact details, just in case.' He extended a hand. 'I'm Buck Reynolds, by the way.'

Julia took his hand and shook it, smiling shyly. 'Julia Grant, Mr. Reynolds.' She fumbled with the plastic envelope she'd brought from the car. 'There's one of my husband's cards in here somewhere. That has our telephone number and address on it.'

Unsnapping the envelope's button catch, Julia went to pull back the flap but in her nervousness dropped the whole lot onto the pavement at her feet. As she impulsively stooped to retrieve it, Reynolds, too, bent down, and in a bit of comic misfortune their heads cracked together.

'Ow!' cried Julia, almost losing her balance. But Reynolds quickly reached a hand to grasp her arm near the shoulder and prevented her from falling backwards.

'You okay?' he asked, shaking his head slightly as if to clear it.

'Yes, I'm … I'm fine.'

Reynolds collected the envelope from the ground with his free hand, then raised himself to his feet, still holding her arm and drawing her up with him. When they stood facing one another again he handed her the envelope and stood watching as she opened the flap and dug around for the card, biting her lower lip in concentration.

'You're sure you're okay?' he asked, concerned. 'You look a little shaken.'

'No, really. I'm fine.' She found the business card and handed it to him. 'Here's it is. It has all our contact details on it.'

He took the card and pulled out his wallet. Taking his own card from a slot inside, he stashed Julia's beside his banknotes and handed her the new one.

'Here's my card. In case you need to contact me for any reason.'

'Thanks.' She took the card and scrutinized it. 'So, Mr Reynolds, you own the landscaping business?'

'Call me Buck, please. Yes, it's my company. I'm an actor, really. When there's any work. Landscaping's my second string. But lately it's become almost a full time job.'

256

'An actor? Wow. I don't think I've ever met an actor. Would I have seen you in anything?'

'Here and there on television. Usually bit stuff. Sometimes a small part in a film. Nothing of note recently, though, alas.'

'Never mind. You're a good-looking man. I'm sure you'll find work again soon.'

'Why, thanks ... Julia. If only the casting directors felt the same.'

Julia smiled, then raised a hand to her forehead.

'You sure you're feeling okay?' Reynolds asked again. 'That was quite a knock.'

She laughed. 'I'm fine. It was just a surprise, that's all.'

He nodded. 'Okay then. Well, I'd better be on my way. I've got an appointment with someone for a job in Wimbledon and I don't want to be late.' He started towards his car door, then turned. 'Do call if there's anything you need. Anything at all that I can help you with.'

'Thanks. I'll do that.'

Buck Reynolds climbed into his van and drove off. For a moment after his departure Julia stood beside her car, staring down at the card in her hand, studying the name on it and the address in Fulham and the telephone numbers.

Three days later, Buck was just climbing into his van in the parking lot of a building supplies outlet when his mobile went. He closed the van door and reached into his jacket pocket for the phone, snapping it open and glancing at the incoming number. It was not one he recognized. He lifted the phone to his ear

'Yeah. Buck Reynolds here.'

'Mr Reynolds. Buck. It's Julia Grant.'

It took him a moment to place the name and the voice.

'Oh, hello, Julia! How're you doing? Is your head all right? From our bump, I mean?'

She tittered, nervously. 'Oh, yes. I didn't even get a swelling. No, that's all fine. That's not why I called.'

'Oh. Good. What can I do for you? Is there a problem with your car?'

'No. The garage is taking care of it for me. The new bumper's been ordered and should be here next week. And you were right. It's only costing me a couple of hundred pounds.'

'Thank heaven for that. So ... why did you phone, Julia?'

'I was just wondering... Could we meet someplace for a coffee, Buck? Just for a half hour or so? If it's not convenient please say so. I just thought it'd be nice if we could ... get to know one another a bit, that's all. You seem such a nice man. An understanding man.'

Buck frowned. What was this? A few yards away a man wearing a hard hat and yellow day-glow jacket climbed out of a pickup truck. Glancing in Buck's direction as he marched towards the store entrance, he raised an arm and waved. Buck waved back, smiling.

'Buck? You still there?'

'Yes, I'm here.'

'I'm sorry.' She sighed. 'I shouldn't have bothered you. I'm sure you're busy. Please forget what I said...'

'No, wait! Julia?'

'Yes?'

'You'd like to meet for a coffee somewhere, is that right?'

'Yes, I would. If you can spare the time. I'll understand, of course, if you think it's not a good idea.'

'No, I'd love to meet you. When were you thinking of?'

'Well, what about ... now? In half an hour? Are you in the middle of something?'

'Nothing I can't put off. Where do you want to meet?'

Julia mentioned a workers' café adjacent to a tube station in an area of south London not far from her home. She asked if he knew it. As it happened he did, and he was nearby. They agreed to meet there in forty minutes and rang off.

She was already at the cafe, sitting at a table on one side, when Buck walked in the door. He waved a hand, then went to the counter to order a white coffee, which he paid for and brought to her table, taking the seat opposite.

'Hey, Julia. How're you doing? It's good to see you.'

She smiled. 'Hello, Buck. Thank you for coming.'

She was wearing a camel hair coat, and her hair had obviously just been done up, the ends curling tidily in at her jawline. She was also wearing makeup. But he couldn't see her eyes behind her heavy, black-rimmed sunglasses.

The lunch hour rush had finished and the café was empty apart from themselves, the white-aproned proprietor having disappeared into a back room. From a distant radio Duffy could be heard crooning her latest single.

Julia stirred her cup of tea.

'So,' Buck began. 'What do you want to talk about?'

'Nothing in particular. I just wanted to … see you again. To know a bit more about you, I guess. You struck me as an interesting man.'

Buck sat back. 'Well, I'm not all that interesting, really. I'm twenty-nine years old. I come from a little town just west of Toronto, and I've been here about ten years – but I think I told you that already.'

'What brought you to London?'

'Drama school. LAMDA. Then I married a girl I met there. A Brit. We were together about eight years. I have a daughter, six years old, Megan. I see her twice a week, and every other weekend.' He pulled out his wallet and flipped the plastic sleeve, revealing a photograph of a blonde girl with her hair in plaits. 'This is her. Taken last year. Cute, huh?'

Julia examined the photo, then handed the wallet back, smiling.

'She's darling. She has your eyes. A lovely girl. You're very lucky.' Julia sipped her tea. 'Do you have a partner now?'

Buck shook his head. 'Nothing serious. I've been involved for a couple months with a Swedish girl I met at a bar, but that's coming to an end, I think. Anyway, there's no future there.' He brought his coffee mug to his mouth and took a swallow. 'What about you? Been married for long?'

Julia took in a deep breath, then blew it out again through her mouth.

'Eleven years. His name is Harvey, my husband. He's a producer of documentary films for television. I was a secretary working in his office. We have one son, Evan, who's ten.' She looked at her watch. 'He gets out of school in forty minutes. I'll have to leave in time to pick him up.'

'No problem.' He took another sip of his coffee. 'Your hair looks nice.'

She lifted a hand nervously to touch it. 'Thank you. I just had it done.' She smiled. 'Not for any special reason, really. I just felt like it.'

'Well, it looks nice. What's with the shades? There's no sun today. Afraid you'll be recognized by somebody?'

'No.'

After a moment's hesitation she raised her hands and removed the glasses. Her right eye and cheek were lightly discoloured with bruising. She had obviously been struck. Buck frowned.

'Wow. Was that your husband?'

Julia nodded.

'Why, because of the car?'

She nodded again. 'Yes. He went ballistic – even though I told him I'd pay for the damage from my own account so we wouldn't lose the no claims bonus.'

'Does he often hit you like that?'

'No. Very rarely. But he has hit me before.'

'I'm so sorry.'

'You needn't be. It was nothing to do with you. Harvey has a terrible temper, and he'd apparently had a bad day. When I broke the news about the car, it was the last straw for him. He shouted at me, called me an idiot for not paying attention and slapped me. He apologized afterwards, of course. He always does. But I can't forget it. Each time it happens it gets harder for me to stay with him.'

Buck leaned forward, frowning.

'Why do you stay? You don't have to put up with that. Why don't you just leave him, Julia? You're an attractive woman. You can find another relationship.'

'I don't want to ruin Evan's home, his family.'

Buck shook his head.

'That's nonsense. Don't you think the boy knows what's going on? Did he see his father hit you?'

'No, fortunately. He was away with a school friend. But he saw my bruises when he came home. I couldn't do anything to hide them. I told him I'd walked into a door, but he knows better. He's very sensitive and intelligent.'

Buck sat back again, crossing his arms and shaking his head, frowning.

'You can't go on pretending everything's okay, Julia. It obviously isn't. If you don't take steps to change things you know it'll happen again. What's to stop him really doing damage to you sometime, huh? These things don't get better – not without help, without counselling. They get worse. Have you asked him about going to see somebody? An anger management counsellor?'

Julia smiled. 'He says he doesn't need counselling. He says it's all my fault – that all he needs is a wife who doesn't continually do stupid things to provoke him.' She shook her head. 'I've given up looking for any sympathy from him. There's never any use in trying to get him to see my point of view, let alone listen to me.'

'Then leave him, Julia. Go to a lawyer. Now, while you're wearing those bruises on your face. There's ample grounds right there for divorce. At least seek legal advice. See what the options are.'

She shook her head with a wry smile. 'I'm forty-one years old, Buck. What would I do on my own?'

'Make a new life for yourself. Forty-one isn't old. Forty-one is young! And you're an intelligent, attractive woman. You had a job before. You could find one again.'

'At my age? It's not easy, you know.'

'Julia, you owe it to your son, you owe it to Evan to get yourself out of that marriage and into a new life.'

She stared down at the table, her lips pressed tightly together.

'Jesus,' Buck said suddenly, sitting back. 'Listen to me. As if it was any of my business. Sorry. I should keep my mouth shut. What do I know about anything?'

'No.' Julia glanced up at him. 'I'm grateful for your advice. That's partly why I called you. Somehow I knew you'd be easy to talk to. That you would … understand.'

'Do you love him, Julia?'

She shook her head.

'I don't know anymore. I think I did once. Sometimes he goes out of his way to be nice to me – usually after one of his flare-ups. He'll bring me flowers and chocolates, and once in a while he'll even take me out to dinner. But that soon dies away again, and then it's back to the usual routine of bad temper and fault-finding. I don't seem to be able to do anything right for him anymore.'

Buck frowned. 'Why did you marry him in the first place?'

'I got pregnant,' Julia replied, blushing. 'He picked me up at an office party, started chatting me up, really paying attention – something he'd never done before. I'd had a lot to drink that night and somehow I agreed to let him come back to my flat. He's an attractive man, quite fit and virile. Played rugby when he was younger. I hadn't many men friends and was flattered that he took an interest in me. With that, and the fact that I was pretty far gone with drink, it was inevitable that … things happened.'

'And a few weeks later you found yourself pregnant.'

'Exactly. To give him his due, Harvey was very considerate and generous when I told him about it. He was a man of honour, he said. He wouldn't leave me in the lurch. We courted for a few weeks, then got married. Evan was born six months later. No one seemed to notice how soon he arrived, or to care.'

'And the marriage was okay?'

'For a few years, yes. Harvey tried hard to be a good husband, and a good father to Evan.'

As she talked she looked down at her hands, rubbing them together on the tabletop.

'Eventually he started to change, began accusing me of trapping him into a marriage he didn't want. From that time on things have just gotten worse. His temper tantrums happen more frequently, and his patience with me has virtually gone.' She looked up at him. 'Do I love him? To be honest, no. Not anymore. But there's Evan. Harvey's a good father to him, and I don't want to ruin Evan's sense of family security.'

Buck shook his head again.

'There isn't any family security, Julia. You know that. You've got to do something about it, one way or the other. For your sake and for the boy's.'

Julia clasped her hands together, taking a quick breath of air, as if drawing a line under the conversation. 'I've said too much. I'm sorry.'

'Not at all. I'm glad you can talk to me. I feel honoured.'

Her eyes found his. 'Thanks, Buck. I really appreciate the sympathy. I don't get it very often.'

'Don't you have a woman friend you can talk to? Someone in the family, or a neighbour?'

'Not really. I don't like airing my dirty laundry before family and friends if I can help it. If I did it might get back to Evan somehow, and I wouldn't want him to suffer any hurt or embarrassment. Kids at that age can be so cruel. If one of his friends found out and taunted him with it...'

'He's going to find out sooner or later anyway. You know that.' Buck drained his cup and leaned forward, placing his right hand over hers on the tabletop. 'Julia, at least think about it, will you? About talking to a lawyer?' He glanced down at his hand on hers, then self-consciously withdrew it and sat back. 'Sorry. I'm just a stranger to you, I know. Just the guy you rear-ended. But in the little time I've spent with you, I feel … drawn to you. As a friend. And what you've told me about your situation is … well, I just don't want you to go on being unhappy. That's all.'

Julia glanced again at her watch, then finished her tea, setting her cup carefully onto its saucer. Then she reached for her handbag.

'I must go.'

Now Buck glanced at his watch.

'Me, too. I've got a concrete mixer turning up at a jobsite in forty minutes.'

They both stood, and moved towards the door. But before he could open it Julia reached out to put a hand on his wrist.

'Thanks for meeting me, Buck. You're a kind man. And your advice is kindly given. It means a lot to me.'

He took her hand in both of his and squeezed it.

'Just think about what I said, will you? And let me know what you decide. If you want to, that is. I'd like to hear from you again.'

Julia smiled.

'Thanks. I'll do that.'

Two days later Harvey Grant announced to his wife that he was leaving the following day for a conference in Birmingham. He was in the development stage of a new documentary, he explained, and there was a meeting with BBC department bosses and accountants to work out the budget for the project. He would be back in two days, he promised.

For Julia tensions in the family circle had settled down considerably since her coffee meeting with Buck. In line with his usual pattern of behaviour after a severe temper attack, Harvey had been especially solicitous towards her, and seemed to make efforts to be an even better father to his son. The evening of the coffee meeting Harvey had been particularly attentive to his wife – complimenting her on her cooking, helping her with the washing up. At one point he'd even pulled her away from the sink and into his arms, hugging her strongly, and declaring once again how sorry he was that he'd lost control and struck her. She had allowed herself to be held, settling herself against his broad chest with sceptical resignation.

The night Harvey was away Julia began to have real doubts about her assessment of her husband's feelings towards her. Perhaps she was wrong about him? Maybe she was being too judgmental? Perhaps he was genuinely sorry for his lapse of control, and did feel true affection towards her, and his earlier complaints about being trapped were simply intentionally hurtful untruths blurted out in the fury of the moment? He'd even telephoned her that evening, had he not, and had told her how sorry he was that he couldn't bring her along on the Birmingham trip? That seemed genuine enough. But there'd never been an occasion before when Harvey had indicated a desire to take her with him on one of his trips. Why should he suddenly change now?

On the Saturday after his return from the midlands Julia was loading whites into the washing machine when she discovered one of his shirts with what looked to be a faint lipstick smudge on the collar. When she lifted the shirt to her nose and sniffed she was certain there was the hint of a feminine scent permeating the fabric. Abruptly she thrust the shirt into the washer, furious with herself for allowing her imagination to conjure such damning evidence of infidelity from nothing. He had seemed so loving towards her of late, after all. And the night of his return he'd made love to her more tenderly than he'd ever done before. Surely these suspicions were groundless?

But a week later, Harvey's newfound interest in his wife seemed to wane again, and on his return home from work one evening he had created a scene in the kitchen – complaining about the clutter on the worktops and shouting at her about what a slut of a cook she was.

When she tried to explain that everything that was out was being used for the preparation of the meal he had exploded in his usual fashion, and with a sweep of his arm had sent everything on the worktops – bowls, measuring jugs and canisters of flour and sugar – crashing to the floor in a jumbled mess. Then he had stormed out, and had not returned until the wee hours of the morning – creeping in and undressing in the dark to take his place on the far side of the bed, turning his back to her and breaking immediately into deep snores.

The following weekend the opening match of the Six Nations Rugby Championship was to be held at Cardiff, and Harvey had announced that he was going to attend. Several people from his crew at work were going, he said, and he'd agreed to go with them. They'd be travelling down on the Friday night, and would be staying on the Saturday night as well, returning home on Sunday afternoon. Even though it meant Harvey missing a Saturday football match at Evan's school – something that Evan was keenly hoping his father would be able to attend, as he was playing as a striker for the first time – Julia was glad to have him out of the house. His moods of late had been trying in the extreme – even Evan had come to her quietly one evening to ask what was wrong with his father. Julia had passed it off as work stress. In the end she'd gone to the school match herself, and had cheered when her son had scored the winning goal – taking him and his mates to the local MacDonalds for a celebratory meal afterwards. She had enjoyed herself. For the first time she remembered Buck's advice in the café. Maybe it was possible she could create a life without Harvey? A life on her own with Evan.

On Sunday morning, after Evan had scarfed down his breakfast and crashed out the door to meet one of his mates for a day of watching footy on television, Julia was washing up the breakfast dishes when the phone rang. She wiped her hands and lifted the handset from the kitchen counter.

'Yes? Julia here?'

'Julia, it's Sam Jacobs. Is Harve around? I'd like a word with him?'

'No, Sam. He won't be back until tonight.' She paused, frowning. Sam was the most ardent rugby fan in Harvey's production team. Surely he would've gone to the Six Nations match with the others? 'Sam,' she went on, 'aren't you in Cardiff?'

'Yeah. We're all here, the whole team. Except for Harve. That's why I wanted to tell him about the game. It was fantastic. He'll be sorry he missed it. He said he had to stay in London for some family do – a football game at Evan's school, wasn't that it?'

Julia felt a wave of nausea rise from the pit of her stomach. She leaned back against the kitchen counter, holding the phone to her ear with both hands.

'Yes. That's right. Anyway, Sam, I'll tell him you called.'

She punched the end call button and stood holding the phone in her hand and staring at the floor, trying to make some kind of sense out of Harvey's deception. But the meaning was now all too clear. The lipstick smudge on his shirt collar, the strange scent in the fabric, the late nights arriving back from work.

Harvey was having an affair.

Buck had given up any thought of hearing from Julia again when, two weeks after their coffee meeting, his mobile rang just after he'd arrived at his flat. He was exhausted, having spent a long day digging drainage ditches by hand along the side of a house in Teddington that he couldn't get to with his excavator. Pulling the phone from his pocket, he snapped it open and sank into his leather armchair in the sitting room.

'Buck Reynolds here. Can I help you?'

'Buck, it's Julia Grant.'

'Hey, Julia! I was beginning to think I wasn't going to hear from you again. How are you? How are things at home?'

'I'm well enough, but things here have taken a new turn.'

'Oh? You want to meet somewhere to talk about it?'

There was a pause.

'Actually I have a proposition for you,' she went on finally. 'Forgive my presumption, and please don't be offended by it. It's not a sudden idea. I've thought about it for some time.'

'Go on.'

'Harvey is having an affair. I'll tell you about it when I see you. He doesn't know that I know about it. I'm going down to Bournemouth next weekend on my own to think things over, and I would be very grateful if you would meet me there.'

'What's happening with Harvey and Evan?'

'Harvey's away in Berlin for the weekend. Evan will be staying with his best friend 'til Sunday night. I've told Harvey I'm going away to visit my sister. He doesn't like her so he won't be checking up on me. Not that it matters if he does. She won't know where I am, in any case. I've booked a double room in a small hotel near the beach. I'd like it very much if you would come and share it with me.'

There was a pause as Buck tried to digest what he'd been told. Julia waited for his response.

'Buck?' she continued when there was none. 'Are you still there?'

'Yeah, I'm here. I'm just a little taken aback by this, that's all.'

'If you think I'm too forward, or if the idea's abhorrent to you, please don't hesitate to say so, Buck. Your friendship is too important to me to ruin by being too demanding. It's just that … well, as you know, I have no one else I can really discuss these things with. And I have come to think of you as someone I can rely on for good advice. And for … well, for moral support.'

'Hmm,' Buck replied. 'Well, I'm not due to have Megan this weekend. I guess I could get away for a couple of days. When're you going down, Friday evening?'

'Yes. I'm driving down after I drop Evan at his friend's house. I should be at the hotel by seven.'

Buck sighed. He wasn't sure about this. It was certainly true he'd found Julia an attractive woman, though older and perhaps a bit more reserved than his usual partners. Still he'd liked her from the moment he first met her at the roadside, and there was certainly no reason on his side not to spend the weekend with her. The on-again off-again relationship with Kirstin had finished in a bitter row the week before. Now there was not the slightest obligation of loyalty or fidelity he owed to anyone. As for Julia, the fact that she'd discovered her husband was having an affair rather pointedly justified her following suit. Buck didn't envisage any kind of ongoing relationship with Julia; that was out of the question. But on the other hand, he saw no reason why he and she shouldn't share a couple of nights together. The idea was actually rather appealing.

'Okay,' he murmured finally down the phone. 'Yes. I'd be happy to spend the weekend with you in Bournemouth. If you're really sure that's what you want.'

'Believe me, Buck, I'm very sure. In fact, I look forward to it.'

Julia gave Buck the details of the hotel and they agreed to meet there at seven Friday evening.

'Thanks, Buck,' Julia said in closing. 'I'll try not to be too downbeat. I really am looking forward to seeing you. And spending time with you.'

'Me, too,' Buck concurred.

Moments later they rang off.

The Bournemouth hotel, The Unicorn, was tucked away in a side street not far from the beach. Julia had booked it under a false name – Mr and Mrs Keith Martin – and together they ascended the carpeted staircase to their comfortably furnished first floor double room overlooking the small back garden and car park.

Julia was carrying a small suitcase which she placed on the chair by the door. Buck's small bag he set on the desk. Unzipping it he drew out a box of chocolates and a clear plastic tube containing a single red rose. Turning, he presented them to her.

'I didn't know if it was appropriate but I thought "what the hell?".
I hope it's all right.'

Taking the gifts she smiled up at him.

'It's wonderful. Very thoughtful of you. Thank you.' Opening the
plastic tube she withdrew the single stem rose. 'I'll just put this in
water.'

In the en suite bathroom was the usual pair of cellophane wrapped
plastic cups. Julia half-filled one of them with water and brought it into
the bedroom, balancing the rose in it against the dressing table mirror
opposite the foot of the bed. Turning the bud so it faced outward she
stepped back to admire her work.

'There. That's lovely.' Buck was sitting on the bed, and she turned
to put a hand on his shoulder. 'I brought something, too. I hope you
like it.'

Moving to her case she withdrew a slim paper bag and passed it to
him. Opening it Buck drew out a bottle of Australian Shiraz.

'I hope you like wine,' she said, producing two stemmed wineglasses
from her case. 'It's a good one. One of my favourites. And it has a
twist top so we don't need a corkscrew.'

He smiled. 'Good thinking. Yeah, I love wine. And Australian
wine is some of the best. I'll open it now so it can breathe. Then we'll
have a glass or two when we get back from dinner.'

Wrapping themselves up against the chilly sea breeze, they left the
hotel and walked down through the gathering dusk to the sea and the
frontage road. Still somewhat shy of one another they didn't touch,
but carried on a light and slightly awkward conversation about Buck's
upbringing in Canada, his education and his marriage, and about his
daughter Megan. Julia obviously wanted to wait till they were more
comfortable to discuss her own marriage issues. Buck respected that
decision by not bringing the subject up himself.

They enjoyed a simple dinner in an Italian restaurant not far from their hotel and returned at about 9:30 to their room. If the landlady suspected anything untoward she gave no sign of it and greeted the couple warmly upon their return, reminding them of the times for breakfast in the morning.

While Buck took their coats and scarves and hung them in the wardrobe, Julia poured the two wineglasses full of the red Shiraz. Turning she offered one to Buck, and the two of them stood facing one another at the foot of the double bed.

'To you,' Buck said, raising his glass and smiling. 'And to a lovely weekend at the seaside.'

'Hear, hear,' Julia responded, with a smile of her own.

They sipped their wine.

There was a slight moment of awkwardness as they both suddenly realized the only place for them to sit down was the bed. But then Buck laughed and gestured to it with a sweeping wave of his arm. 'Please. Make yourself comfortable.'

'Thank you, kind sir.'

She moved to sit on one side of the bed.

Buck moved to the other side and settled himself at the head, sitting back against the headboard.

For a moment nothing was said as they sipped their wine. When one caught the other's eye they smiled, still obviously a little nervous about the situation. Finally Buck spoke.

'So tell me about what's going on. If you want to, that is.'

And she did. Lying on her side across the bottom of the bed Julia filled him in on the events of the last couple of weeks, starting with Harvey's unusually attentive behaviour in the weeks following the slap incident – before it changed again to his usual bad temper – then telling him of the discovery of the scented shirt with the lipstick stain, and of catching Harvey out in his lie about going to the Cardiff rugby match. From time to time Buck interjected a comment or raised a question – suggesting, for instance, that Harvey's sudden attentiveness could simply have been the result of a guilty conscience, which Julia discounted, as she didn't believe Harvey had a conscience anymore, as far as she was concerned anyway. Then Buck asked if she had any idea who the other woman was? Julia wasn't certain, but she suspected that it was Harvey's PA, Shirley, with whom she'd spoken on the phone several times, and who had always seemed somehow deliberately offhand and cool with her. Julia went on for nearly half an hour, finally closing by saying that she didn't know what she was going to do now – feeling torn between the two options of confronting her husband with his affair and taking the consequences, or of keeping quiet and simply carrying on as she had been, forcing herself not to be hurt by his rejection. Buck scowled at that.

'That's no good. You can't ignore his infidelity, Julia. It's got to be brought out into the open. He's treating you like dirt. You're the mother of his son, for Christ's sake. You've got to show him that you're not a fool, nor a doormat to be walked over with impunity. You have a right to happiness, too, you know?'

Julia's face crumpled and she brought a hand to her eyes.

'That's easy to say, Buck. But he's so much stronger than me. I don't know that I have the backbone to confront him. He can be very frightening.'

Buck leaned forward, resting a hand on her skirted thigh. 'Of course you do. And you have to do it, for your sake and for Evan's. You won't be alone in this. Not if you get a lawyer behind you. With the evidence you have against him Harvey wouldn't stand a chance contesting a divorce case, and he'd have to provide for you and Evan in the settlement.' He stroked her thigh reassuringly through the fabric of her skirt. 'I'll be around to give you moral support – you know that. And if he threatens you physically, you only have to call me and I'll be there in a flash.'

She reached out to grip his hand. 'You're very good to me, Buck. So understanding. That means a lot to me right now.' She sat up, facing him. 'Hold me, please. I need your strength right now. Please.'

And Buck pulled her to him, stretching out on the bed and cradling her against him, stroking her back and shoulder with one hand, and bending eventually to plant kisses on her forehead, her hair. Finally he lifted her face and kissed her on the mouth, a kiss that began tentatively but which built slowly in intensity and confidence. Julia felt her scruples melting. Giving way to the slumbering passion he'd rekindled within her she willingly opened herself to him.

The next two days were spent restfully – in walks, quiet meals at seafront restaurants, and a fair amount of time in bed, for they had found a special compatibility in their lovemaking – something that was new and wonderful for Julia. Harvey had never been the most tender or giving of lovers, and he'd been her only man till now. Buck on the other hand was young and thorough, and took the time and effort necessary to bring her to levels of pleasure she'd never dreamed existed.

There was no need to discuss the marriage anymore. That ground had been covered as well as it could be at this juncture. Now it remained for Julia to take the next steps. Whatever her decision, it would depend on what she found once she returned to London. But for the rest of the weekend the two friends blocked out all other considerations and revelled in their time together, exploring Bournemouth and one another like a pair of young lovers on an away day.

At home the following week Julia was pleased to see that once again Harvey seemed in a better, lighter mood. While he remained in this state she found it hard to confront him with his unfaithfulness. Perhaps he had wound up the affair and it was now a thing of the past? She could not know for sure, but so long as he did nothing to worsen the situation she was content to let things lie.

As the weeks passed Julia phoned Buck from time to time for ten minute conversations, just to keep in touch. But there was no element of compulsion about it for her. Indeed it was often a week or more between their telephone contacts.

Though Buck was sceptical about Harvey's apparent change he was tactful enough to keep his reservations to himself. It was, after all, Julia's life and Julia's choice, and so long as she was not hurting he was content to leave sleeping dogs lie. In any case he was pleased she sounded so relatively upbeat.

One weekend when Harvey and Evan had both made plans to be away Julia phoned Buck, and when, in the course of their conversation, they realized that Saturday evening was free for both of them, Buck had asked her to meet him for dinner, and to spend the night at his flat. Julia had considered the offer and accepted.

The evening had been relaxed and pleasant, for both of them. Julia had enjoyed seeing the space in which Buck lived, and had felt comfortable there. And they had lain together in his double bed as easily, and as lulled by their mutual contentment, as they had been at the hotel in Bournemouth. But something was changing, subtly, and even without voicing the thought they both knew this would be the last time they would share such intimacy. With this meeting they had taken that part of their relationship as far as it could sensibly go, and though it'd been a thoroughly positive experience for each of them – and perhaps even necessary at the beginning as an antidote to the despair Julia had suffered over her fractured marriage – the realities of their separate circumstances rose up now, urging the return to a purely platonic relationship. Certainly neither of them would at any stage have said that they felt 'love' for the other – that was not the nature of their mutual attraction. It was more that they had simply come together as friends, and had for a moment willingly and spontaneously overstepped the normal bounds of friendship in response to a particular need felt by each of them. Both had always accepted that sooner or later the physical phase of their relationship would dwindle away. And now, it seemed, that moment had been reached.

Still, Julia knew, Buck's tender attentions to her, in bed and out, had done an enormous amount to bolster her self-esteem. And she knew now that this rediscovery of her own strengths as a woman – her ability to attract and to please – had done much to bolster her courage to face, and eventually to resolve, the uncertainties of her troubled marriage.

But before she could bring herself to put into effect her newfound self-confidence an event occurred which was to change everything.

One sunny June morning a couple of months after her final tryst at Buck's flat, after Evan had left to take part in a school cricket match, Julia turned from a sink full of breakfast dishes to find Harvey standing in the doorway behind her, his hands in his pockets and an expression of nervous apprehension on his face.

'Julia, there's something I have to tell you,' he said finally. 'Could you leave that for a bit and come into the sitting room?'

Raising her eyebrows, Julia dried her hands on the kitchen towel and followed him into the lounge at the back of the house, its windows overlooking the long garden. Harvey settled himself on the edge of his armchair, and Julia perched on the sofa across from him. For a long moment Harvey didn't speak, but sat leaning forward, his elbows on his knees, rubbing his forehead with the tips of his fingers as if searching for exactly the right words to begin.

'There's no easy way to say this,' he said at length, dropping his hands, 'so I guess I'd just better lay it on the table.' He looked up at her. 'I want a divorce, Julia. I've met someone else and I want to spend my life with her. I've given it a lot of thought. For a while I believed my interest in this woman was only a passing thing. But it isn't. It hasn't been. I find that I love her, and I want to be with her now more than anything. I'm terribly sorry to have to bring such pain to you, and to disrupt Evan's life. And you can be sure that I'll be more than fair in providing for both of you when the divorce is complete. I'm quite happy for you to file against me for adultery, but I'd rather you didn't involve … my new partner. I can provide another name you can use, who will swear to the truth of the allegation.'

He had been rubbing his hands together throughout this speech. Now he gripped them tightly and looked up at her again, with a look of desperation in his eyes.

'I'm so sorry, Julia. I don't feel very good about myself. I know I'm a cad. I've been a far from perfect spouse over the years, and now I'm committing the worst offence a husband can commit. But … it isn't working with us anymore. You must know that, too. Surely it's the best thing for both of us.'

There was a pause as the two of them stared across the room at one another. Julia's face was impassive, her eyes firm. Finally she spoke for the first time.

'This comes as no surprise to me, Harvey, to speak truth. I've known for some weeks that you're having an affair. I won't embarrass you by telling you how I know, but suffice it to say that you were not very clever about masking your indiscretions. I'm only glad Evan didn't discover it accidentally through your blundering. Am I surprised that you want a divorce? Not really. We haven't been a couple for some time. In fact I've been very close to seeing a solicitor myself. I was certain I could find the grounds, with or without your co-operation. So this declaration does not come as a shock to me. In fact it comes as a kind of relief. At least now the need for lying and deception will be over. Now perhaps I can make a happier life on my own, without having to pretend an affection that is no longer there.'

She dropped her head, shaking it as if to clear her mind of conflicting thoughts.

'There is one thing I would ask of you,' she continued after a moment. 'If you're serious about this new relationship, promise me that – for her sake – you will seek help to control your temper. I can't bear the thought of another woman having to endure the physical and verbal abuse you've visited upon me over the years.'

There was a long pause. Then Harvey rose to his feet, hands in pockets.

'Okay. You're right. I shall seek anger management counselling. And I'm sorry you had to suffer because of it. It's certainly a part of myself that I don't want to bring to my new relationship. I'll work on it. In the meantime I'll leave it to you, Julia, to contact a solicitor and set the wheels in motion for the divorce. As I said, I won't contest it if you file on the grounds of adultery. When you're ready I'll provide the details of a co-respondent.' He paused for a moment, looking down at her. 'I suppose it'll be best if we break the news to Evan together, if you're okay with that? Of course he doesn't have to know all the grisly details.'

Julia nodded, her face still an impassive mask.

'Then we'll do it tonight, after dinner. Evan's almost eleven. So long as we keep any bitterness from him he should be fine with it.'

Harvey left the house for the day and Julia continued with her household duties. After lunch she found time to phone Buck's mobile, to tell him the news. He was pleased to hear the whole thing was finally out in the open, and assured her that she'd be much better off on her own. While in her rational mind she believed that was true, a part of her was still terrified at the idea of coping with life as a single mother. But her association with Buck over the preceding weeks, and the influence of his assured, reasonable approach to things, had taught her she was actually stronger than she'd thought herself. In spite of a few doubts about what the future would offer in terms of work, for the most part she remained confident, and indeed optimistic.

Over the coming months events moved swiftly. With Harvey's co-operation, the divorce went through in the minimum amount of time, and the terms of his settlement with Julia were as generous as he had promised. The family home was sold, and the profits split between them – leaving Julia with more than enough to relocate out of London – in St. Albans, the town she had known as a girl.

She was pleased to see that Evan – after the first pangs of disruption were lived through – had managed to cope very well with the relocation to a new school and a different circle of friends.

Shortly after moving into their new house Julia found a position as a receptionist in a doctors' surgery. A modest start on the employment ladder, but a start at least. Life, in short, began to shape itself into a much more attractive menu of possibilities. Buck had been right. Getting out of her painful marriage had been the only answer.

Slightly over a year from the date of the chance accident that'd first brought them together, Julia telephoned Buck to say that she was coming to London for some shopping, and asked if he would be free to meet. He confirmed that he could make himself free and they agreed to rendezvous at St. Pancras station after Julia had finished her errands, and to find a nearby café. Accordingly on the afternoon of that day Julia stood at the front of the station and waited until she saw Buck's blond head bobbing above the crowd of pedestrians coming and going along the pavement.

After a quick embrace and kisses on both cheeks the two friends walked a block or two until they found a café to their liking, and went inside.

Buck got their drinks, while Julia selected a corner table near the front window. Two other tables on the far wall were taken with couples, but their chat was quiet.

Sliding the two cups onto the tabletop, Buck sat down opposite her, echoing the same positions of their first café meeting.

'So,' he said, 'what's the news? Evan's doing okay in the new school?'

'Very well,' she replied. 'His work doesn't seem to have suffered at all from the move, and his marks are excellent. He's doing great. Even Harvey says so.'

'That's fantastic.' Buck sipped his coffee. 'And you, how're you doing?'

'Fine,' she chirped. 'Actually I've started a new relationship and I wanted you to know about it. He's someone I met through amateur dramatics – a divorcé like myself, about my own age, with a daughter a year younger than Evan. His name's Charlie. He's in insurance.'

Buck nodded, smiling. 'That's great news. I knew you'd land on your feet, Julia. I told you as much. No wedding bells in the offing yet?'

'Heavens no!' she scoffed. 'I've just got my freedom. I'm not about to give it away so soon. No, we're both quite happy to maintain our separate households, and to spend as much time together as we can with things as they are. We'll let it ride like that for a time and see how things develop.'

'Very smart.'

Julia sipped her tea.

'How about you, Buck? Are you seeing anyone?'

'Actually I am. A lady named Kim. Met her through a friend of mine. She's in fashion design. We've been going out for a few weeks now. Matter of fact I've asked her to move in with me.'

'Wow. Serious then?'

'Could be. A man's got to settle down sometime. Megan gets on well with her, too. This could be the one.'

'I hope so. I'll keep my fingers crossed.'

There was a pause as they sipped their drinks. Finally Julia reached a hand across to lay over Buck's on the tabletop.

'I know we don't see much of one another now, Buck. That's to be expected, I think. But I just want you to know how glad I am that I rear-ended you that day a year ago, and that I screwed up the courage to contact you again. Somehow I knew you would help me. And you certainly did that. You've been a tremendous influence in my life. I shall always be grateful to you.'

Buck looked embarrassed but smiled through it, putting on a cod western accent. 'Shucks, ma'am. I was only doing what comes naturally.' Dropping the accent, he continued: 'You're a lovely person, Julia. In all ways. It wasn't hard to respond to you. I'm glad we came together too, and if I was able to be of use to you then I'm a happy man.' He laid his other hand on top of hers, and pressed down lightly. 'Anyway, whatever happens I want us to stay in touch. You're very special. I'm pleased that I helped you to realize that.'

When they finished their drinks Julia reached for her handbag and they both rose to leave. But at the door, Buck turned to her.

'Walk back with me to my van, will you? It's parked around the corner. There's something I want to give you.'

Intrigued Julia acquiesced, and they left the café, strolling together through the crowds thronging the pavements.

When they reached the van Buck stepped to the back door, unlocked and opened it. Reaching inside he pulled out a small ball of fur at the end of a leather lead. Cradling it in his arms, he turned to her.

'This little guy needs a home. He's a Jack Russell. A friend of mine's dog had puppies and he's looking to place all of them in a happy environment. When I heard that I knew there couldn't be any happier place right now than with you and Evan.'

He handed the puppy over and Julia took him into her arms.

'He's lovely, Buck! Does he have a name?'

'He does. It's Dylan, after the Welsh bard. I hope you like him.'

'Oh, I do! Evan will be over the moon!' She looked up at him. 'Thanks so much, Buck. For everything!'

• • •

Human beings are a pretty shambolic lot in the way they conduct their lives. They choose the wrong careers and are miserable their entire working lives. They make marriages that are ill-fated from the start. They live by rules that cannot ultimately be adhered to without restricting themselves within a straitjacket of moral rectitude and self-righteousness that denies any spontaneity, any justifiable exceptions.

Is there a moral high ground in this story? Is Julia's infidelity just as bad as Harvey's? Is it worse?

Does it matter?

What mattered was that because of a chance accident Julia Grant found a confidant at the exact moment in her life when she needed one – a confidant that helped her find the courage to confront and surmount the serious problems she then faced. She found a kind man who was also a wise man, and that changed everything for her. The fact that she and Buck became lovers is ultimately of no consequence, except to them. In the face of what was enabled through their coming together – Julia's newfound self-esteem and her confidence to deal positively with her stalled life and the collapse of her marriage – her 'little infidelity' with Buck Reynolds was certainly neither socially, ethically nor morally reprehensible.

It's easy to assign guilt in such a situation. To be judgmental. But it's also wrong. I suspect there are many such cases around us that we know nothing of. And even if we did – so long as no one suffers as a result there's really only one just response: tolerant acceptance and understanding. Even celebration. Everyone's life is a voyage, and no one can know where the winds will take us.

Be grateful for the journey, with all its unexpected twists and turns.

And enjoy it.

Life is a gift.

(London, 2010)

About the Author

(Photo by Bob Bailey)

William Roberts is an American actor, writer and voice artist resident in the UK for over forty years. Born in Oregon, he was raised and educated in northern California, and still proudly carries a US passport. He currently lives and works in London, enjoying his writing, flying his small airplane around Europe and watching his grandsons grow.

Also by WERoberts

The Humanist

When a young man's body is found near a remote northern California town sprawled over jagged rocks at the base of a seaside cliff, the authorities dismiss the death as an accident or suicide. But there are suspicious circumstances surrounding the tragic event. Sent to investigate, crack San Francisco reporter Arnold Rednapp soon discovers that the boy's unorthodox beliefs had turned a large section of the small town against him, leading the journalist to suspect a community-wide conspiracy to hide the truth of what happened. Rednapp's suspicions are hardened when he himself receives anonymous threats...

A gripping, intriguing tale of detection with a strong cast of memorable characters that offers just a bit more than the usual.

Available on Amazon as a quality paperback, in Kindle format and as an audiobook read by the author.

An Ill Wind

After witnessing the recovery of a mysterious mutilated body in a public park in Northern California, San Francisco reporter Arnold Rednapp becomes embroiled in an investigation involving drugs, gangs, pedophilia, political corruption and murder, and follows a trail of clues that extends the full length of California and deep into Mexico. As he closes in on the villains, their desperate efforts to avoid capture result in a climactic finale that brings the lives of Arnie and several of his closest friends to within a whisker of extinction.

A tense thriller, filled with memorable characters and plot twists, that moves inexorably toward its breathtaking finish.

Available on Amazon as a quality paperback, in Kindle format, and soon as a downloadable audiobook read by the author.

Printed in Great Britain
by Amazon